Children of the Hector

*Family photograph believed to be
Elizabeth Ann Fraser (Annie)*

Children of the Hector

A novel by

Pamela Edwards & Ann Louise Stevens

Children of the Hector is a work of fiction. It is based on the lives of a real family and other real people of the eighteenth and nineteenth centuries. However, the personalities and characteristics of these people have been created by the authors. All characters, real and imagined, historical events, places, dialogue, letters and situations are used fictitiously. Any resemblance to persons living or dead is entirely coincidental.

Book and Cover Design by Vancouver Desktop Publishing Centre

Cover Illustration by Ashton Creative Design, Pictou, Nova Scotia

Maps by Teresa MacKenzie, Art and Design, Pictou, Nova Scotia

Photo Courtesy of Isabel Purney (Cox) Baker and Anne Gorham Blakeney

Eastern Chronicle, Thursday, September 6, 1888, Publisher S.M. Mackenzie, New Glasgow, Nova Scotia, Vol. XLVII No. 34. Courtesy McCulloch House Museum and Genealogy Centre, Pictou, Nova Scotia

ISBN: 978-1-9992896-0-7

Published by Pamela Edwards and Ann Louise Stevens
Printed in Canada by Marquis Book Printing, Quebec

To our families with love and appreciation

And

To Hugh and Sophia Fraser, and all other immigrants,
past and present,
who have made Canada a better place

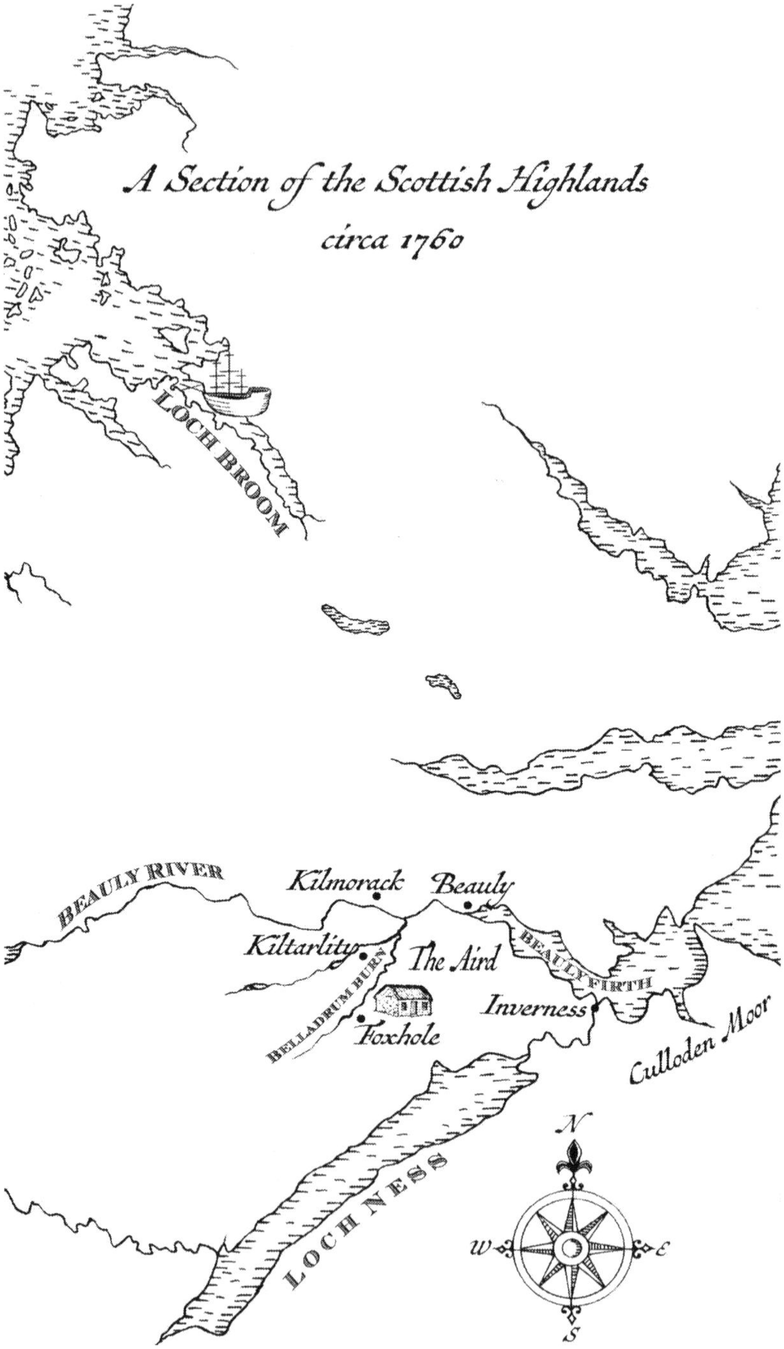
A Section of the Scottish Highlands
circa 1760
LOCH BROOM
BEAULY RIVER
Kilmorack
Beauly
Kiltarlity
The Aird
BEAULY FIRTH
BELLADRUM BURN
Inverness
Foxhole
Culloden Moor
LOCH NESS
N
W
E
S

The Pictou County Area circa 1870

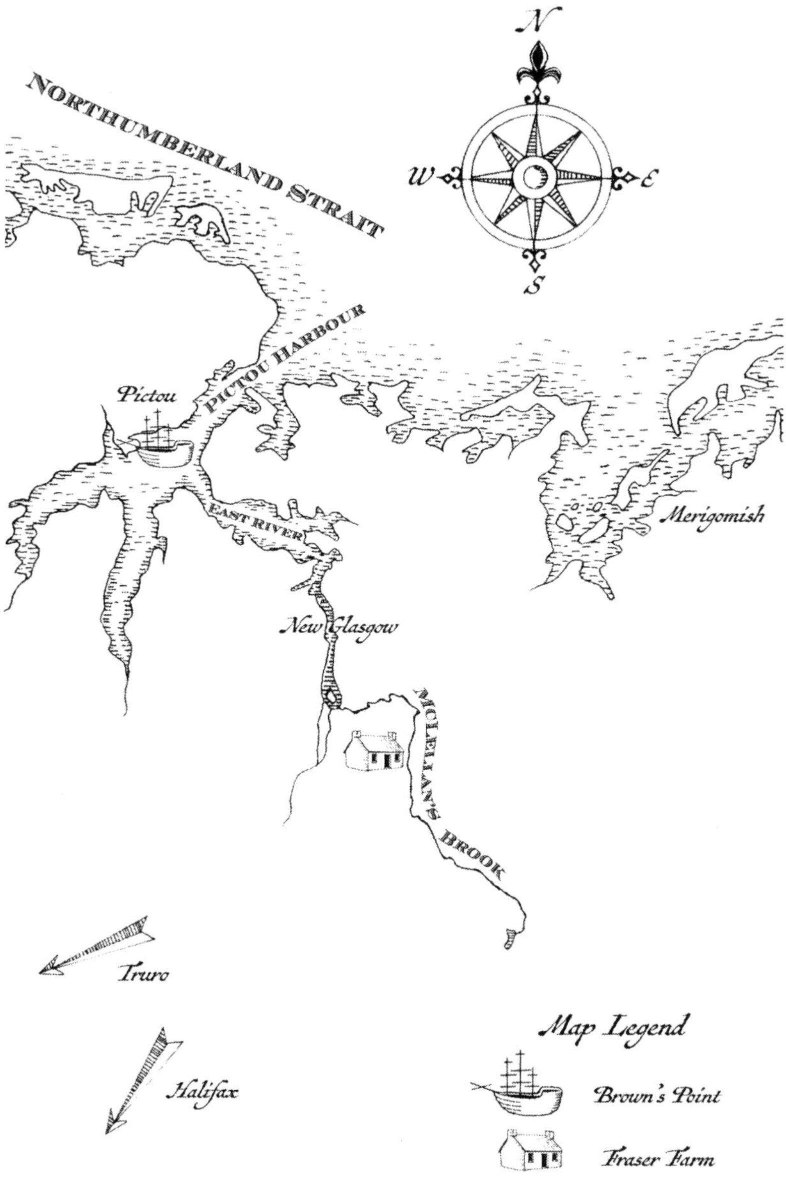

Eastern Section of Jamaica 1823

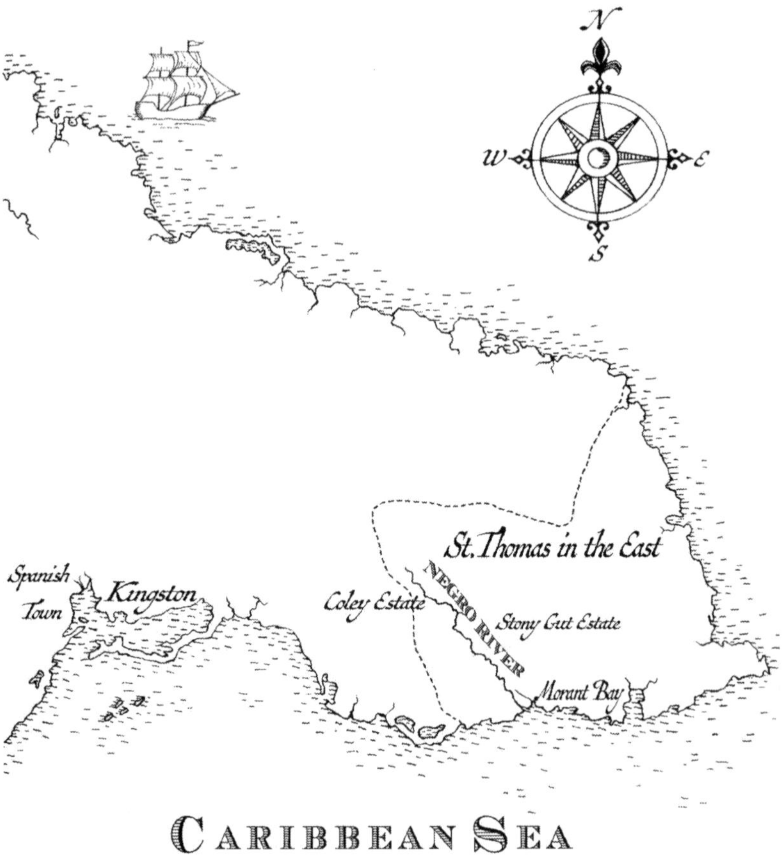

Shaded area shows St. Thomas in the East

THE FRASERS

HUGH FRASER* - SOPHIA MCPHERSON*
Children: Jane Fraser*
JOHN FRASER
Mary Fraser*
Donald Fraser*
Alexander Fraser
Margaret Fraser
Hugh Fraser
Sophia Fraser
Ann Fraser

JOHN FRASER – Jannet Murray(1)
Children: Hugh Fraser

JOHN FRASER – CATHERINE FRASER ROSS*(2)
Children: Marron Fraser
Sophia Fraser
David Fraser
Alexander Fraser
Walter Fraser
Jannet Fraser
EDWARD SMITH FRASER
John McPherson Fraser

JOHN FRASER – Elizabeth Matheson(3)

EDWARD SMITH FRASER – ELIZABETH BISHOP
Children: Edward C. Fraser
Mary Fraser
ELIZABETH ANN FRASER (ANNIE)
Alexander Fraser

ELIZABETH ANN FRASER (ANNIE) – DUNCAN ROSS
Children: William Henry Ross

LOUISA ROSS (LOUISE)
Roderick McGregor Ross
Richard Ross
Isabella Ross
Josephine Ross (Josie)

OTHER PROMINENT CHARACTERS

Donald McPherson, Sophia's father (fictional)
John Ross, Agent of the Philadelphia Company*
Rev. Malcolm Nicolson, Minister of Kiltarlity Parish
Hugh and Christina MacLeod*
John Patterson, Perthshire Merchant*
John Speirs, Captain of the *Hector**
Walter and Christy Murray*
Samuel and Martha Blair and family (fictional)
Rev. James MacGregor
Richard Lane, Overseer Stony Gut Estate (fictional)
Thomas Howe, Bookkeeper Stony Gut Estate (fictional)
Rev. W. Stearns, Island Curate, Trinity District Church
John Eccles Ward, Doctor, Executor of Edward Fraser's Will
Louisa Fraser, cousin of Annie Fraser

*Came to Pictou, Nova Scotia aboard the *Hector* in 1773

UPPER CASE indicates direct ancestor of author Ann Louise Stevens

The Eastern Chronicle

New Glasgow, Nova Scotia
September 6, 1888

PERSONALS

Mrs. Duncan Ross, and daughter, Josie, left here on Saturday last, to visit her brother, Mr. Edward Fraser in Boston. It is over 30 years since Mrs. Ross and her brother saw each other.

Prologue

Boston, Monday, September 3, 1888

I did not seek this reunion. I did not want to see him again and relive all the pain of the past. This was the brother who had abandoned me when I was a child, even as he had promised to be with me always. A promise he had made to Mama and Papa. A promise he had broken. But this was the same brother whom I had once adored, the one who had looked after me, who had protected me when we left Jamaica. The same brother who had comforted me and loved me when we first arrived in Nova Scotia.

When his letter arrived, asking me to visit him, it suggested failing health and the need to right the wrongs of the past. He promised, finally, to share our story, our family secret, the reason why I never saw Mama again, why she never came to Nova Scotia. And Papa's story, too. I knew then that, despite some reservations, I had to go. This could be my last chance to find out. To learn the truth about my family.

And now I was standing at the ship's railing, with my daughter Josie at my side. I recognized Edward right away, there on the wharf. His brown curls were streaked with grey, but less so than mine, I noticed with a touch of envy. His face was not the Edward's that I remembered. It was heavily lined: creases of age, of sorrow, or both? But it was his eyes that gave him away.

When he looked up and recognized me, the love in them took me back to my childhood. He smiled and waved. I smiled in return as Josie pulled at my arm.

"Is that him, is that Uncle Edward? The man who is waving?"

"Yes, that's him. Let's go back to our cabin and gather our bags." I drew her away from the railing.

When we disembarked, Edward came forward and hugged me warmly. I responded, with just a little reticence.

"I am so happy that you agreed to come," he said. Beside him, his wife, Ellen, smiled and then turned her attention to Josie.

The rest of that day passed in a blur. During the carriage ride, Josie kept up a stream of high-spirited chatter, and I was grateful for the distraction, a chance to collect my thoughts. We arrived at Edward's home, one in a series of row houses, with a small well-manicured front yard. There we were greeted by Edward's grown children, Ima and Howard.

That evening, after a cheerful family dinner, we retired to the front parlour. An exhausted Josie fell asleep not long after, sprawled across my lap. I put her to bed and then returned to the parlour to find it quiet and dimly lit. Edward alone remained. Two candles burned on a side table. The only sound was the ticking of the grandfather clock in the hallway.

"Ellen has gone to bed," said Edward. "She's been very busy these last few days preparing for your arrival and she knows we need time to ourselves."

"She is so kind, so thoughtful," I murmured, as I took the chair opposite him.

We sat in silence for a few moments, not sure how to begin, how to bridge the decades of hurt and misunderstanding.

Then Edward leaned forward and said earnestly, "I never wanted to leave you in New Glasgow, Annie, but I had no choice! You must believe that! Uncle Alex wanted me gone."

"I know that now," I replied slowly, "but I didn't understand then. I was only eleven when you left. I felt abandoned, first by Papa, then by Mama, and then by you. I had lost my whole family. And you had broken your promise to stay with me."

"I know, Annie. All I can say is how sorry I am. I know it must have been very hard for you. But in your letters I sensed contentment or at least acceptance. And when you visited me, when you were about fifteen, if I remember correctly, you seemed happy enough and no longer asked about Mama. So I tried to forget about the broken promises to you and to Mama and Papa, and the lies I had to tell for so many years. You see, Annie, I did know, even before we left Jamaica, that Mama would never come."

"Oh, Edward! You knew?"

"Yes, Annie. I knew, but Mama and Papa made me promise to keep this from you. You were too young to understand when we left."

His voice broke then, and he looked away. When he looked back at me, I saw his tear-streaked face.

"I have longed to share this with you," he continued slowly. "You deserve to know the truth. I believe that Mama and Papa would want you to know."

I nodded but could not speak. My heart had started to pound. Suddenly I was afraid of the very truth I had waited so long to hear.

"Papa also wanted me to tell you about our family, to tell the story of the Frasers. He told me to tell you when you were much older. I think you're old enough now."

He smiled then, as if this joke could ease the tension, but I just nodded, willing him to go on.

"The story of the Frasers was very important to Papa. He wanted us to know who our ancestors were and to tell their story to our children." Edward looked over at a desk by the window. "I have something for you, something that Papa gave me, a piece of Fraser history, but that will come later. First, our story. It began over a hundred years ago."

He looked over at the desk again, as if seeking inspiration. When he began to speak, his voice was wistful.

"I remember sitting on our verandah in Jamaica, one hot summer evening. Papa was lying on a cot under a mosquito net. All around us was the hum of thousands of insects. Do you remember that sound, Annie?"

I nodded wordlessly, afraid to break the spell, as the long-forgotten Jamaican night seeped into the room. As long as I live, I shall never forget that sound.

Edward continued. "Papa's voice was low and weak. I realized later that he knew he was dying. He started by telling me how close he was to his grandfather Hugh back in Nova Scotia, how he was closer to him than anyone else. He said the family story started with Hugh and his wife, Sophia, our great-grandmother. Papa said he never knew her; Sophia had died before he was born. Their story began in the Highlands of Scotland in 1773. It was a time of terrible hardship. Hugh was only thirty-two when he had to make the biggest decision of his life."

Part One

1773 – 1779

Chapter One

It was a clear night with just a breath of wind, but bitterly cold nonetheless. Hugh Fraser wound his cloak tightly about himself as he stepped out of the kirk. He murmured farewells to the other men as they moved silently past him, anxious to get to the warmth of their own hearths. Hugh stopped and looked up. And the stars held him: tiny, bright beacons in a calm sky, such a change from the howling winds and raging snows that had torn across the land for days on end. Until tonight.

"Please be a sign," he muttered to the heavens, "that our voice will be heard, that change will come."

Behind him the heavy door of the kirk banged shut and he turned to face Reverend Malcolm Nicolson, minister of Kiltarlity Parish.

Nicolson smiled at him. "Away home, Fraser, too cold to tarry," he said, then turned without waiting for a reply and hurried to the manse nearby.

But still Hugh did not move. It was more than the gift of a quiet night and starlight that held him. It was the need to organize his thoughts. He must decide what to say to Sophia, how to convey the results of this meeting and his fears for their future. Nervously, he ran his fingers through his thick brown beard.

He took a deep breath and strode purposefully up the

winding path that rose from the glen toward the farmhouses perched on the hill over-looking Belladrum Burn.

He passed half a dozen or so cottages, longhouses of fieldstone like his own. Each was a glowing taper in a dark landscape. The fires inside provided the glow, and through the opening at the top of each thatched roof spirals of smoke escaped to the night sky. He looked beyond them. Thanks to the starlight, he could see the smudgy outline of the distant treetops along the crest of the hill.

It took him another twenty minutes to reach the collection of dwellings that made up Foxhole Farm. He welcomed the time to think about what he had heard at the meeting. More than anything, the crisis was forcing him to think of this land, his home, in a way he had never done before. Although he had travelled very little outside the Aird, he had seen nothing that matched its beauty. And it was common knowledge that these gentle rolling hills were perhaps some of the most fertile in all of the Scottish Highlands. Inverness, the Highland capital, was only fifteen miles to the northeast. As a young boy, Hugh had once accompanied his father to the great town. And conveniently close by was the market town of Beauly, at the head of the Beauly Firth, where Hugh had attended the weaving school.

This ancestral land of the Lovat Frasers was the only home that generations of his family had ever known. Could he be forced to leave? Surely never!

He reached a level area just below the crest of the hillside, where there was a cluster of three rectangular stone cottages. Hugh's younger brother William and his family lived in one, and their father lived in the largest, along with Hugh's two unmarried sisters. In addition, all three households included an assortment of youthful servants: household and field help. As tenant farmers, the Frasers of Foxhole were poor, but there were many truly destitute who hired out their children through necessity.

As he came through the door, he almost bumped into his

eldest, eleven-year-old Jane, who was attempting to wrestle a bonnet out of the hands of her younger sister, Mary.

Startled, Mary looked up at her father, and the momentary distraction allowed Jane to pluck the bonnet from her grasp. With a flourish, Jane presented it to her mother, who was sitting by the fire.

"She put it on one of the sheep outside!" announced Jane. "And tied it on tight so it wouldn't fall off!"

"Oh, Mary, what were you thinking?" demanded Sophia in frustration at her ginger-haired daughter, who was now glaring at her older sister. Then to Jane she said, "Put the bonnet on the trunk, dearie."

The youngest, Donald, an eighteen-month-old, sat in the lap of Margaret, a young helper, sucking his thumb. He didn't look up at Hugh.

Nor did six-year-old John, who was stacking bricks of peat by the fire. But Hugh heard him mutter, "Silly girls."

At that moment, James came through the door. "Shall I bring the animals in now, sir?"

Hugh nodded, then said, "Aye, and pull out the pallets now for the night, will you, James?"

The twelve-year-old moved quickly to do his master's bidding. A good lad and a good worker that, thought Hugh. And a good example to young John.

"Come away to the fire now, Hugh," said Sophia as she motioned him to his chair. Her eyes met his with a question in them.

He sat down, stretched his hands towards the warmth and said quietly, "We will speak when the children are asleep." It pained Hugh to look directly into his wife's eyes. Once a striking blue, now they seemed washed of all colour. Her light brown hair hung limply around a pale, tired face.

It had been a hard winter for all of them, but Sophia had suffered the most. Only months ago, she had been expecting another child, but it had come much too soon and the child had died. She looked older than her thirty-one years.

As Hugh studied the faces of his children around the fire, he knew they were all hungry. They had taken a meagre meal together before he had left for the kirk. There was some buttermilk, some bannocks of oats mixed with water, and the usual potatoes.

And they were amongst the more fortunate of Kiltarlity, thanks to the modest income he made from his weaving. Hugh prayed they had enough food to last until spring, until he could get some buyers for his weaving or some commissions.

After the children and servants were settled on their pallets, Hugh and Sophia moved to the other side of the fire. Sophia took their sturdiest chair and, with a candle at her elbow, took up John's trousers to mend.

"He is outgrowing these, too," she murmured, without looking up. "He will be tall like you."

They sat in silence for a time, Hugh staring into the fire, Sophia focused on her mending.

The earthen floor of the cottage was crowded with a scattering of stools and chairs, a trunk, a bench, a table and a wooden bed frame for the parents. Over the fire, a large cooking pot hung suspended from a crook. Sitting along the length of one wall, Hugh's large hand loom dominated the room. The area close to the fire was cozy in the dead of winter, in a dwelling that was cold and damp even in the finest of weather. There was more space at the back of the cottage, separated only by a woven screen. This was where the animals were housed in the cold of winter.

"Most signed," Hugh began. "Only two did not. Perhaps they had no wish to offend. But for me there was no choice." He sighed and stared into the fire.

"What did the petition say?" asked Sophia hesitantly.

"It is humbly put. It says we can't endure yet another increase of the rents. It pleads with their Lordships to reduce our rents, to understand that we have lived on credit till there is no more. It says that unless the rents are lowered, many of us will be forced to leave our land, to quit the only home we have ever known—" he stopped, his voice unsteady.

Sophia rose and put an arm around his broad slumping shoulders. "No, Hugh, surely it would never come to that?" she whispered.

He looked up at her. "I fear it could. We can't go on much longer. Savage winters, harvests drowned in rain, rents that rise and rise again. Can you remember a time when we believed our young might have a better life than ours? This land has become accursed."

"Hugh! You can't say that!" Sophia was frightened now. "That is blasphemy!"

He stood up and put his arms around her. "May the Lord forgive me. But I must be harsh, my love, to warn you. There's no future here. As you know, many have left already to find a better place than this. We *must* think of it. For the sake of the children, if not for us."

She broke away from him, trembling. "How can you think I could ever leave my home, my family! Everything I hold dear! And where would we go?" His heart sank at her defiant tone.

"Many are taking ship for the Americas," he replied. "We could have land of our own there."

"I have heard talk of the Americas," said Sophia angrily, "a place full of savages and wild animals. You would wish to take us there?"

"My love, you can't believe all you hear. They are tales told by those who have never been to such places."

"My point exactly!" cried Sophia. "They are lands unknown to everyone! How can you consider taking us to such places, to risk our very lives?"

"But, Sophia, it's a risk to remain here. We would have a better life there."

"Would!" spat Sophia, and then turned away from him. He waited. The peat fire crackled, as she turned back to face him. The set of her jaw and the anger in her eyes took him aback.

"No," she said flatly. "I will never leave my home and my family. Never!"

"And I promise I will never make you do something you can't abide." He held out his arms. "Come here, my love."

She went to him reluctantly, and he felt the tension in her body.

"Don't worry." He smiled down at her. "Perhaps the petition will be acted upon. Most in Kilmorack and Beauly have signed, too. Reverend Nicolson says one hundred and seventy-six tenants in all have signed. He and Reverend Fraser of Kilmorack have written a piece to support our plea. With their backing and such a grand sum of signatures, perhaps we shall have a favourable reply."

Sophia said nothing. She simply sat down again and resumed her sewing. Hugh sat down and stared morosely into the fire. He had sought only to reassure her. He did not believe his own words. History had taught him otherwise.

The past. The disaster at Culloden Moor, near Inverness, almost thirty years earlier, had changed life in the Highlands forever. The battle there had been the last attempt of the Jacobites to overthrow the English king, and restore the House of Stuart to the throne, in the person of Bonnie Prince Charlie. In 1746, the rebel Jacobites, many of whom were Highlanders, were soundly defeated by troops loyal to the Crown. Afterwards, the government wished to punish those who had risen against the King, but all Highlanders suffered, even those who had taken no part in the rebellion. Suspicious of wild Highlanders and their Gaelic culture, the Crown sought to destroy the clan system. Everything of value to a Highlander's way of life was stripped away: his tartan dress, his clan chiefs, even the playing of the pipes.

Life on the land became precarious. Each year saw ever-higher rents on land divided and subdivided, again and again.

And the short-term leases held by the tenant farmers

could be cancelled at any moment. Harsh winters and frequent famines rendered life a miserable struggle for mere existence, and Hugh saw nothing to change that pattern, a way of life he had known since childhood. His own father, John, like the rest of his neighbours on the Belladrum Estates, were tenants of the clan chief, Simon Lord Fraser. His Lordship had joined the rebellion and, as a result, all of his lands had been forfeited to the Crown and were now administered by the Board of Forfeited Estates. As a weaver, Hugh was a skilled craftsman, but the poverty of all meant few buyers and fewer commissions for his work. Like all tenants, he and his family struggled to grow what food they could and feed their few animals. Hugh feared that the petition for redress was the final act. If the rent burden was not lifted, there was only one choice open to them. To leave.

Chapter Two

February brought no change. Frequent snowstorms and bitter winds kept the Frasers confined indoors for much of the time. Their clothing, hair and skin became thoroughly soot-blackened and their eyes were continually irritated by the smoke from the fire.

On days when the winds calmed and the snow stopped, Hugh organized the children and servants in fighting the ravages of winter. He, John and James used plaited straw ropes weighted down with stones to keep the thatched roof intact. Jane, Mary and Margaret were tasked with running hands along the cold stone walls and stuffing the cracks with mud. Mary did as little as possible and complained constantly.

"I'm tired," she whined one day, "I can't reach high enough anyway."

"Margaret and I will check the higher walls, you check all the lower walls," said Jane wearily, then raised her voice. "Don't sit down! You have not done all four walls yet!"

Jane looked over at her mother, who was checking their store of food. Sophia looked up in irritation. "Mary! We must all do our share! Now, stop whining and keep at it!"

Mary pouted and folded her arms across her small chest, but moved away quickly as Sophia turned and glared at her. She shook her fist at Mary, who retreated to a corner and hid behind Margaret.

"It's enough that I must worry about how little we have left to eat," cried Sophia, "I will not listen to your mewling, too! Are you trying to drive me mad, lassie!"

Hugh had heard Sophia's raised voice from outside and came through the door. He saw Mary clinging to a stunned Margaret, and a white-faced Jane. He motioned for the girls to leave, and they melted through the door quickly.

"Sit by the fire, my love," he said quietly. He sat beside her and rubbed her back. Finally he felt her body relax. She leaned against him.

"Mary is a minx and a trial for any mother, but I should not have lost my temper so," she said. "She's only four, after all."

"You're tired and worried. This winter has been especially harsh, for you most of all. Don't blame yourself." He cupped her chin in his hand and smiled at her. "I do not. And Mary needs a wee scare now and then."

It was a subdued group who huddled around the fire after supper. The night was still, with almost no wind. Hugh could see that Sophia's outburst had cast a pall that still lingered.

He watched Jane and Margaret cast nervous glances over at Sophia, who seemed absorbed in her sewing. John and James seemed relaxed enough, but they were normally quiet lads. Mary sat very still and seemed to be humming. Hugh decided to break the silence.

"Mary, what are you singing?"

Mary stopped and looked up at her father in surprise.

"She's humming the cradle lullaby," Sophia said, and she smiled at her younger daughter. "Don't stop, my wee minx." Then she began to sing softly and soon they all joined in, even James. Only John did not.

Hugh closed his eyes and allowed the warmth from the fire and the soothing lullaby to fill him with contentment. He was blessed. This was home.

Sophia sang two more lullabies and then asked if they

wished for a tale. Hugh loved the reaction which was always an excited "Aye, please!" Sophia's mother had told them to her and her brothers and sisters. Now she passed along the same gift to her young.

"Once, long ago, in a faraway glen in the distant north," she began in a whisper, "there lived an old shepherd who was plagued by a water sprite."

Hugh sat back happily and let her words wash over him. He loved to study the children's faces as they listened to the tales.

Even Mary would devote her full attention to her mother at these times. She glanced into the corners of the room, as if the flickering shadows cast by her father's loom were part of the magic of her mother's tale. Jane, just as intent, would stare into the fire as if the characters were to be found there. Donald would cling to his mother's skirts, hiding his eyes from the dancing shadows that so excited Mary. Only John's eyes remained locked on his mother's face. And she, in turn, gazed at him.

There's a special bond between those two, Hugh thought.

Near the end of February, despite the threat of yet another storm, Hugh made his way to the kirk one dismal afternoon. He told Sophia where he was going and why. She said nothing.

This time he had company. His younger brother, William, was curious to hear what the guest speaker had to propose. They walked down the hillside cautiously, as the path was slippery with snow. Hugh wound his cloak more tightly about himself against the bitter wind. At the bottom of the hill, where the path levelled out, the going was easier, and they could walk abreast.

William spoke first. "Do you know this agent who is to speak?"

"Aye, a little. Father has heard of him. John Ross is a respected merchant from Loch Broom."

"I wonder if there will be many there to hear him," said William.

Hugh nodded. "I believe there will be a fair crowd and one open to the scheme. After all, Ross successfully conducted two hundred Scots to Boston for The Philadelphia Company just three years ago."

"But there's no guarantee that life will be better in the Americas," said William. "If only we knew what awaited us there..."

"There's far less guarantee that things will improve here," said Hugh. "There has been only silence from the Board about our petition. I'm not alone in believing that nothing will be done to lessen the rent burden."

"Well, if you ever did decide to go," said William, "and got word back that it was worth it, perhaps I would consider it and follow you."

Hugh bit his tongue. It had always been thus. William would take no step until a safe path had been cleared by his older brother or someone else.

Sensing his brother's feelings, William added quickly. "And you have an advantage, of course. I can do no more than farm. You have your weaver's skill to count on wherever you go."

He was silent for a moment and then added, "Mother was so proud of you. First in our family ever to learn a skill," he paused. "You know she favoured you."

Hugh did not answer, surprised by this turn in the conversation. Yet he knew there was some truth to it. Suddenly, he wondered if Sophia favoured John, just as his mother had favoured him.

"She fought for all her young equally, if you remember rightly," he said curtly, "especially when Father had had too much drink."

William stopped and looked directly at his brother. "Aye, perhaps, but if Mother were still alive, I know what she would say. 'If anyone could take on such a venture and make it a success, it would be Hugh. He has the heart and mind for it.'"

Hugh was taken aback and had no response. At that moment, they came within sight of a group of men on the path also making for the kirk, so fell in silently behind their neighbours. William's words had embarrassed him, but he had to admit that he felt somewhat flattered, too.

As he looked ahead and saw even more figures, he was pleased that his prediction was accurate. There would be a large assembly that afternoon. And as he entered the kirk, he felt trepidation but also a twinge of excitement.

A dark afternoon was becoming an inky, starless evening by the time the meeting ended. Hugh made for home on his own, as William had stopped to talk to his brother-in-law from Kilmorack way.

Hugh was impatient to share with Sophia the details of the meeting. It would be difficult. He would wait until the children were asleep.

Once the young were settled on their pallets, Sophia joined him by the fire, taking up her sewing. Outside, the wind had picked up again. The steadily rising howl seemed to mimic Hugh's mounting anxiety, as he struggled to find the right words. Would this be the start of another battle between them?

"Let me tell you of the meeting, my love," he began.

She did not look up.

"The speaker was John Ross, a highly respected merchant."

When Sophia shot him a sharp look, he added quickly, "The words of Reverend Nicolson, not me. Ross is an agent of The Philadelphia Company and he came to describe the Company's generous emigration offer. There was an advertisement in the Scottish papers about the scheme which he explained to us." Hugh stopped and waited.

"Go on," she said coolly.

"The offer is one hundred and fifty acres of free land and a year's free provisions in the colony of Nova Scotia. The price of ship's passage is modest; for berth and—" But Sophia cut him off.

"How do you know that they will honour those terms once we get there?" she demanded.

"There will be a signed contract."

"And what of the savages there—a contract doesn't matter when we are all dead before the year is up!" Her voice rose.

Hugh reached for her hand, but she pulled away from him and stood up. "I *cannot* believe this is my husband speaking. You would put your family in harm's way, take such a risk?"

"Sophia, I would never do that. But there is many a man from this entire area prepared to go. Even my own brother, even William may consider it." Hugh smiled. "And you know he's afraid of his own shadow."

"Jest all you like. It makes no difference. The children and I will remain here in our home. Go if you must!"

"Surely you can't mean that, Sophia. We go as a family or not at all."

"Then it's settled. Not at all."

"My love, I understand your fears, truly. But this is more than just an escape from hardship. It's a chance to gain something we have never had, never will have here. Our own land. Not leased, not rented. Ours."

"But at what risk, Hugh? I think you want this only for yourself." She stood there trembling, and it was the fear in her eyes that betrayed her feelings.

They faced each other for a few moments of dreadful silence, then Donald started to cry. Sophia went to her youngest to soothe him and did not return to the fireside. Hugh was stunned. He had made matters worse.

It was just a few days later that Sophia's father, Donald, arrived with a small sack of potatoes. "We have no need of these," he said.

Sophia did not believe him but accepted them gratefully. She pushed her father gently into their best chair and begged him to take a cup of buttermilk.

"No, dearie. Save it for the children."

He motioned for his namesake, Donald, to climb onto his lap and then asked, "Where are the others?"

"Hugh has gone up to the kirk, along with John and Jane, to help with small repairs. And Mary is outside with the sheep."

"Granddad!" Mary came racing in through the door. She leapt onto his lap, successfully dislodging Donald. After wrestling Mary's jacket and wet shoes off, Sophia watched with great tenderness as her father arranged both children, one on each knee, and soothed Donald's hurt feelings.

Her father was a compactly built man. His grey beard and full head of hair outlined a weathered face with laugh lines that seemed permanently fixed. His eyes were a deeper blue than his daughter's and those of his grandchildren, save Mary. His wife's death, a year ago, had devastated him. Aching joints and weak lungs plagued him, but he never complained and always arrived with a smile, a gift and a cheerful word. The children adored him, as did Sophia.

He took out two straw-woven figures from his jacket pocket and handed one to each child. "Yours," he said to Mary, "is a Queen, your namesake, of course, and yours, my wee laddie, is a water sprite."

Mary thanked him, and Donald beamed, then both slid off his lap onto the floor to play with their new toys.

"Now, my precious girl," he said, "sit down. We must speak. There is no talk but of the emigration scheme. Many are for it and have signed already. I know your Hugh will be considering it. If I were a younger man, with a wife and children, I would consider it, too."

"*You* would leave this land, you of all people!" cried Sophia. "I do not believe it!"

He took her hand and patted it. "Calm yourself, lass. We must speak of it. There's no future here for the young. Each year is worse than the one before. You can't stay. This emigration plan is the best chance for all of you."

"I can't believe my own father would give up and run away." She looked away from him.

"But it's not running away, it's going *to* something, something much more than you have here. It's not defeat."

He paused to regain his breath, then added grimly, "For thirty years we have been beaten down without mercy. Go to a place where you are laird of you own land, where you can wear the plaid and hear the pipes with pride!"

Mary and Donald had stopped playing when they heard the harsh tone in their grandfather's voice. Mary stared wide-eyed at her mother, while Donald drew close and grabbed her skirt, hiding his face in its folds.

"But I can't leave you, I can't—" Sophia began to weep.

He drew all three of them to him and held them tightly. Gently he said, "Know that I would go with you if my health allowed, truly. And then there are Margaret and Ellen, and young Donald's family, too. They need me still."

He began to cough and waited once again to regain his breath. "I believe you must go, for your own sakes, but for mine, too. I will miss you, but thank the Lord each day that you will be living a better life than this." He paused, then added, "Listen to your man. Talk to your sisters, too, hear what they say. Do it soon."

Ellen and Margaret arrived at the doorstep the very next day. Between them they lugged a bucket of goat's milk.

Hugh took it gratefully and, without a word, ushered them to the fire, where Sophia sat stirring a pot of oatmeal, with Donald at her feet.

She raised her eyebrows at her sisters. "Did Father send you?"

The younger of the two, Ellen, grinned and said playfully, "Oh no! I came to see my wee Mary."

Hugh smiled. "She is outside bothering the sheep, I fear. Your influence, no doubt."

Ellen laughed, "I can't deny it. She has my red hair and spirit to match!"

Margaret shot Ellen a disapproving look, then touched Sophia's arm, as she sat beside her. She was a taller, more angular version of Sophia, but... not nearly as bonny, thought Hugh.

"Father thinks you need to speak of this emigration scheme with us, your sisters, who know the fears and uncertainties you have as a woman." She glanced at Hugh as she said this.

He nodded. "Aye, I believe that's best. I was just on my way out..." He trailed off as he went through the door.

"I couldn't consider it as a woman alone," continued Margaret, "I'm too set in my ways, too fearful of unknown places, but if I were married and had the future of children to consider, perhaps I would think differently."

Sophia was surprised. Never would she have believed that staid Margaret would ever entertain thoughts of leaving.

Ellen broke the silence. "Well, I'm betrothed and must consider my future and those of children that might be, so David and I have spoken of it, of course."

"And what does David say?" asked Sophia eagerly.

"He doesn't wish to go... now. He shares a croft at Tenakyle with only one brother, so believes we could make a living there."

"So you will not go!" said Sophia, triumphantly.

"No, I didn't say that," said Ellen. "We won't consider it. Now. But we may... at a later time."

"At a later time!" cried Sophia, rising to her feet. "It's not real to you, it's like a tale I tell the little ones! Could you leave your home, your father, your family, and never see them again? Ever? Could you cross a great sea to a strange land full of savages and wild animals?"

Neither sister replied.

"I didn't think you could!" Abruptly Sophia stooped to pick Donald up from the floor and wrapped a blanket around them both. Without another word, she stalked out of the cottage with him. She left a stunned silence behind her.

Hugh had heard the door slam. He looked up to see Sophia striding off through the pasture, down toward the burn. She had Donald in her arms, but that did not slow her determined pace.

Hopeless, he thought, as he leaned against the door. She will never see the merits of emigration. My arguments have only driven us apart. Leaving Scotland would break Sophia's heart, but I know it's the right thing to do. He sighed and straightened his shoulders. But it's our only hope. Somehow I must convince her.

Chapter Three

Hugh trudged slowly home from Beauly. It was about four miles away, and he was tired after a long day of knocking on the doors of family, merchants and even the weaving school, in search of commissions for his work. All to no avail. A cousin, Kenneth, had offered him one of the fish he had caught that morning in the Beauly Firth, and Hugh was grateful. At least he could present Sophia with something for his efforts. It was almost sunset, and the track was not as muddy as it had been that morning. A stiff wind started blowing. It was surprisingly biting for spring, and he quickened his pace.

Expectant faces looked up as he came through the door, faces and hair now scrubbed of the black soot that had been like a winter skin for months on end.

"A fish for supper!" cried Mary and she jumped up to touch it, red curls bobbing against her pale face.

"Not tonight. For tomorrow," said Sophia as she took it from Hugh and wrapped it in a cloth. "Our supper is ready now."

Mary pouted, and everyone ignored her, except John, who shot her a disdainful look. Hugh noticed it and resolved to talk to Sophia that evening. He had avoided any sensitive subject for months now, but John was becoming too full of himself.

After supper Sophia told Jane and John to go to the well.

John smiled at his mother, "I can go on my own, Mother."

"No," said Hugh. "You'll need your sister's help. The full bucket will be heavy."

"But Jane is just a girl, not as strong as me. I will go on my own or with James."

"Don't argue with me!" said Hugh angrily. "James is busy. Go with your sister. Do as you are told!"

John looked up at his mother in surprise, but picked up the bucket by the door and walked out, with Jane dutifully following.

"That was a bit harsh, Hugh," said Sophia.

"I don't think so, and we will talk of it later," said Hugh, nodding toward Mary who was staring at them.

Later by the fire, the children were falling asleep before Sophia had finished her first tale. "Time spent in the spring air has worked like a tonic for them," she murmured.

They carried the two youngest to their pallets, and Jane slipped drowsily under the blanket with Mary, while John went to his own bed. Then Hugh and Sophia settled themselves in their respective chairs by the fire. She took up her sewing.

"What is it you wish to talk about, Hugh?" Sophia asked guardedly.

"I'm concerned about John's attitude toward his sisters and brother, especially his sisters," Hugh began. "He shows some arrogance, I fear. He thinks he's better than they are." He studied Sophia's face. "Do you not see it?"

"Arrogance?" repeated Sophia. "I don't see that. He's just a boy finding his way. He's only six, for pity's sake."

"I wonder," began Hugh, choosing his words carefully, "if you favour him a little and he feels... better than his brother and sisters."

"I favour all my young equally!" cried Sophia hotly.

Hugh looked toward the sleeping children. "Hush, my love, a little softer."

Sophia looked up at him. "Where has this come from, Hugh?" she whispered.

"My mother favoured me over my brothers and sisters, and they felt it," he said.

Sophia looked surprised. "Did William tell you this?"

"Aye, and I had never thought of it. Perhaps that's why we have never been close. I don't want that to happen to our young."

He was silent for a time and then added, "Please, just consider my words, Sophia. That's all I ask."

She nodded. "I don't agree," she said firmly, "but I will think on it."

He didn't press the issue. He was more concerned about her feelings after the visit of Ellen and Margaret, which had so angered and upset her. He hadn't seen the two sisters again in the cottage, and Sophia didn't speak of them.

For several months now, Sophia had been moody and quick to anger. Their painful quarrels about emigration were only the most recent upset. He was sure that the loss of the baby in the autumn troubled her still. He loved her so and knew that she loved him, too. And yet she always seemed on the verge of erupting angrily. He prayed that with winter's end her grieving for the loss might be over. Perhaps then she might be healed enough to listen to reason, to consider more calmly the emigration question.

As April turned to May, winter loosened its grip. The wind that blew down the glen did not bite as it once had. The sunshine was still weak, but seemed to linger. The children were happier in the warmer weather. But a dwindling food supply overshadowed the promise of spring for Hugh and Sophia.

After yet another trip into Beauly, Hugh returned one afternoon to find Sophia alone in the cottage.

"All gone, even Donald?" he exclaimed in surprise.

"Aye, Father fetched them all to see his new lambs. Jane is minding the wee one there." She pointed to the bannocks by the fire. "I've made good use of my time." Then she looked at him and smiled.

He kissed the top of her head. "That's a marvellous sight to see," he said, "a smile on my wife's lips." Then he bent to kiss them, too.

"Don't get carried away," she laughed and pushed him away.

"And laughing, too. My prayers have been answered." He guided her to her chair and took the one beside it. Gently, he took her hands and pressed them to his lips.

"Dearest Sophia, I have missed your smiles so much... and your love. I know losing the babe was terrible for you. And I know how much the talk of emigration has upset you."

"Hugh, I have missed you, too, especially our time by the evening fire. But I'm still angry with you, forcing me to accept leaving as the only answer. You say that if we stay our children may die of starvation. But they may just as easily perish at sea or in the wilderness over there."

"Sophia, we have no choice. I can't sell my weaving or barter it for seed. Our animals are too weak to produce much. We can't plant a crop for next year. We could even starve before the year is out."

"There must be another way, Hugh. Perhaps move to another farm? We could send James and Margaret away. We could hire Jane out—"

"No, Sophia! Listen to yourself. You could never send Jane away. Your fears are mine, too. I can't leave my homeland lightly. I fear the journey, but I fear remaining here more. There's no choice. You say we might perish if we go. But I fear we'll perish if we stay."

"Dear Lord, how has it come to this?" Sighing deeply, she covered her face.

Hugh judged it best to be close, but to let her be. They sat like this for a long while in the quiet of the empty cottage. The baaing of sheep was a weak, distant sound.

Eventually Sophia sat up. She pushed stray hair away from her face and smoothed her dress. He was relieved to see her eyes clear and dry.

"I had a visitor today," she said in a steady voice, "my cousin Mary. You know Mary McIntyre, from Beauly way?"

"Aye."

"She and James are thinking of going. She came to talk to me about it."

"What did she say?"

"We talked of our children. We spoke of our love, our fears, our hopes for them. She said what you have said, what my father has said, what my sisters have said. For our children there's only one choice: to leave."

She looked down at her hands, and this time her voice was unsteady. "And we spoke of the babe I lost. I told her what I have never told you. Even in the worst of my grief, I kept thinking, it was for the best, because how could we feed another mouth? I hated myself for such a blasphemous thought."

Hugh moved closer and put an arm around her shoulders. He squeezed them gently but said nothing.

After a few moments Sophia sat up straight. He saw a familiar look of determination in her face. "Cousin Mary has given me confidence," she said softly. "She feels as I do, she wants to put her children first. For them I must be strong."

Then she locked her eyes on his, and her gaze was steady. In a firmer voice, she said, "But mark my words, Hugh Fraser, *you* are accountable to this family. This is your choice, not mine."

She took a deep breath and said more gently, "Hugh, you're a kind man, a good husband and father. Despite everything, I love you so. If you believe we should emigrate, we will go."

He could not answer right away. He held her tightly,

fighting to control his emotions so that he could reply in a steady voice.

"You will not regret it, I promise you, my love. I will make a far better life for us in the new world, you will see!" Laughing, he lifted her off her feet and twirled her around.

"Come to your senses, man, and put me down!" But she was laughing, too.

He set her down gently and sat beside her. "Let me tell you what I heard at the meeting in Beauly today," he began excitedly. "John Ross, you know the agent I spoke of, said that there are already close to two hundred committed passengers for the *Hector*, the brig that will carry the new colonists to Nova Scotia. Many in this area have signed on to go, as you know, as well as some from much farther north, from Sutherland and Loch Broom. According to Ross, the ship will soon be filled."

He stopped then and took both of her hands deliberately in his. "Now is the time to make a decision, my love." He looked directly into her eyes and said slowly and very softly, "Are you sure?"

Sophia held his gaze and lifted her chin. That familiar cocky pose almost made him grin.

"Aye, I am ready to commit to this scheme," she said firmly. "I will put my faith in you and in the counsel of my father and sisters. And my cousin, too." She smiled. "But I will hold you to your promise of a better life, Hugh Fraser. Don't you forget it."

And so Hugh went to Reverend Nicolson to tell him of their decision, to ask his blessing and to send word to John Ross that they wished to enrol in The Company's scheme.

After that, events moved swiftly. There were animals and a loom to sell, their tenancy to surrender, family to see and belongings to sort and pack. There were preparations to make for the journey to the embarkation point of Loch Broom, fifty miles away. They would carry little with them on the trek north. It would be made on foot.

They were leaving an old life behind; they hoped to find most of what they needed in their new home. But Hugh reverently withdrew the Fraser plaid from its hiding place and bundled it for the journey. It would accompany them, along with a few items of special value: Sophia's wedding shawl and the quilt made by Hugh's mother many years ago.

Mary was excited about the plan and asked questions constantly. When would they leave? What was the sea like? What animals would they have there? Jane, who was anxious about any change, kept her feelings to herself. And Donald was simply confused by all the fuss.

However, six-year-old John's reaction was dramatic.

"I won't go! I want to go to school with cousin Alex! You can't make me go!"

His tears and his anger surprised Sophia. Her stoic boy never cried. "Oh John, you will like it there. You will go to school and make many new friends, I promise. Your cousin James McIntyre is going too." She hugged him tightly. "And we'll be together. That's most important of all."

She looked at Hugh for support, and he repeated much of what she had said. But he knew that it was more for her benefit than John's. Sophia's words were the ones that would sway John. Or not.

Hugh could see that Sophia was upset by John's outburst, but was relieved that her resolve did not falter. John did not voice his feelings again, but became sulky and irritable. He is much like his mother, thought Hugh.

He watched as Sophia forced herself to concentrate on the work at hand. He knew she was determined to avoid thinking of what the future held and especially of how she would face leaving her father. Together she and Hugh visited Donald's cottage to plead with him to reconsider accompanying them. But he was adamant.

"I will miss you all so, but I'm too old to go. Sixty-four is too great an age to be sailing across the seas. I would be a burden, and these old bones could not take it. I hear the winters in Nova Scotia are worse than ours. No, I am better here in my croft, with Margaret to look after me."

Sophia got down on her knees beside his chair and gripped his arm. "Father, I can't imagine leaving you. Please, please, give it more thought, I beg you. There's still time to change your mind and come with us."

Donald looked into her desperate eyes and shook his head sadly. "Please, dearie, don't do this to yourself. I can't come with you. I've lived too long. I'm a Highlander and will spend what time I have left in sight of these hills."

He looked to Hugh for support, and Hugh moved quickly to Sophia to help her to her feet. "Come away, my love. Your father is tired and we must get back ourselves."

He nodded to Margaret, who had stood off in a corner, twisting her hands nervously, unwilling to meet his eye. He led a tearful Sophia through the door and out into a sunny afternoon.

At the end of June, word reached Kiltarlity that the *Hector* had sailed from Greenock with about a dozen Lowlanders aboard and was making its way north, up the west coast, to Loch Broom.

It was time to make immediate preparations for their journey. Hugh had delayed their departure to give Sophia as much time as possible with her father. They could delay no longer.

Hugh sought out Reverend Nicolson. The minister had offered to furnish him with a letter of recommendation so that authorities in the new land would recognize the bearer as a highly respected man.

Then disaster struck.

Chapter Four

John had been listless and without appetite for several days, but both Hugh and Sophia had assumed it was his unhappiness about leaving. Preoccupied with preparations for the journey, they had given his malaise barely a passing thought and John had complained to no one of his nausea and backache.

But he collapsed one morning as he brought in a water bucket from the burn, and Sophia rushed to his side as he attempted to rise, only to fall back, too dizzy to stand.

As she gathered him close to her, she was horrified by his hot skin and flushed face. His body trembled and he groaned.

"Mama, I'm so cold," he whispered.

She wrapped him in a blanket and sat with him by the fire, cradling his head on her lap.

"Jane, a cup of water for your brother."

Jane had been afraid of what she had just seen but now sprang to life, relieved to have something to do. She brought a cup of water from the bucket by the door.

Holding the cup to John's lips, Sophia coaxed him to take a few sips. Then she looked up. "Now run to find your father, Jane. I think he's in the far pasture with Uncle William."

To John she spoke softly, soothingly, trying to keep the panic out of her voice. "There, my pet, rest. You've been working too hard."

When Hugh arrived, he registered the terror on her face right away.

"Hugh! He's burning hot!" she cried.

They stared helplessly at each other, their thoughts the same. They had to leave within a day or two to face an arduous journey. How could John endure such a trip in this condition? He was too big to carry.

And what *was* his condition? They struggled to blot out the awful possibility that first came to mind. Smallpox was the greatest nightmare for all Highlanders, the scourge that carried off so many of the young. If indeed it was smallpox, the spots would appear soon.

"Please, dear Lord, no," Hugh heard Sophia whisper as she held her boy tightly to her. He stood by, helpless, his mind numb.

They didn't have long to wait. The spots appeared the very next evening, with his fever still high. The other children were kept away; in fact, Sophia demanded that Hugh keep his distance too. She insisted that she alone would nurse John.

The following day her father arrived with a tonic to ease John's fever and some of Margaret's bannocks for the rest of the family. He spoke gently to his daughter and grandson, then moved to where Hugh was standing. They conferred quietly for some time. Then the older man made ready to go, kissing the heads of Jane, Mary and Donald in turn.

"I'm away, dearie," he called to Sophia. "The Lord keep wee John and all of you. Listen to what your man has to tell you." Then, with a wave in her direction, he was gone.

When the other children fell asleep, Hugh moved close to the fire, careful to keep his distance from Sophia and John. They sat in silence, as Sophia gently caressed her son's forehead.

When John eventually drifted off to sleep, Hugh spoke softly. "We must speak now of what to do. Your father has offered to take John when we leave. He and Margaret will nurse him back to health. He gave me his word that he would send John to us or bring him, himself, at a later time. You know John is too ill to travel and he would never be allowed on board. We have no choice, as you know."

Sophia's eyes blazed. "I don't believe what I'm hearing!" she hissed at him. "You can't think I would leave my son now, even in my father's keeping! He could die!"

Hugh shook his head. "Sophia, we have no choice. We must leave him here. He will be well cared for. We have a few days only, at the very most, before we must start our journey north. It may take John weeks to recover. By then, the ship will have left without us."

"Then I must stay behind. We all must!" She was shaking now.

"We can't," he pleaded. "We have no home here anymore. Roderick and his family will move in here soon, to take over the tenancy. We've sold our animals. We have no seed for next year. And I have sold my loom. We've nothing left. I've paid our passages on the ship. Please, my love, you must understand this."

Sophia shook her head. "Oh, Hugh," she wailed, "you ask too much, to leave my boy behind. I can't do it." Then she looked up at him, sharply, "Perhaps you can do it. After all, you think he's an arrogant child."

That remark struck like a blow and stunned him for a time. Silently he looked down at his sleeping son. Surely she didn't know what she was saying.

He said softly. "I promise you, it will break my heart, too, to leave my boy. But I'm thinking of him, as well as our other three. Our one chance for a better life is now. Only now. We must take it, for the sake of all of them. Please."

"Dear Lord, I can't bear this!" she cried, sobbing as she rocked her feverish boy back and forth in her arms.

Hugh stood up and hovered above them both indecisively, then turned away. He knew there was nothing more to be said. For now, he must let her be. He moved to their bed at the back and lay down. But he could not sleep. Everything had gone so terribly wrong.

The next morning Hugh walked down the path toward the kirk just after sunrise. Reverend Nicolson was waiting for him with the letter of recommendation.

"How is your lad?" he asked anxiously.

"His condition is unchanged," replied Hugh wearily. "My wife is distraught, but I see no choice but to leave. Her father will care for the boy. We put our faith in him and the Lord and trust that John will join us in Nova Scotia sometime later."

Reverend Nicolson put a hand on Hugh's shoulder. "Be strong, Hugh. Know that I'll watch over your lad and your wife's family. As painful as it is, you are taking the right path, the only one open to you."

He handed the letter to Hugh.

"There's no pleasure in saying farewell to a man such as yourself," he continued. "Too many good folk forced from this land, through no fault of their own."

Then he put out his hand. "Go with my blessings, Hugh Fraser, and may the Lord keep your family safe."

Hugh gripped the other man's hand. "My heartfelt thanks to you."

Nicolson's words had helped, and he walked home with some resolve restored. When he entered the cottage there was activity but no murmur of voices. All was quiet.

Sophia sat with John on her lap, bathing his face with a cloth. She did not look up. With the loom and much of the furniture gone, the cottage seemed larger. But it was a sad and empty place, he thought.

"His fever is less now," said Sophia tersely.

Hugh felt a stab of relief, but could tell by her voice that she was determined not to hint at improvement or hope. So he simply nodded.

He noticed that the spots he saw on John's face and hands had blossomed into pustules. Sophia had rarely left his side and had said nothing to Hugh and little to the other children.

Hugh supervised the children in bundling their remaining possessions: clothes, food, bowls, spoons, some small farm implements, their few toys and keepsakes. All was now ready for the morning. All the other families bound for Loch Broom had left days before. The Frasers had to depart the next day or risk arriving too late. The *Hector* would sail without them. Sophia's father arrived at dusk to spend their last night with them, as she had requested.

During the night, Hugh watched as Sophia and her father whispered together. Finally Donald settled by the fire and closed his eyes.

With John sleeping in her lap, Sophia gently snipped a lock of his hair, tied it with a bit of string and tucked it into her bodice. Only after he saw Sophia lie down and fall into a restless sleep did Hugh allow himself to relax.

He had barely drifted off, when the children stirred with the sunrise. It was a calm, warm morning with the promise of sun. Silently Jane prepared the breakfast, while Hugh gathered the bags and bundles by the door. Uncharacteristically subdued, Mary sat by the fire holding wee Donald's hand. Both watched their mother minister to John. They ate the meal in silence.

When Sophia spoke she addressed her father. "His fever is less this morning. Give him sips of water often and bathe his brow when you do. See if he will take some broth tomorrow. Margaret will be in soon. Please move him to your cottage only when he's fully recovered, no matter what cousin Roderick may say. And tell John his mother left because she had no choice, but will see him soon, she promises that with all her heart." Her voice shook at these last words but she did not break down. Then she added, "Love him, Father, please love him for me."

She turned to her other children. "We have a long way to

go, so we should make a start. Kiss your Granddad goodbye. Say a prayer for your brother."

She held her sleeping son gently one more time, kissed his forehead, then said, "I'll be outside."

Carrying sacks and bags and strapped with bundles, they walked away from their home minutes later, Hugh carrying Donald.

The rising sun highlighted the green summer fields of early July and the gentle slopes dotted with sheep and cattle. They moved silently along the path down the hillside and along toward the bridge over Belladrum Burn. As they crossed, they heard the water gurgle below and birdsong in the nearby trees. None of them looked back.

Hugh welcomed the good weather for their journey, but he felt it was a torment, too, to see his home so achingly beautiful this one last time. He would never again witness glorious sunrises or watch the alternating play of light and shadow move over the hills. He would never again see his pastures glistening with frost, or misted with rain, or white with snow. With his free hand he reached into his jacket pocket and fingered the leather pouch there. It held a handful of soil. He had collected it the day before. He needed a keepsake of the land, of this precious place and the life he was giving up. He took a deep breath and withdrew his hand. But it is not *my* land and never will be he reminded himself. Pray God our new home is even half as lovely. He glanced at Sophia, but her face was a mask; he could read nothing there.

They made good time that first day. The track was well-established, the sun was warm and the slopes they climbed were gentle.

Each glen provided a burn for drinking water and an opportunity for Donald and Mary to paddle. They slept that first night in the open. Although the weather continued to hold, the following day was more difficult. Sophia's lack of sleep while nursing John had exhausted her.

Jane was an invaluable support, involving the young

ones in games, stories and songs, and sometimes carrying Donald. They stopped often. By the following day, the track was rougher and the hills steeper. In the distance they could see towering fir-clad peaks.

Over the next two days, as the terrain became rockier their pace slowed. Jane became too weary to entertain with songs and games and reacted angrily to Mary's whining. Hugh reprimanded them both, while Sophia remained silent.

It rained on the sixth day. The track became muddy and slick, adding to their woes. Mary's whines turned into a steady wailing. All save Donald had painful blisters on their feet, but even he cried intermittently in Hugh's arms.

As they rose from a brief rest around noon, Jane lost her footing and went down with a cry of pain.

"Are you hurt, dearie?" cried Sophia, crouching down beside her.

"My ankle," gasped Jane.

"Can you stand on it?"

"I... I think so."

Sophia helped Jane to her feet, as she tested her weight gingerly on her right side.

"She will need support," said Hugh. He looked at Sophia. "I'll help her walk, if you are able to carry Donald."

Sophia nodded and their eyes met. Hugh felt a stab of pain. He was asking so much of her. He turned away and hooked his arm securely around Jane's back to take the weight off her right side. They limped on slowly, following Sophia, Donald and Mary on the slippery track.

Hugh smiled down at his daughter, but his thoughts were uneasy. And he feared that Sophia was near the breaking point. He looked around at the rough, unfamiliar terrain. How much farther was it? Would they get there in time?

Chapter Five

Then a godsend.

He heard the creaking of a cart before he saw it through the rain on the track ahead. It was a family from Glen Urquhart, also making their way to Loch Broom and the *Hector*. James Grant, a miller, kindly allowed Jane, Mary and Donald space on the cart with his two youngest children, who were perched atop their possessions. Hugh, almost faint with relief, said a silent, fervent prayer of thanks.

A few hours later, with the rain still falling softly, they climbed a ridge and stopped at the summit. Below lay the long body of water known as Loch Broom, with slim bands of farmland hugging the shore. A fieldstone kirk stood on the flatlands at the head of the loch, surrounded by hills of summer green.

"The parish of Reverend James Robertson," announced Grant, adding, "He is a man much admired for both his physical and spiritual strength."

Hugh's relief was overwhelming. He looked over at Sophia, but her face was empty as she stared at the scene below. She had not said a word directly to him during the entire journey. Perhaps silence is her only means of keeping her feelings in check, he thought.

They made their way carefully down the steep incline.

There were makeshift shelters dotting the flatlands

around the kirk set up by the *Hector* passengers. With a soft rain still falling, Hugh and Grant quickly set about erecting their own shelters. As they did so, some local women approached and, with true Highland hospitality, offered the two families bowls of milk or whey.

The *Hector* was expected to arrive soon and, as all prospective passengers were likely present, Reverend Robertson held a service for them, to bless their journey and to offer communion. There were so many that he was forced to hold the service outdoors in the kirkyard as the rain continued to fall.

Afterwards, Hugh helped Sophia lay out a cold meal, then settled the two youngest in their shelter. They were asleep within minutes. Jane and Sophia lay down soon after. Hugh sat at the entrance to the shelter and gazed out at the temporary village and the loch beyond, the hours of daylight stretching long into the night at this time of year. Only a few fishing boats bobbed in the distance. Then he, too, settled down and found sleep.

Hugh was the first to wake next morning, as sunshine streamed onto his face through the shelter's opening. He looked out over the flats and bog onto the calm waters of the loch. Well out from the shore, a ship lay at anchor. It was a dark three-masted brig, with white trim along the black topsides and black gun ports painted above the water line. It had to be the *Hector*, their ship, their passage to Nova Scotia, to a new and better life.

He woke the girls, leading them outside to see this wonder, this thing that none of his children had ever seen before. Mary danced and clapped excitedly, but Jane was silent, her body tense. She moved back to stand with her mother, who had joined them with Donald on her hip. She, too, said nothing.

The Highlanders dismantled their shelters and waited patiently by the shore. Throughout the day, a small boat rowed back and forth between ship and shore, ferrying the passengers and their belongings out to the *Hector*. During the entire embarkation process, a Sutherland piper, John William MacKay, strode along the shore proudly playing the forbidden pipes. At dusk it was the turn of the Frasers and Grants to board, among the last to do so.

Once helped onto the deck, they followed a sailor who led them down a ladder into the hold. Hugh's spirits sank with each step, as the fresh sea air was replaced with an ever-strengthening fetid stink. He led the way down, helping the girls from below, then taking Donald from Sophia and carrying him the rest of the way. When their eyes adjusted to the gloom, they saw a cramped space filled with three-tiered bunks made of rough-hewn wood planks. There was little headroom available on each berth and just enough space to move sideways between the bed frames. The open hatchway provided the only light. The smells of salt water-soaked wood, tar, urine and old freight were overpowering. Overhead, a few fish oil lamps hung from the bulkheads and below were a number of covered wooden buckets.

Pointing to the nearest bucket, Mary asked loudly, "What's that for?"

A sailor turned and grinned at her, making a mock bow, "Your chamber pot and puke bucket, my lady."

He winked at Sophia. "Don't empty them to windward!"

She shuddered and looked away from him, then said anxiously to Hugh, "There's barely room down here for forty souls. Do you know how many of us there are?"

"One hundred and eighty-nine passengers, so the captain says." He smiled encouragement and gave her hand a squeeze.

"Dear Lord, surely not," she said, as she looked around in dismay. "And half that number young ones, I'd wager."

Then she said briskly to Jane and Mary, "Quickly, girls, we must find a place for ourselves. We are allowed two bunks. There, in the corner, next to the bunk with the hanging blanket."

The girls sidled between the bed frames and placed their bundles on the two lower bunks.

Mary pulled back the blanket on the adjacent bunk, and it revealed a woman suckling a newborn baby. The woman's face was thin and pale, framed by curly red hair, much darker than Mary's.

"Oh, Mary!" said Sophia, then to the woman, "I'm sorry."

But the woman smiled and waved away Mary's indiscretion. She introduced herself as Margaret Fraser, originally from Inverness.

Margaret told them she was one of those who had boarded the ship at Greenock. Only days into the voyage north to Loch Broom, she had given birth to a daughter, Jean. "With the captain's help," she added shyly. Her husband had died only three months before.

"How could you face this on your own?" Sophia blurted out.

"I have my other girls with me, and my cousins from Sutherlandshire are on the ship, too," said Margaret.

Sophia was appalled. She, at least, had a husband with her.

While Hugh, Sophia and Jane stowed the rest of their belongings and put up their own privacy blankets, Mary's attention was drawn to a section of uneven hull beside their bunk. She began to pick off slivers of rotting wood with her fingers before Hugh saw her and stopped her. He hoped Sophia had not noticed. His misgivings about this vessel were growing. It seemed old and in poor condition. He was determined at all costs to hide his fears from Sophia.

The next morning the ship weighed anchor at dawn. As the *Hector* slipped down the long loch toward the open sea, piper MacKay stood on the deck playing the sad lament of farewell. The wail of the pipes expressed, as nothing else could, the pain in so many hearts as they said goodbye to their homeland. Hugh and his family were amongst the many crowding the railings as their last sight of Scotland receded into the distance.

But the captain did not allow them to linger on deck. He directed the mates to hustle them below. When many resisted, they were told that its shallow draft made the *Hector* unstable. Passengers would be allowed on deck only at certain times of the day and only in the calmest of seas. Captain's orders.

And so that first day at sea was spent in the gloom, despite the bright sun above. Reprieve from the claustrophobic hold came only at dusk, when they were allowed on deck to empty the buckets and take an evening meal of barley soup and oat bread prepared for them by the ship's cook. Thereafter, women passengers would take turns cooking on deck, preparing meals over fires in small sandboxes.

"They seem happy enough," said Hugh to Sophia, as he watched the children race up and down the deck, released from their prison below.

"Aye," agreed Sophia guardedly. She may have spoken hardly at all and shown little emotion, but he could read her well. He knew that the sea terrified her and that their uncertain future troubled her. But he also knew that it was John's fate that caused her the greatest anguish. He could well imagine the questions with which she was torturing herself. Would he live? Would she ever see him again? And underlying all these terrors was the blame that she harboured. Sophia had made it clear who was at fault for her misery.

That night Hugh prayed desperately as he lay on his hard bunk. He prayed that, after weeks of fear and hardship, this voyage might be a respite for Sophia. For all of them. He prayed that John would live. He prayed that John would understand their decision. No, his decision. Then he thought of the voyage. Surely it could be no worse than the last few weeks had been?

Chapter Six

During that first week at sea, Sophia had little time to brood. She was too busy. It was her responsibility to manage the family's rations: one pint of water a day for each passenger over the age of eight, and the weekly rations of three pounds of salt beef, four pounds of bread and four pounds of oatmeal. Like the other women, Sophia used sea water to wash their clothes, as the water ration did not extend beyond what was needed for cooking and drinking. In addition, she found it a constant challenge to control and amuse three children in such a confined space. The chores taxed her physically, and that she welcomed. After an exhausting day, sleep came more easily at night.

Sophia looked forward to her turn cooking. On deck, the fresh breezes and salt air removed the smell of the hold that clung to all of them. And she could chat with the other women as they went about their tasks, in a way she was unable to do with her husband. She was allowed on deck with the same group of women each time, and Christina MacLeod was one of them.

Christina and Hugh MacLeod and their three daughters were from the rougher reaches of the northern Highlands. Christina described it as a region very different from the gentle and fertile countryside of Sophia's home, the Aird. The two women found much that they had in common; Christina, too, had opposed her husband's wish to emigrate.

"But he wore me down," she confided to Sophia, as they prepared a kettle of beef stew one evening. "All but my own parents counselled me to go, for the sake of my children. I felt I had no choice."

Sophia nodded grimly. "Aye, it was the same for me, but how do you feel now?"

Christina shot her a look of surprise. "Now? Why, what is done is done. I... we must make the best of it."

"How I wish I could feel that way, but I am still so, so... angry!" cried Sophia. She felt tears coming and she shook her head, frightened that she might lose control.

"What is it?" Christina whispered anxiously and put her arm around her friend.

The warmth and kindness in the other woman's voice undid Sophia. In a convulsive gush, she released what she had held back for so long. She told Christina everything. About John. And she showed Christina the precious lock of hair that she had clipped from her son's feverish brow and kept in her bodice. The only part of him she had left.

Christina was shocked. "My poor pet, what agony you have been through! Cry as much as you need." She held Sophia tightly against her body, rocking her like a baby.

"You are a far stronger woman that I am," Christina continued. "I couldn't have done what you did. But I believe you did the right thing. One day your boy will thank you for being so brave."

The warmth of the other woman's body and the soothing flow of words were like a comforting blanket. Calmed but embarrassed, Sophia sat upright, wiping away tears and pushing unruly strands of hair away from her wet face.

"I am so, so sorry. Thank you for listening and for your kind words."

"Don't be sorry, no need to thank me," said Christina

smiling. "We'll help each other. Agreed? If we face this together, we'll endure."

Sophia managed a weak smile as she nodded. "Aye, together."

From then on, Sophia came alive only in the evenings when she spent her brief time cooking on deck with Christina. She found that sharing her thoughts, with someone who made her feel safe and understood, brought her more relief than she had felt in a long time.

Christina told her that her husband had collected scraps of oatcakes tossed away by some of the passengers. "Hugh says they claimed the food was mouldy," said Christina, "but it's such a waste." Sophia nodded in agreement.

Then she grinned like a young girl. "When the men talk amongst themselves in the evenings, they think we're not listening, too busy with the children or our mending, but we hear everything!"

Christina laughed. "Aye, that's true. I have heard some of those old soldiers, who have had experience in the new world, talk of unpredictable savages and dense forests there. In low tones, mind, so as not to frighten *the women.*"

Sophia's face fell. Talk like that did frighten her. Christina reacted quickly and said lightly, "Did you hear the prediction of James MacIntyre? He has been on many a sea voyage. His counsel was to enjoy this part of the voyage with the fair seas. He said," and she mimicked his deep voice, "'Savour it as you would a honeymoon, a brief and happy time that cannot last.'"

Both women laughed.

Sophia had said nothing to Hugh of her new friendship, but knew that he had made his own friend in a younger man, a bachelor, John Patterson, a Lowlands merchant. She noticed them spending more and more time talking together each evening. It struck her as an odd friendship, with such a vast difference in class and means between the two.

Patterson was an educated man who spoke English and,

unlike many Lowlanders, Gaelic as well. He was the lone immigrant on board who owned rental property in Scotland. Sophia wondered why he would choose to leave and what he and Hugh could possibly have in common.

James MacIntyre's prophetic words came to pass during the second week of the voyage. The fair weather came to an end, and heavy rain began to drum against the ship. The winds strengthened, and the seas became rougher. In the hold, parents held tightly to their children as belongings rolled across the floor and the waste buckets tipped and sloshed their foul contents into every corner. The creaking of the old brig rose in volume. As the ship rolled constantly, many passengers succumbed to unrelenting seasickness.

Sophia and Hugh were both determined to fight it. On those few evenings when the captain permitted passengers on deck to prepare meals, they ignored the children's protests to be left on their bunks and took them on deck. They all needed a break from the stench and sounds in the hold.

And they did feel better in the open air.

Even after several days, when the seas calmed and seasickness abated, conditions in the hold did not improve. In the neighbouring bunk, Margaret Fraser seemed to be suffering from more than seasickness. She cried persistently for water and was racked with aches and fever.

With help from Margaret's cousins, Sophia cared for her and her newborn, Jean. She insisted that Hugh fetch Captain Speirs, who quickly diagnosed dysentery in Margaret and several others. But worse was to come.

Sophia had instinctively kept her children away from a mother and daughter who had developed suspicious fevers not long after they had sailed. She had warned Christina to do the same. Now they talked of it constantly.

"You think it could be smallpox, then?" asked Christina.

"Aye," said Sophia. "The fevers seem so very much like John's."

"A disaster if so," said Christina, looking about the hold, "so many young ones in such close quarters."

With John's illness so fresh in her mind, Sophia was distraught, but not surprised, when she was proven right by the spots that appeared first in the feverish daughter. She prayed that by keeping her own and Christina's children away from the girl, they might be spared the dreaded disease.

The nightmare really began when the infection spread rapidly, mainly amongst the children. For Sophia, each newly stricken child brought back the horror of John's illness. But she was determined to do what she could. As was Christina.

Hugh pleaded with Sophia to avoid the sick.

"My love, you can't save them all. Think of your own children and yourself. You'll succumb to the disease or wear yourself out! Think of John. He'll need you when we are reunited."

"No! I must help!" she insisted. "I must do for them what I could not finish with my own son."

Her voice wavered a moment, then grew stronger. "I nursed him and didn't become infected. Keep our three away from this as much as you can."

Sophia and Christina worked with the stricken, who lay pitifully on their bunks, feverish, covered in pustules, too weak to do more than accept sips of water. Soon Mary MacIntyre, Sophia's cousin, joined them in their work.

Hugh did as he was asked and kept the children as far away as possible. Donald was distressed by his mother's absence, but Sophia noticed that Jane took over. Even Mary tried to entertain her little brother with silly faces and antics. Their efforts helped to sustain Sophia. As long as they survive, she thought, perhaps I can put up with anything.

But when the first child died, a little boy of four, it still came as a terrible blow. Sophia felt almost as heartbroken as if it were John who lay lifeless before her. How could I have lost this little one, she thought, as she wept silently beside his bunk.

Christina's support and comforting words pulled her together. Mary McIntyre joined the two of them in washing the little body and wrapping it tenderly in canvas. When they had finished, the boy's father carried his son up on deck.

The captain conducted a brief service. Then the body, weighted with a ballast stone, was slipped over the side. During the service, Sophia stood rigidly, gripping Hugh's arm.

Afterwards, Hugh spoke to her tenderly.

"You did your best, my love. It was God's will."

"Hugh, you don't understand. I want to believe my son has survived. But with the death of this one, so like my John, I don't know anymore. If I couldn't save this one, perhaps John, too, has not survived!"

Hugh did not reply. He turned away, but not before she saw the hurt in his eyes. But she couldn't help it. She had felt removed from him for a long time now.

Christina approached, took Sophia's hand and looked into her eyes with a question. Sophia nodded. Together the two women made their way back down into the hold. There was still much to be done.

There were many more repeats of that deck-side service in the weeks that followed. Three children in one family died of the disease, two on the same day. Sophia nursed them all, but did not weep for any of them. She never cried again after that first death, even when her own cousin Mary succumbed.

Weeks passed and gradually the number of new cases lessened. Margaret Fraser had recovered from dysentery, and both she and her baby had avoided smallpox infection.

Exhausted, pale and thinner, Sophia and Christina stood together in the quiet hold. Most passengers were up on deck. A few children lay peacefully on their bunks, weak but apparently out of danger.

The two women hugged each other, silently celebrating the fact that no new cases had been reported for three days and that their own children, thus far, had managed to avoid the disease.

"Could this nightmare finally be over?" asked Christina softly.

"Perhaps," replied Sophia. "If so, we've done it together, as you promised me, so long ago."

"So long ago," laughed Christina. "That was just a few weeks ago! But it does seem as if we've been fighting this battle forever."

"Aye, it does. You gave me the strength to fight. I could not have done it without you." As Sophia reflected on her words, she realized it was true. She needed Christina more than she needed Hugh. She had lost her son because of him. Of course he suffered, too. But right now her own feelings threatened to overwhelm her. She had nothing left to give him.

Chapter Seven

By early August the smallpox epidemic seemed to be over. The captain allowed passengers on deck more frequently to help prevent further outbreaks.

One sunny afternoon, Mary spotted something in the sky and jumped up and down, waving her arms.

"A bird! A bird! Look, a bird!"

All eyes followed her upraised arm and soon many others were shouting excitedly. Captain Speirs announced, with a rare smile, that this sign could mean that land was near, perhaps ten days to two weeks away. Applause broke out amongst those on deck, but Sophia could not help frowning. Weeks yet to go? She had hoped it might be a matter of only days.

Next to her, Hugh said, "Just a wee bit longer, my love, but soon, soon this will be over."

She made no reply.

The mood in the hold that night was lighter than it had been since that first sunny week at sea. But the mood darkened the next day. Early that afternoon on deck, Sophia watched as James MacIntyre, an experienced sailor, pointed out to Hugh a series of angry black clouds forming on the horizon.

"A storm is coming," he shouted above the rising wind.

Soon after, the captain directed all below, then ordered

the sails reefed and the hatches battened down. By late afternoon, those in the hold could feel the winds buffeting the ship and hear the sea pounding the hull. The full force of the hurricane hit later that night. Below, in the gloom lit only by wildly swinging oil lamps, passengers huddled together on their bunks, holding tightly to each other and the bed frames.

The wind's howling became deafening. Rain and sea water splashed regularly into the hold through the leaky hatch, as monstrous waves broke freely over the deck above. The ship's shuddering and pitching sent belongings, and sometimes people, tumbling into the narrow spaces between the bed frames, where they were coated with the contents of the overturned buckets. Some prayed, some sang hymns, some cried and many vomited where they sat or lay. Then the oil lamps went out, and the darkness was complete.

On the bunk, Sophia felt Hugh's body tense, as he tightened his grip on the girls and the bed frame. She clutched Donald tightly to her chest. She stroked his face and sang lullabies softly into his ear, trying to block out the sounds around them. The sounds of hell. Hugh has brought us to this, she thought. We're all going to die.

Sophia did not remember falling asleep, but she must have, as she awoke with a start, lying on the bunk with Donald curled beside her. The storm continued to pummel the ship and the clamour in the hold was as deafening as before.

Fear and despair surrounded her in the darkness. Eventually she escaped it all by drifting off into another restless sleep. Waking, then dozing, over and over again, she had no sense of the passage of time. With the darkness complete, there was no way of telling when day followed night. Disoriented, she began to believe that they were trapped in a never-ending nightmare.

The next time she opened her eyes it was to a stream of light filtering through the hatch. It was still and quiet. The ship was rolling gently. I'm dreaming, she thought, and closed her eyes again. When she dared open them, she knew it was not a dream. Hugh stood beside her bunk.

"It's over," he said, and helped her to her feet. She reached down to pick up Donald, while Hugh roused the girls.

Sophia, weak from lack of water and food, carried Donald as she staggered over to the ladder. John Patterson was waiting there. Together, he and Hugh helped her and the children up the ladder and onto the deck.

The unaccustomed sunlight struck her like a blow as she emerged into the open. Slowly Sophia sank to her knees with Donald and allowed the warmth of the sun and the sea air to revive her. The girls followed her example. Eyes still shut, she heard Patterson speak to Hugh.

"Are you well, my friend, no bones broken?"

"I am," said Hugh. "And the children and Sophia, too. We are as exhausted and as shaken as you are, but whole, I believe. My thanks to you for your help, John."

Sophia stood up and studied the younger man's face. She read the concern in it. His pallor was as unhealthy as his fellow passengers', but he looked resolute as well as kind. This is a good man, she thought.

"My thanks to you for you assistance, Mr. Patterson," she said, stepping forward.

Patterson bowed slightly and said, "It is a pleasure, Mrs. Fraser."

Behind her, Sophia could sense Hugh's satisfaction in her words. Soon after, all aboard were instructed to gather on deck for a service of thanksgiving.

A few unlucky passengers had broken bones when they had been thrown from their bunks during the storm, and they remained below with those still suffering from seasickness or recovering from smallpox. Uncharacteristically enthusiastic, Captain Speirs praised the Lord for their deliverance and heaped accolades on his crew for their skill during the storm.

Then he paused, and when he spoke again his voice was sombre.

"I must warn you of more hardship to come. This storm has blown us off course; our voyage is now much extended. Our supply of food and water is my primary concern. The bread has been soiled by sea water; only salt beef is left. Our water is fit to drink only when some vinegar is added."

He did not finish, as a loud voice interrupted him, "We must turn back... we are blown almost back to Scotland, surely!"

Sophia looked around but could not see who had spoken. But the speaker's call prompted others to shout "Aye" and "It's true!"

The captain raised his hand for silence. "No!" Beside him, agent John Ross nodded his head grimly.

The captain continued, enunciating every word slowly. "My orders are to sail this ship to Pictou Harbour, then on to Falmouth and Boston. Those are my orders, and I will not deviate from them. Keep in mind that *I* am the sole master of this vessel!"

He paused and then added in a lighter tone, "I can report that we are far closer to the New World than to the Old. Now there is much restoration to be done by crew and passengers alike, so let us begin."

There were a few muttered protests, but most passengers wearily went below to salvage belongings scattered, soiled or damaged by the effects of the storm.

Christina squeezed Sophia's hand. "I see the doubt in your face," she told her friend, "but we can't go back now after we have been through so much. We'll face it together, as we've faced everything else."

Sophia smiled in return, "Aye. Together." Christina always lifted her spirits.

Later that day, Christina's husband judged it a suitable time to produce his sack of mouldy oatcake scraps and share them amongst his fellow passengers. Many were sheepish, but all were grateful.

The next few weeks were blessedly uneventful. With fair

seas, good weather and few smallpox patients, most passengers were able to escape the unhealthy hold and spend part of each day on deck. The Captain had relaxed his rule to appease his long-suffering passengers.

Mary's exuberance quickly returned, and below deck she alternately entertained and frustrated Donald with games of hide-and-seek. Jane, however, became even quieter. Sophia tried to talk to her, to encourage her to join in the children's games and in singing hymns and songs, but was unsuccessful. Christina suggested Sophia give Jane time. But Jane's withdrawal worried her mother.

Then, in early September, the battered little ship entered the mighty Gulf of St. Lawrence and from there slipped into the Northumberland Strait. All passengers were allowed on deck to welcome landfall after so long at sea.

Sophia, however, rejected Hugh's pleas to join him and the children on deck to witness this first sight of the New World.

She insisted on staying below, sitting with Hugh MacLeod by the bunk of her dear friend Christina, who was becoming weaker by the hour.

Sophia had refused to believe it at first, but now accepted the terrible truth that her friend had fallen victim to smallpox. She held Christina's limp hand and gently bathed her feverish face.

On September 15, after almost twelve weeks at sea, the *Hector* skirted Pictou's sandbar and entered her broad harbour. Under a shining autumn sun, curious Highlanders lined the ship's railing and caught the scent of pine trees drifting toward them. They had noticed a scattering of wooden dwellings along the harbour's edge and now peered anxiously as approaching figures wove through the dense forest toward the shoreline.

Once again Sophia was not present on deck with her family. She sat dry-eyed beside Hugh MacLeod. They were both putting off the task of wrapping Christina's body in canvas. Sophia carefully studied the look of peace on her dear friend's face. This was how she wished to remember Christina.

Hugh MacLeod broke the silence.

"Go up on deck to share this moment of arrival with your family," he said softly.

Sophia shook her head. "I prefer to be here with Christina. And I would only dampen their spirits."

Through the open hatch she heard the captain's call to drop anchor. John William MacKay chose that moment to pipe a thanksgiving to mark the end of an epic journey and the beginning of a new life.

For Sophia, however, the music brought no comfort. To her it was a lament for all those who had lost their lives, for Christina, for Mary and for the sixteen others who had succumbed to smallpox on the voyage. And for survivors like us, she thought, it marks the loss of our old life, not the promise of a new one.

At that moment, she felt Hugh MacLeod's gentle touch on her shoulder. "It's time."

She opened her eyes and roused herself to perform one last act of love. Together they wrapped Christina tenderly in canvas. Two sailors carried her up on deck.

Sophia joined her family there. Christina's body, accompanied by her husband and daughters, was on one of the first small boats to leave the ship. Sophia's eyes followed the little boat that held the MacLeods, as if it were vital that she alone see them safely to shore. The sickest and weakest *Hector* passengers were ferried ashore next. The rest waited patiently along the ship's railings, taking in their new surroundings.

Sophia shifted her gaze to the shoreline. She saw a few log houses close to the water. Each was centred in a small cleared patch dotted with stumps, where trees had been felled to create some space. Beyond this settlement stood a vast forest. It was like a wall of trees that marched to the horizon in every direction. The trees themselves seemed impossibly tall. It was a dark forbidding place, even in the sunshine, so different from the soft open contours of the Aird's heather-clad hills. So different from home.

Sophia became aware of Hugh beside her. He gave her shoulder a gentle squeeze, then said to the children, "Soon it will be our turn to take the boat ashore. Hoist your bags and be ready."

Chapter Eight

And so the Fraser family was rowed ashore, one of the last families to leave the *Hector*. Their first steps on dry land were unsteady. After all those weeks at sea, they tottered on the wharf. All but Mary, who skipped to the end of the pier, then clambered confidently along the rocky shore, laughing as she swayed this way and that. Jane was sick after taking only a few cautious steps on dry land. A wailing Donald preoccupied Sophia and instinctively she rocked him.

Strangers came forward to assist them and offer milk and bannocks. Their smiles were warm and welcoming but the language strange. English. Sophia sat with the children near the water's edge to enjoy this first meal on dry land. She noticed Hugh and the other men talking and gesturing with the strangers, and soon the men were busy erecting shelters along the shore line, using tree branches. Once the frames were in place, women of the settlement provided blankets to cover the lean-tos and provide some warmth within. Sophia watched all this activity with little interest. By the time a warm afternoon gave way to a cool autumn evening the shelters were ready.

Like the other exhausted *Hector* passengers, Sophia, Hugh and the children crawled into theirs and allowed exhaustion to claim them.

When Sophia awoke the following morning, she was stiff

and chilled to the bone, despite the warmth of Donald nestled against her.

As she sat up, moving her sleeping boy gently aside, she saw Hugh sitting by a fire at the entrance to the shelter. John Patterson was standing beside him. Hugh glanced her way, and the worry on his face was replaced by a smile.

"My love, come to the fire. John has brought some water and tea leaves from the settlers and some bannocks, too. And the tea is brewed."

She moved to the fire slowly and held her hands to the flames. Looking about her, she saw the same ominous forest she had seen the day before. She felt a sense of despair. Despite the fire's warmth, she shivered.

"What is this place? And who are these people?"

John handed her a cup of tea and said, "They are Ulster Scots. They came here from the American colonies several years ago. There are sixteen families here in Pictou. And they speak no Gaelic, only English."

"This is Pictou?" cried Sophia. "This is it?" She met Hugh's eyes. "This is the promised land you've brought us to? And others are here before us? What of our land?"

Hugh and John exchanged glances. Then Hugh said, "John and I plan to find John Ross, the Company's agent, this very morning and learn the answers to all those questions. Everything will be as promised. Don't worry."

He and John left soon after. Sophia prepared more tea and served the bannocks to her sleepy children.

She was too restless to remain by the shelter, so she and the children walked along the shoreline. Mary ran ahead, skipping and jumping, noisy as ever, while Jane hung back, holding Donald's hand, content to match his toddling pace. The long line of shelters they passed reminded Sophia of the temporary village at Loch Broom. How long would they have to remain in a rough lean-to this time?

Turning away from the shore, she approached a settler's log house and studied it. It was smaller than her stone house at home, and the meagre patch of cleared land that surrounded it did not look fertile. What crops were fit to grow here? How could they possibly survive in such a place? A woman appeared at the door, with a small child clutching her skirt, and she smiled at Sophia. She had a thin pinched face and ragged strands of hair that hung from her bonnet. Abruptly she disappeared and returned with an empty bucket. She offered it to Sophia with a smile and said something in English.

Sophia thanked her in Gaelic and said "Sophia," pointing at herself. The woman replied, "Sarah." The two women stood awkwardly a moment longer still smiling at each other. Then Sophia turned away and led the children to the harbour. Perhaps they could find something there for a meal.

When she returned, Hugh and Patterson were sitting by the fire. Both rose when she approached. Mary ran forward with the bucket.

"Look what we found on the beach, Father. We dug them up!"

"Clams," said Patterson, smiling. "Well done, lass!"

Sophia smiled at Patterson, then looked quickly at Hugh. "What have you learned?"

"It's not good news," said Hugh wearily. "We spoke to John Ross. He says he has been misled by the Company. There's no temporary accommodation, and the provisions promised are not here. Ross has been told that they will arrive later, when the *Hector* returns to Pictou from the southern colonies."

Too stunned to speak, Sophia stared at Hugh until he looked away.

"No!" she cried, "It can't be! What are we to do? How can we live?"

Patterson stepped forward. "Mrs. Fraser," he began, "there is a storehouse here. Dr. Harris, one of the agents of The Philadelphia Company, manages it. We can buy provisions there."

"Buy!" exclaimed Sophia, "With what? We have very

little money left." She turned to Hugh. "We'll have to return home."

"I am sure the settlers here will do all they can to help until the *Hector* returns—" Patterson broke off and looked at Hugh. "I should take my leave now." He nodded to Sophia and walked away.

"I've spoken to many others this day," Hugh said. "We all agreed that we must see our allotted farm land now, to set up our own accommodation on it. That promise at least has not been broken. The Company surveyor, Mr. Robert Patterson, will show us tomorrow."

"This is a godforsaken place," Sophia said harshly. "When the *Hector* returns, we should leave... if we are still alive." She turned away from him, her mind reeling.

Later, sleep would not come. The night before, exhaustion and numbness had brought oblivion. Now Sophia lay beside a sleeping Hugh, her body tightly wound by fear and anger.

Hugh should not have done this to us. Why had she agreed to come? How would they ever survive? Perhaps with Christina at her side, she might have been able to cope, but now... Then the anger turned to anguish as she thought of the boy she had left behind. It always came back to him.

The next morning, Hugh left early with the other *Hector* men to accompany Robert Patterson into the forest to see their farm lots. He did not return until well after midday.

She watched him approach and noticed his head down and body hunched forward. Like a chill wind, fear swept over her and she pulled her shawl more tightly about her.

"Where are the children?" were his first words.

"Jane has taken them to the harbour." Sophia sat down then, exhausted by the effort to put on a brave face.

For a moment both were silent. Then Hugh sat down beside her. His face was pale. He took a deep breath.

"Robert Patterson took us deep into the forest, perhaps two to three miles from here. There was no track, so the going was difficult. You can see how dense this forest is."

Sophia nodded but said nothing. Hugh continued in a monotone. "What Patterson showed us were uncleared swaths of forest. It's not arable land and miles from the harbour or any water source. How we could wrest farmland from that impenetrable forest, the Lord only knows."

He looked at her then. "Sophia, I am heartsick at this betrayal, but even more so for you. You've suffered so much." He paused, then added, "Now for me to tell you this."

Sophia sat stunned. She heard his words but was having difficulty absorbing yet another terrible blow. She saw the torment on his face. Then she erupted angrily.

"After arriving to no provisions and no proper shelter, how could you have believed that there was good land just waiting for us. Like some well-deserved gift!"

Sophia knew that these words would hurt him, but she could not help herself.

He looked up at her then, and she saw that his face was haggard. "You're right," he said in a low voice. "I wanted our own land. I believed it was the right thing to do."

"Well, then, Hugh Fraser, you must fix this. You must do something or we will all die!"

He stood up and clenched his fists. "And I will, I promise you." His voice became hard. "To a man we have refused the allotments. It was not the land promised, so they have broken the contract. They must provide other, acceptable land. Ross will deal with the Company on our behalf. Till then, I will improve this shelter, make it sturdier."

"And what will we do about food?"

He looked around as if there were an answer nearby. "We must make do; we still have a little money. I'll buy some provisions at the storehouse and perhaps the settlers will help us until the provisions arrive on the *Hector*."

"Oh, Hugh, I can't believe what I'm hearing! Can you still believe them when they say that provisions will be coming, after all the lies they've told?"

"I must believe it! What other choice do I have? Please,

Sophia, don't give up hope. I'll go to the storehouse to buy food now. And build us a better shelter. In the meantime, Ross will negotiate better land for us."

He looked directly at her as he said these words, but she turned away. "If the *Hector* ever does return," she said quietly, "I intend to leave this god-forsaken place and go home."

Hugh was as good as his word. He returned a few hours later with a sack of provisions, including a cooking kettle and a woodsman's axe that he had borrowed from a settler.

"John Patterson and I will work together," he said brightly. "He also plans to build a more solid shelter."

Sophia looked doubtfully at the massive trees that surrounded them. "If we ever get some land here, how do a Highlander and soft Lowlander tackle such monstrous trees as these? You have never wielded an axe such as this in your life, Hugh. The crooked spade and hoe of the Aird are far different from this."

Hugh smiled. "Then I will learn!"

Sophia had to give him credit for his spirit. He and Patterson worked tirelessly all day to cut down a single tree. Over the course of the next few days they attempted to cut the tree into useable logs. Sophia went about the back-breaking and unrelenting daily challenges of fetching water, boiling it, washing clothes and preparing meals.

With the children's help, she searched for food where she could: clams and fish along the harbour and berries and a few wild greens in the forest.

She was determined to stay focused on these physical tasks.

If she could wear herself out, she would sleep like the dead and avoid dreaming. Perhaps then she could banish any thoughts of those she ached for: John, Christina and home.

One morning, after returning to their shelter with Jane, lugging a bucket of water from the nearby stream, Sophia was surprised to see Hugh sitting beside Mary and Donald by the fire. John Patterson was nowhere to be seen. With Jane's help, she carefully lowered the bucket to the ground. She felt her hands shaking, and when Hugh looked up at her, his eyes confirmed her fears.

"Jane, once the bucket is emptied, take it to the harbour to dig for clams," she said, "and take Mary and the wee one with you." She saw Jane's mouth open to protest, then close again.

When the children had gone, Sophia busied herself at the kettle, refusing to look at her husband.

"I sense it is more bad news, Hugh. Tell me now."

"John heard this news from James Grant," began Hugh, wearily.

"James has learned that John Ross has fallen out with Dr. Harris and Robert Patterson, the Company men. He has resigned as our agent. We'll get no more help from him."

"So there is no hope. The scheme is dead." Sophia's voice was brittle. "We have no choice but to return home."

As if he had not heard her words, Hugh continued. "James intends to take his family to a place called Truro, where he can find work and proper shelter for the winter." He looked up at her. "Truro is a town, a true settlement known for its hospitality. It's forty miles west of here, through the forest. John Patterson agrees that is the best idea for a family such as ours."

"So John Patterson makes decisions for us now, does he?"

Hugh rose to his feet. "No, of course not. I simply respect the man's advice and believe I... we should consider it. We must talk of what course to take now. I fear it may take too long to build a proper shelter before the winter comes."

"And what does Patterson himself intend to do?" demanded Sophia.

"He says that as a bachelor, with no wife or young to consider, he will stay. As a young man on his own, he can cope with winter in a rough lean-to."

Sophia placed her hands on her hips. "I do not intend to trek miles and miles through that forest to another unknown place. I would not risk our children. I wish to remain here to await the return of the *Hector*."

She saw the disbelief in his eyes. "What if the promised supplies are not aboard, and just another lie of the Company," he began, "as you have told me you believe?"

"If the supplies are aboard the *Hector*, then it will have been the right decision to remain. If not, we will board the ship to return home."

"But Sophia," began Hugh desperately, "returning on the *Hector* isn't possible. We haven't the money for it and no passage booked. And we have nothing to return to. There are only two choices open to us: to remain here in the hope of provisions arriving, or to go to Truro."

"How can you say we have nothing in Scotland?" she cried. "John may be alive! Our families are there. Look about you. We have far more there than we have here."

Hugh stared at her, his anger mounting. After a few minutes of silence, he said quietly, but coldly, "We will stay. We will await the arrival of the ship. Now I must get back to work." And he walked away.

Chapter Nine

Two days later, the Grants, along with several other *Hector* families, left Pictou to walk westward through the forest to Truro. Hugh, John Patterson and the other remaining men continued the task of improving their shelters as best they could. It was now apparent that the Americans who had offered their help at first, along with their axes, were fast losing their compassion for the newcomers.

Patterson explained the change in mood to Sophia and Hugh one day, when he arrived to share a meal with them.

"Many settlers tell me that they do not understand why our men have refused the land," he began. "They say they have wrested arable land from the forest here and believe we can do the same. I have explained that our men have no experience with the forests here, or the tools, as these Americans had before they came. And the land on offer is in the middle of a dense forest, not along the harbour."

"And what of the fact that we have been lied to, our contract broken?" Sophia demanded.

Patterson shook his head. "Despite that truth, they see us as ungrateful. To them, we are becoming a different people in more than just language. I fear that soon they will no longer share their food or help."

Things had been better between Hugh and Sophia since

the decision to remain had been made. But it was more like a truce. Both of them were preoccupied with the daily struggle to stay warm and dry and find food. There was little time or inclination for tenderness.

Tensions grew as October came to an end, with the ship due at any time. One frosty morning, while Sophia was busy washing clothes in a bucket of heated water, she heard shouting in the distance, and then people started running toward the harbour. It must be the *Hector*! She scooped Donald into her arms and ran in the same direction. There was a large crowd already on the wharf when she arrived. Her heart skipped a beat when she caught sight of the familiar ship out in the harbour. A small boat had already reached the shore and was being unloaded. The provisions!

She saw John Ross push his way through the crowd toward the unloaded goods. Then she lost sight of him, but heard his voice clearly.

"Sirs, these people have been waiting patiently for too long now. They are hungry, almost starving, some of them. Please distribute the provisions at once, as promised!"

There were cheers and shouts of agreement. Then another, louder voice rose above the rest.

"Ross and all of you who came on the *Hector*, listen to me! I am Dr. Harris, agent of The Philadelphia Company, along with Mr. Robert Patterson here beside me. Know this, by refusing the allotments, you have broken the contract with us. Accept the land offered and you shall receive provisions. If you do not, the provisions are forfeit and will be distributed only to those who can pay!"

There was a moment of shocked silence, and then pandemonium erupted. With roars of anger and disbelief, the crowd began to sway and move as one. Sophia was jostled, even as she stood on the outer edge. Realizing the danger, she retreated with Donald tight against her chest and walked back to the shelter, her heart thudding painfully. Jane and Mary rushed to meet her, throwing their arms around their mother.

"What's happening?" gasped Jane. "We heard the shouting!"

"Only men arguing about provisions from the ship," said Sophia, in as calm a voice as she could muster. One glance at Jane told her that her words had not reassured her elder daughter.

When Hugh returned later, he found them sitting by a fire that had been built high and was blazing. They sat huddled together, Sophia singing lullabies. Her eyes met his. I know, her eyes told him. Not now. Later.

He nodded.

That night, after the children had fallen asleep, Sophia and Hugh sat silently at the entrance to the shelter for a long while. Both stared into the fire, absorbed in their separate thoughts.

Along the shoreline, many others sat by their own fires, trying to come to terms with the day's events. The giant trees surrounded them like sentinels, unmoving in a windless night.

Sophia felt oddly calm. Untroubled. It's over, she thought. The worst has happened. There are no more arguments to be had, nothing more to be said. We have no choice but to go home. She was about to say so, when Hugh broke the silence.

"I bought all the provisions I could get at the storehouse before the agents locked the door," he said quietly. "I was amongst a small group who did. But now we have no money left." He lapsed into silence again, as if to allow this information to sink in. Then he continued in the same monotone.

"Although I've worked very hard to improve our shelter, I can't complete it before winter comes. I'll make it stronger, but it will not be proper protection against the ice, snow and winds of a winter here. So I fear we have no choice. We can't stay."

He stopped again but, with her eyes still fixed on the fire, she said nothing. She was waiting for him to finish, to say the words she longed to hear.

"So we must make for Truro soon," he concluded. "There are many others I have spoken to who are planning to go. We won't be alone on our journey."

She turned slowly to face him, eyes wide, in astonishment.

"Truro!" she gasped. "Surely you can't mean it! There is only one answer. To go home, Hugh. Home to Scotland." She paused and shook her head. "How can you not see that?"

It was his turn to register shock. "Sophia, you know that it's not possible. I've told you before: we have no money, no place on the ship. We can't go back."

"What about your friend John Patterson? He is a man of means, perhaps he can arrange it?"

Hugh shook his head. "No, it's not possible," he said firmly.

Sophia lowered her head into her hands. I think I shall go mad, she thought. In a small voice that shook she said, "I can't do this anymore, Hugh. I'm worn out. I'm sick to death of this place. I'm sick to death of everything that has happened. I want to go home. I want to see my John again. Please, Hugh, take me home."

He gathered her trembling body into his arms and held her close.

"My love, I'll take care of you," he whispered in her ear. "Let me do the fighting for both of us. For now. Until you're strong again." He felt her body go limp.

"I promise you we'll have our own good land here. I'll build us a proper house. We'll welcome John into it. I'll make a good life for all of us here, I promise you that. Sleep now and think no more of anything."

And she slept.

When she awoke, she did not know where she was. All she knew was that she was cold, so terribly cold, and her body was shaking uncontrollably. She heard someone moaning, then a cup was put to her lips.

"Take some sips, my love," said a soothing voice. Hugh's. "You're feverish. Jane has gone to get more blankets. Just rest now. Rest."

Sometime later she awoke to find her body no longer trembling, but she was hot, too hot. She attempted to throw off the blankets, but did not have the strength. The cup was placed against her lips, and the same soothing voice encouraged her to drink. She dreamed that John came to her, but when she put her arms out to him, he drifted away out of sight. Her screams did not bring him back.

Sophia awoke again and lay very still. She could feel the heat of a nearby fire on her cheeks. Under the blankets, her body was warm but no longer ached. She felt exhausted, as if even opening her eyes would demand more effort than she had.

She did not know how much later she opened her eyes, but when she did, she saw Hugh sitting by the fire, his back to her. He was staring at the wall of trees, the same view she had from the shelter's entrance. Jane was sitting beside him stirring the kettle, and she noticed Sophia's open eyes.

"Mother!" she cried, jumping to her feet. "You're awake!"

Then Hugh was at her side, gently touching her forehead. "Thank the Lord, your fever has broken. My love, you look so much better."

His smiling face seemed to fill her whole field of vision. "Jane, some water for your mother."

Donald toddled over to Sophia as Jane brought the water. Sophia took a few slow sips. Even that little bit refreshed her. Donald nestled his body against her side.

Sophia heard Jane say that there was meat stew for later and then she drifted away again, this time into a deep restorative sleep.

It was a loud voice that awoke her next. She did not open her eyes, but this time she knew where she was. She knew that voice. It was John Patterson's.

"Hugh! The storehouse has been robbed! Colin Douglas and Donald Macdonald entered the store when the agents were there and demanded their provisions. When the Company men refused and ordered them to leave, Douglas and Macdonald overpowered them, tied them up and took their guns. Then they took what supplies they believed were their due and left!"

Then she heard Hugh's voice. "I know these men," he said quietly. "They were neighbours of mine, from Kilmorack and Beauly."

"Aye," said Patterson, "and they were helped by another Beauly man, Rory Mackay, who described it all to me. It was he who released the Company men, after the other two were well away into the woods!"

"They are good men, you know," said Hugh, "but driven by desperation."

"I agree," said Patterson. "They left a paper accounting of what they had taken, signalling they would repay the Company. That is not the mark of criminals. The Company has brought this on themselves."

"But John, I fear what will happen next."

"As I do. The Company could even send for the garrison in Halifax," Patterson replied grimly. "And the American settlers will not look kindly on what has happened, let alone the rage of Harris and Robert Patterson directed at..."

"All of us, no doubt," Hugh finished for him.

There was silence between them, and then Patterson spoke again. "I believe you need to reconsider your decision to stay, my friend. It will be a difficult time here; feelings will run high. I will manage, but a family man like yourself..." He did not need to finish.

More bad news, thought Sophia. But she was surprised how little troubled she felt about this latest disaster. My body no longer aches. My fever has gone, as have my nightmares. For now, that is enough. But I'm so very hungry! I'd like some of that stew.

She learned that John Patterson had provided the meat, a deer, for the wonderful first meal she enjoyed when she was able to sit up.

Patterson shared the stew with them and told her that Sarah had supplied the potatoes and turnip.

"She has a soft spot for you," said John. "She alone, of all the settlers' wives, offered help during your illness. It was her herb mixture that Hugh and Jane used to fight your fever."

The following day, Sophia felt strong enough to leave her bed. She was determined to thank Sarah. She asked Patterson to accompany her, so that Sarah would understand her words of gratitude.

They found Sarah behind her cabin, hanging blankets over a rope strung between trees.

She welcomed them with a smile and directed them to a bench at the front of the cabin. Patterson declined the offer of some milk and then told Sarah what Sophia had asked him to say. Sarah smiled and touched Sophia's arm gently. Her face lit up when, in halting English, Sophia said, "Thank you." Sarah spoke a little longer to Patterson, in a more serious tone this time. Then he and Sophia took their leave.

As they walked away, Sophia was impatient to learn what Sarah had said.

"She was very pleased with your visit and your expressions of gratitude," began Patterson.

"No, no, John, I mean after that, when you both spoke so seriously."

Patterson stopped. "I do not wish to trouble you further, after what you have been through."

"John!" cried Sophia. "I am recovered. And I must know what is happening. Please!"

They continued walking. John offered his arm to her and she took it.

"She warns that most settlers do not feel as she does. Even her husband distrusts us now. Most of them no longer want us here, fearing that we are taking more than our share of the resources, and doing nothing in return except complaining or resorting to thievery."

"Do you think they would ever... harm us?"

"I don't believe so, but the storehouse robbery has outraged them. Soldiers from the garrison in Halifax may arrive any day."

"Soldiers!" cried Sophia, stopping in her tracks.

"Yes, but you are in no danger of arrest," he said with a smile. Then it faded. "But this place is becoming more troubled. Too many mouths, too little food, and winter is coming. Many *Hector* people have already left for other settlements."

"You think we should go too, John? That's how you have counselled my Hugh."

"Aye, but I have merely agreed with his thinking. He is a good man. He wants his family safe and fed, but respects your feelings, more than most husbands would. He does not wish to force you."

Sophia sighed. "Have no fear, John. As much as we have argued, in my heart I know he truly wants what is best for us."

When they returned to the shelter, she found she was worn out, so went to lie down. Later, with Jane's help, she prepared a meal. All the while, Sophia thought of what she would say to Hugh that evening.

She began by asking about the *Hector*.

"The ship left some time ago, not long after you became ill."

"I thought as much. I know now that it wasn't possible for us to go."

"I'm so glad you understand that, my love."

"I do."

They were silent for awhile. He does not wish to raise the subject, to upset me, she thought. It must be me. She looked down at her hands.

"I think I've been at my wits' end for a time, and it led to my illness. But I'm better, my thoughts are clear. Today I heard from Sarah, through John Patterson, how the settlers feel about us. I know of the robbery. I've listened to John. And I've considered carefully your words, Hugh, even though I rejected them at first." She looked up at him then.

"I know we must leave here, at least for the winter." Then more firmly she added, "So let's prepare for the journey."

Hugh moved to her, wrapped his arms about her and gently kissed the top of her head. "My love," was all he said.

They learned that there were two other families who would join them on their journey to Truro. Hugh built a wooden sled, with Patterson's help, to carry their belongings. On the third morning after the decision to go, Sophia went to say goodbye to Sarah.

The two women embraced, and Sarah pushed a warm bundle of newly baked bannocks into Sophia's hands. In English, Sophia offered her thanks, then said in Gaelic, "Farewell, my sister."

They were ready to leave. About two thirds of the *Hector* passengers had already left for other settlements, so there were few friends left to bid them farewell. Except John Patterson.

"I know I shall see all of you again, soon," said the younger man as he shook hands with Hugh.

Sophia carried Donald, with Jane following her, clutching a bundle in one hand and Mary's hand in the other. Behind them, Hugh pulled their laden sled.

Even though Sophia was fearful of what lay ahead, she was not sorry to leave.

Pictou had been a cruel disappointment, despite Sarah and the early kindness of the settlers. She regretted leaving such a loyal friend as John Patterson. She knew it must be even harder for Hugh.

As they trudged westward into the forbidding forest, Sophia thought wearily, another long trip into the unknown.

Would it be another nightmare journey like the trek to Loch Broom, or worse, the hellish sea voyage? As these thoughts threatened to overwhelm her, she stopped a moment to fight off the panic. And what of Truro? Would it prove to be a haven? Surely, as a more developed settlement, it would be better than Pictou. Please Lord, let it be so.

Chapter Ten

It was quiet in the forest. The dead leaves on the forest floor muffled their footsteps. The November sun was weak and unable to penetrate the towering evergreens. It was dark even though it was morning. Luckily there was little wind, but it was very cold and Sophia could see her breath with every step. The narrow track forced them into single file. She knew from Walter Murray that only the marks blazed on trees every so often kept them on the right path. He was at the head of the line; he had agreed to lead the way. His family followed him, with the Mackenzies directly behind them. Sophia and the children completed this trio of families, with Hugh at the rear, pulling the sled.

According to the Pictou settlers, the trip could be made in a little over two days. But with children it would probably take twice as long. And they did have to stop often to allow the little ones to rest. Sophia, who was carrying Donald much of the time, was thankful for the frequent stops. All of them were grateful for one particular piece of advice the settlers had given them before they left.

As the Indians had taught them, so the Americans showed the newcomers how to wrap layers of cloth around their feet to create Indian-style moccasins. They kept out the cold and cushioned their feet against the rough terrain.

They carried no cooking pots with them, so there was no

warm food or drink, just small amounts of salt beef, dried fish, berries and some bannocks donated by a few sympathetic settlers. At night, they slept in hastily built lean-tos made with boughs of deadfall and leaves that did nothing to keep out the cold. On the third day it snowed, a blowing snow that found its way under shawls and blankets and stung eyes, ears and noses. The little group now shuffled along the snow-covered track, each wrapped up in a private misery of exhaustion, cold and hunger.

On the morning of the fourth day, when Sophia believed she could not take another step, they stumbled out of the forest and into the settlement of Truro. As she looked about her, Sophia's relief turned to a flicker of hope. It was much larger than the settlement at Brown's Point, with many log houses and an air of permanence that Pictou lacked. These people, she thought with admiration, have won their battle against the forest.

While the little group stopped to take in their new surroundings, Walter Murray cleared his throat and announced with some fanfare, "This is Truro. It is ten years old and is home to about one hundred and fifty families."

He led his weary group to a wooden building, which stood at the edge of the settlement, where he said Reverend Morrison waited to shelter them temporarily.

And Reverend Morrison and his wife confirmed their reputation for hospitality right away by welcoming them warmly into the manse.

While the travellers rested, the women on benches, the others on the floor, some women of the settlement appeared to prepare a hot meal.

After the meal, Sophia rested her head against the rough log wall. Jane and Mary dozed on either side of her on the bench, while Donald lay fast asleep on her lap. The luxury of a full stomach and a warm, drowsy body had never given Sophia so much pleasure. Out of the corner of her eye, she noticed Hugh approach the minister. I will wager he wishes to show Reverend Morrison his letter of recommendation as soon as possible. It was her last thought before falling asleep.

When Sophia awoke, it was to feel Hugh kneeling in front of her on the floor. The children slept on. His eyes were bright and on her.

"I have much to tell you," he whispered. "I showed Reverend Morrison the letter, and he said it was an excellent recommendation. When I told him I was in need of a position here for the winter, he said he knew just the place for us." He stopped and waited for her response.

"Good news, Hugh. Go on."

"He said that on the morrow he would introduce me to Samuel Blair, in the meeting house. He believes that Mr. Blair is in need of assistance and would welcome a man with such an excellent reference. What do you think of that!"

Hugh sat back and looked at her expectantly.

"What is a meeting house?" asked Sophia, sleepily.

"Oh, Sophia, are you not pleased with my news?"

"Of course I am, Hugh. But we must wait to hear what this Samuel Blair has to say before we raise our hopes."

His face fell, and Sophia regretted her words immediately.

"You've done well to move so quickly to find a place for us. Truly. I don't mean to cast doubt on your efforts, but you know how afraid I am to hope. We've been promised so much and then been so cruelly treated."

Hugh nodded. "Aye, I know that. But this time, I feel I can put my faith in the Reverend." He paused. "And, shrewish wife, a meeting house is their name for a kirk."

The next day, as they sat side by side in the meeting house for the Sabbath service, Sophia could feel the tension in Hugh's body, despite his confidence of the day before. For her part, Sophia found the service a comfort, although the language was unfamiliar and the place so unlike the ancient stone kirk of home. But to be part of a worship service again after such a long time was a solace, and she found herself wondering if the faint flutter of hope she felt yesterday was the same as Hugh's.

Once the service was over and they were standing outside, Hugh asked her to take the children back to the manse.

"Reverend Morrison has asked me to wait here alone at the door of the meeting house. He will join me after he has had a chance to speak to Samuel Blair."

Sophia smiled encouragement, then hustled the children away. But her smile faded as she turned away from him. No point in entertaining false hope.

When Hugh came back to the manse, the grin on his face announced the good news before he could. "Samuel Blair has agreed!" he declared excitedly. "We will work on his farm for the winter, in exchange for food and shelter. He can offer us accommodation in his barn."

"Oh, Hugh, that's grand news! The first bit of good news we've had since we arrived." This time her smile and reaction were genuine.

"Aye!" Hugh took her hands and kissed them. "But we've no time to waste now. Mr. Blair wishes to leave for his farm within the hour. Gather your things. We must hasten to join the Blair family at the meeting house."

After thanking the Morrisons for their hospitality, they gathered their few belongings and were at the meeting house within half an hour. While they waited by the sled, Hugh told Sophia and the children the few things he had learned about the Blairs.

"They own a farm a few miles from here on the Salmon River. They have six children, two boys older than you, Jane. Reverend Morrison speaks very highly of Mr. Blair as a fair Christian man, so I believe we will be in good hands. Remember, they have no Gaelic, only English, so listen well. It will be up to us to learn as much English as we can."

Mary jumped up and down and cried, "Here they are!"

Sophia looked up to see a large family approach. A burly

man with sandy-coloured hair and a full beard walked alongside two sturdy-looking young men with the same colouring as their father. Behind them were three younger children. And finally, lagging behind all of them, was a tall, slim, woman, heavy with child, holding the hand of a toddler close to Donald's size. Samuel nodded to Hugh and then pointed to his wife and youngest saying, "Martha and Ann." Then he pointed to his children, moving from tallest to shortest.

"Samuel, Robert, Mary, Andrew and Betsy."

Mary Fraser ran forward to stand in front of Betsy, who looked close to her age. The latter looked up at her mother uncertainly. Martha smiled and said in English, "Welcome, all of you."

The language was alien, but the tone was warm, so Sophia stepped forward and smiled into Martha's kind blue eyes.

"Thank you," she said in halting English and then in Gaelic, "You're most kind. We are happy to meet you." She pointed at herself. "I am Sophia."

Then Hugh introduced himself and the children.

Without another word, Samuel started walking briskly past the meeting house on a track that led into the forest. Everyone followed.

With their long strides, he and his two eldest sons were soon well ahead, leaving behind the younger children and the two mothers, each carrying her youngest. As before, Hugh brought up the rear, pulling the sled.

Martha stumbled on a tree root, almost dropping Ann, but Sophia caught her just in time.

"Thank you." Martha squeezed Sophia's arm and smiled, then coaxed some loose strands of brown hair back into her bun with her free hand.

Sophia pointed to Martha's stomach and asked in Gaelic, "How long to wait?"

Martha held up three fingers and said in English, "About three months."

They heard the river before they saw it. With a wide smile, Martha turned to Sophia.

"Soon," she said.

Not long after that, they came into a clearing. Open land led down a gentle slope to a river. Farther along, they saw a log cabin perched on a slight rise above the river, with another larger building beyond it. There was cultivated land on both sides of the cabin.

Sophia stopped and stared. The forest was only a backdrop here, not a menacing wall of green. Not like Pictou at all, she thought. No tree stumps. And it appears very fertile.

Samuel led them first to the larger building, a barn. There were a few pigs, sheep and chickens in a penned area beside it.

Mary ran excitedly to the sheep pen, leaning over the fence to touch one. Inside the spacious barn, two cows and a horse were in stalls. Above was a hayloft. Samuel pointed to the loft and said something in English. Sophia and Hugh looked at one another. This was obviously their accommodation. In unison they offered their thanks in English.

Samuel smiled for the first time and gestured toward the cabin. Then he looked at his eldest, Samuel, and issued some instructions. The younger Blairs started pulling items off the Fraser sled. Mary understood right away and joined in. Jane looked up at Sophia uncertainly, but young Samuel smiled at her, touched her arm and gestured for her to help him.

Sophia smiled and nodded at Jane. Then she and Hugh turned away from the barn and followed Samuel and Martha to the cabin.

Inside the sturdy log house was a large front room with a spacious hearth and a small bedchamber behind. Above was a sleeping loft.

Martha put Ann down beside the hearth and gestured to Sophia and Hugh to sit on a nearby bench. In a small pot she began to boil some water. "Spruce tea," she said.

She poured thick amber-coloured syrup into the tea, then ladled cups out for all the adults. The tea had a strange sharp tang but was sweet.

"Mm," Sophia murmured and smiled at Martha. "Very good!" she said in Gaelic. Martha looked pleased.

When the children returned, Martha motioned for all to sit on the benches around their large table. Samuel bowed his head and gave what sounded like a blessing. Then Martha served a stew which had been simmering in a large pot. Sophia found the taste unusual but delicious. There was silence while everyone attended to their meal. Martha passed around bannocks which helped scoop up every last drop of gravy.

"Mmm, that was good!" declared Mary in a loud voice. Hugh and Sophia were embarrassed by her outburst, but Martha laughed and said in English, "I'm pleased you liked it."

And so they settled in. The drafty barn loft was a vast improvement on the makeshift shelter they had endured in Pictou. Mary was excited by the animals and had to be coaxed up the ladder each night. She was often down below early in the morning before her parents were awake, talking to the sheep, patting the horse or chasing the hens. Each day started at dawn with the men and boys tending to the animals and going to the river for water, while the women prepared the fire and the morning meal.

When the men returned, there was a huge breakfast of potatoes, meat, eggs, bannocks and often stewed fruit. The adults drank spruce tea and the children, milk.

After that, Sophia and Martha, with the older girls' help, spent the rest of the day washing, cooking, milking and collecting eggs. They also spent many hours preserving harvested vegetables and the berries and apples they had gathered earlier that autumn.

While the women worked indoors most of the day, the men and older boys, Samuel, fourteen, and Robert, eleven, were outside, cutting wood, making cabin and barn repairs and hunting. The deep snow had not yet made the woods impassable, so they travelled into the forest and along the riverbank searching for game.

After the miseries and the uncertainty they had endured, Sophia felt that they had traded a nightmare world of chronic hunger and cold for a world of plenty and security. During the first week, she wondered constantly if she might wake to find it all just a dream. It had been such a long time since she had seen Jane relax and smile and had heard Donald laugh. And she loved working alongside Martha.

Martha's generosity and patience were like a balm on a wound. Although language was a barrier, they seemed able to read each other easily. It reminded Sophia of her easy friendship with Christina.

But John was never far from her thoughts. His absence was an ache that never went away. Deep down, she still blamed Hugh for having to leave John and subjecting them to such misery.

But Sophia knew he was trying so very hard. At night in the barn, she needed to share her thoughts with him. After the pressure of attempting English all day, it was a relief to speak Gaelic again. And it was obvious that he needed to talk with her just as much. Working alongside Samuel, he said, was an education beyond value.

"I am learning how to fell trees the right way," he began, "and to hunt animals like..." and here he stopped, before attempting in awkward English, "*moose and deer*." They both laughed at the sounds of those peculiar words.

"He has shown me how to bury the meat in the snow to preserve it. All of this will serve me well when we have our own land."

These nightly conversations, however, were brief. Exhaustion carried them both off to sleep too quickly.

With the light fading by late afternoon, the evening meal was taken once it was no longer possible to work outdoors. It was a repeat of the substantial breakfast.

Afterwards the men sat by the fire while the women knitted, sewed and attempted conversation. Then Samuel would read aloud from the Bible, and Martha would use the story to teach a little reading to the children.

The younger Blair children showed the Fraser children how to play games with sticks or stones as markers, but often dozed by the fire after a busy day. Samuel and Robert sat apart, whittling wood, considering themselves too old for children's play.

"I love our time in the evening," Sophia told Hugh one night, about a month after they had arrived, as they were lying on their pallets of straw. "Martha is not only a kind person but a good teacher. Do you notice that our English is improving?"

"*Yes*," he said seriously, in English, then laughed with her, drawing her close.

"I want to learn to read, too," she continued. "I shall ask Martha if I may join the children when she teaches them to read. Do you approve?"

"Aye, wife. You will make an apt pupil. Watch that your children do not become jealous of you!"

She pinched his arm and laughed.

Sophia's new-found contentment came to an abrupt end the following day. As she and Martha cleared away the remnants of the morning meal, Martha drew her close, out of earshot of the younger children who were with them.

"Sophia," she began softly in English, "Are you with child?" She patted her own much-distended belly.

Sophia was stunned. She thought she had understood the words, but no, she must have misunderstood. Surely it could not be? She shook her head.

"No, it's not possible," she replied in Gaelic.

Martha smiled and put her arm around her shoulder. "I have seen some signs. Think on it."

Sophia stared at Martha transfixed. She understood the words, but could not accept their meaning. But it *was* true. It must be months now since she had last bled. She had not thought about it; she was too busy adjusting to life on the Blair farm. A cold fear gripped her heart.

“I don’t want this now,” she cried. “It’s hard enough to face this new life. Please, no, it must not be!”

Martha did not understand the Gaelic, but understood her distress.

“Come, sit down by the fire,” she said gently. “You have nothing to fear. You’re here with us. You have me to help you.”

Martha’s soothing words eventually calmed Sophia.

“You’re right, my dear Martha, I can face this if you’re with me.” She gripped her friend’s hands tightly. “I must accept it.”

That night, as she lay on her pallet beside a sleeping Hugh, she touched her thickening waist and sensed for the first time the tenderness in her breasts. Martha knows me better than I know myself, she thought. I’m blessed to have another such friend.

But she was not prepared to tell Hugh. Not yet. How would he react to the news? Would he be as troubled as she was?

Chapter Eleven

A series of December snowstorms started not long after, confining them all indoors for much of the time, the women and younger children in the cabin, the men and older boys in the barn. The crush of bodies in so small a space frayed everyone's nerves. The children, especially, found it difficult to remain cooped up inside. Even the older Blair boys became testy and took it out on the younger ones. Well aware of the tension in the household, Sophia told herself once again that it was not the time to tell Hugh about the baby.

By Christmas morning the snow drifts reached halfway up the door. Young Samuel and Robert cleared the snow away to allow the door to open, as they had done every few days for weeks. But the day itself was blessedly clear and sunny, though extremely cold.

Samuel provided snowshoes for Hugh and the older children for the trek to the Christmas service. He hitched the horse to a sled to pull their wives and youngest children. Inside the Truro meeting house it was very cold, but the mood was warm as they sang hymns, listened to Reverend Morrison recount the Nativity story from the Bible and prayed for the well-being of their community. There were several *Hector* families from Pictou there, those determined to attend this service, despite the difficult journey.

When Sophia heard of the dire conditions in Pictou and

learned of the death of the young daughter of one of the storehouse robbers, her fears resurfaced. She offered a fervent prayer of thanks for their decision to leave Pictou. She addressed it to the Lord, but she knew Hugh deserved her gratitude, too.

On their return, Sophia helped Martha prepare a special meal of roast mutton. With help from Hugh and the boys, Samuel had killed the sheep the day before. The meat was roasted on a spit, with drippings caught in a pan, much to the interest of the youngest children, who had to be continually shooed away by Martha.

After the meal, Samuel and Hugh enjoyed a cup of spruce beer. Then Samuel told stories of their previous life in a place called New Hampshire, as well as tales of their dealings with the Indians. Sophia loved listening to the gentle cadence of his voice, even though she, like Hugh, could understand only a little of what he said. She suspected that Mary could understand most of it. Sophia was invited to sing and sang a few soft Gaelic laments, and her girls joined in.

Later that night, as they lay on their pallets, with only the rustling sounds of the animals below, Sophia knew the time had come to tell Hugh. But before she could speak, he reached out to clasp her hand and said, "The Lord has been so good to us. I feel only peace and contentment."

"Aye," she replied. "I'm so grateful to be here, too. And the children are happy." Then she sat upright abruptly and faced him. "Hugh, I must tell you that I am expecting a baby, again."

Hugh sat up slowly and faced her. He said nothing at first. His reaction is the same as mine, she thought. He is troubled by this news, too. Then his face dissolved into a broad grin and he hugged her tightly.

"That's wonderful news, my love. I'm a happy man. It's a sign from the Lord. A new life for us here, in this new world."

"Your face didn't give me that message at first," Sophia said slowly.

"True. You read me well. My first thought was another

mouth to feed. Then I remembered. We're no longer in Kiltarlity. We're here in this wonderful place."

"I would like to feel as you do, but I can't," she said. "I still feel it's an added burden I must face. Me more than you. But Martha has reassured me. I know that as long as I'm here and have her near me, I can cope."

"But, my love," said Hugh, this time with concern on his face, "we must leave here in the spring to find our own land. That's my agreement with Samuel. We'll likely be on our own land when the babe is born."

Sophia pulled away from him. "I want to be here when my child is born. I can't do it without Martha. I won't do it in Pictou. Please, Hugh. I beg you."

"When will the babe be born?"

Sophia took a deep breath, trying to calm her rising panic. "Martha and I believe it'll be sometime in June."

Hugh was silent for a time. Then he said slowly, "Samuel has already brought up the subject of our departure in the spring. He has suggested May. He says that all the snow should be gone by then, and it'll be warm enough for us to travel and to make a start on our land."

Sophia drew the blanket around herself tightly. She could not stop shivering. Her voice shook.

"I shall stay here until the child is born, Hugh. Martha has promised to help me. I shall stay."

Then she lay back down and said no more.

Late in January, after yet another snow storm, Martha sent her two eldest boys to Truro one morning to bring the midwife. Sophia was surprised, as she had noticed no signs of labour. Martha just smiled at her.

"After six children born, I know my body well. It will come before this day is over."

And, sure enough, a few hours later, Martha's labour

started in earnest. In preparation, Sophia boiled water and prepared clean blankets and insisted that Martha take to the bedchamber to rest.

By early afternoon, the boys returned with Rebecca Burns from Truro. Rebecca was tiny, no taller than nine-year old Mary Blair, but efficient and masterful. She took charge, banishing everyone from the bedchamber. Sophia wanted desperately to help, to be with her friend, but Rebecca was adamant. A few hours later, the wail of a newborn woke Sophia and the youngest children, who had been dozing by the fire. No one dared enter the room, but soon Rebecca appeared with a bundle in her arms.

"A boy," she said. Then, directing Sophia to hold the newborn, she muttered that she had to see to the mother. It was only much later that Rebecca invited them into the bedchamber, the father first, to see mother and baby together. Samuel reappeared, with a rare smile on his face, to announce "James" as his new son's name.

Martha sensed Sophia's disappointment when she saw her. "It's better this way. Rebecca knows her business well. She has birthed all my children. Please don't be sad."

Sophia understood. She reached down to kiss the baby's downy head and gently squeezed her friend's arm. "I am happy... you and babe well," she said slowly in English.

"*Aye,*" mimicked Martha in Gaelic, and then winked. It was a good imitation. They both laughed.

From that time on, the winter weeks blended one into another, both women busier than ever.

Sophia assumed as many of the household chores as possible, so that Martha could be free to suckle James and snatch moments of rest during the day. Despite the cold, the deep snow and frequent snowstorms, only the youngest, along with Jane, remained indoors most of the day. Everyone else spent the greater part of the day in the barn. It was just too crowded for both families to be in the cabin except at mealtimes. The men and older boys were busy with farm chores, while Mary, Betsy and Andrew wore themselves out playing in the barn and in the snow.

Sophia was relieved to have been at the Blair farm for the birth of James. It gave her confidence that when her time came she could manage it in this new unfamiliar setting. She and Hugh had not spoken again of her determination to stay with Martha for the birth of her own child. She was sure he did not want to upset her by raising the subject and, as time passed, she became convinced that his silence meant that she would have her way. They would delay their departure.

In the meantime, Sophia's confidence grew as she learned many crucial skills from Martha. She learned how to brew peppermint tea to soothe sore throats and calm Jane's upset stomach. She learned how to prepare the sap of the balsam fir as a salve for cuts, scratches and mouth infections. Martha promised that once spring came the two of them would escape the confines of the cabin. Together they would forage for healing plants along the riverbank and in the forest. Sophia looked forward eagerly to these excursions.

Early spring was a dangerous time, as Samuel Blair kept reminding them. He was a man of so few words that his warnings were taken seriously by both his own family and the Frasers. The ice on the river thinned, making water collection and fishing difficult. Then the spring ice melt and rain combined to turn the river into a swollen torrent. In mid-April, as if to validate Samuel's fears, the son from the neighbouring farm fell into the river. Robert was with him and attempted a rescue. But he lost his balance and fell in, too, and both boys were swept down the river. Their shouts alerted the others. Samuel, Hugh and young Samuel raced along the riverbank in pursuit. Robert managed to grasp a large tree branch protruding from the bank and held on until the men arrived to pull him out. The other boy was nowhere in sight. His body was found many days later. The tragedy of his death shocked all of them. The near loss of Robert was terrifying. Badly shaken, Samuel became even more taciturn and Martha anxious and withdrawn.

Sophia felt her friend's distance acutely. The long period of security and contentment she had known since arriving at the Blairs had come to an end.

As April came to a close, the weather was foul. Melting snow had reduced the tracks and cultivated fields to muddy quagmires. Frequent rain and high winds made outdoor work miserable.

Everyone seemed on edge, from youngest to oldest. Never had the living space seemed so inadequate, so cramped as it was now. Sophia could see that even Hugh's natural optimism was being stretched to the limit. She confronted him about it one evening when they were alone.

"Hugh, I know how awful things have been: the drowning, the weather... but it's more than that with you, isn't it?"

He was silent for a moment, choosing his words carefully.

"It's time to move on," he said quietly. "The Blairs have been more than kind, but I fear we have stayed long enough. Their cabin was never meant to house two families." Their eyes met, and he held up a hand. "Please, my love, hear me out."

Sophia's heart was thudding, but she nodded.

"When Samuel and I went into Truro for supplies today, I met Walter Murray and Colin Mackenzie. They are planning to go back to Pictou next week, to investigate land along the rivers that flow from the harbour. This is not the land that was shown to us last autumn. I plan to join them in the search for some land in this new area, land that we may claim as our own. Samuel supports the idea. I'll go alone. You'll stay here with the children."

Sophia's relief was overwhelming. "Thank the Lord,

Hugh. You know I don't wish to leave here, not yet. And you know how I feel about Pictou." She shivered with distaste. "How do you feel about returning there?"

His face lit up. "Oh, it doesn't concern me at all. In truth, I'm excited. I have been restless for so long now. I ache to find some good land, to truly make a start to our new life. And I know my family are in excellent hands, so I can't wait to be gone!"

He laughed and caressed her belly. Then he became serious. Taking her face in both hands and moving it close to his, he whispered, "The sooner we lay claim to our own land, the sooner we can arrange for John to join us." Then he pulled back to study her reaction.

"Aye," she said but turned away. She knew he was right, but the thought of leaving Martha to start again elsewhere was terrifying.

A week later, fortified by Martha's spring tonic of dandelion tea to "cleanse the blood," and a week's supply of food, Hugh set off for Truro to meet Walter and Colin. From there, the trio planned to trek through the woods to Pictou.

Sophia rested a hand on her swollen belly and waved as she watched him walk away. She smiled. His stride was jaunty, like that of a youth. He was a man on a quest. She wished him well with all her heart. But she felt a stab of guilt. She was relieved to be staying behind. She did not want him to hurry back. Take your time, she thought. Enough time that I may still bear this babe here, with Martha.

Chapter Twelve

It was more than two weeks later that Sophia heard a child's cry from outdoors. She stopped stirring the stew in the iron kettle and moved awkwardly to the door. Outside, the early morning mist still lingered, and she could hear voices but could not see anyone. The snow at her feet was slushy and the air damp and cool. She felt Martha's hand on her shoulder, as her friend joined her silently, sharing her anticipation. Was this the day that Hugh would return?

Still Sophia saw nothing, but heard the same voice again. It was Mary's.

"He's back! Father is back!"

Then out of the mist materialized Hugh, with Mary trotting beside him, pulling on one arm. His clothes were soaked, his hair and beard matted, but Sophia surprised herself by embracing him fiercely, despite her swollen belly.

Hugh laughed. "I'm so very glad to see you, but away now, all of you. Give me a chance to get to the barn and put on dry clothes. I will join you by the fire as soon as I can."

He nodded to Martha, who smiled at him warmly and said, "You'll need a hot meal after such a journey."

Later, after Hugh had enjoyed a bowl of stew, some bannocks and tea, he was ready to relate his story. Everyone gathered around him expectantly in the cabin's main room. Only Samuel's two eldest boys were not present, away helping their neighbour, the man whose son had drowned the month before. Sophia had studied Hugh as he ate. Even after only two weeks, he appeared leaner, toughened. Most of all he seemed excited. She shifted in her chair again in discomfort due to an aching back.

In mostly Gaelic, but with as much English as he could muster for the Blairs, he made only passing mention of the hardships of the trek there and back. Then he leaned forward and, focusing directly on Sophia, described the lands bordering the three rivers that emptied into Pictou Harbour.

"The soil is fertile along those riverbanks, and the rivers, which abound with fish, allow easy transport to the harbour. The trees there are good and strong for building and might be suitable to sell as timber. Walter, Colin and I are of one mind and plan to settle in that area."

He stopped and took Sophia's hand. "My love, I traipsed up the longest of the rivers, the East River, to the head of a brook. It's called McLellan's Brook, after John MacLellan, who has already settled there. You remember the MacLellans, from the *Hector*?"

She nodded and he continued.

"I have marked some fine land along the brook for us, just near theirs. Our own land. Our new home. Just by settling on it we can lay claim to it." He stopped as his voice became unsteady, then took a deep breath. "I built a shelter on high ground above the brook. Then I hastened back without the others. I knew we must get there soon to be settled before your time comes."

Sophia's words were caught in her throat. She knew how important this was to him, to them, but her fear was greater. Fear of leaving this comfort and security. Fear of giving birth without Martha. But she could not deny him his triumph, so she smiled and nodded but did not trust herself to speak. Even Mary was silent, sensing the importance of her father's words.

It was Samuel who broke the silence. He stood up and clasped Hugh's hand.

"Well done, Hugh! You have chosen wisely. May God grant you and your family prosperity on your new land."

The next few days were hectic. Hugh was anxious to return as soon as possible, and Samuel supported the need for haste.

While Hugh, along with the two eldest Blair boys, went to Truro to buy and barter for provisions, Sophia gathered up their belongings. She steeled herself to bid farewell to the woman who had not only become her dear friend, but on whom she depended so much.

Jane withdrew into herself once again. Sophia knew she was anxious about yet another change, but this time she sensed anger in Jane as well.

When she tried to talk to her, Jane cut her mother off and cried loudly, "I don't want to go. Why must we move again?" Then she burst into tears and ran from the cabin. Sophia was startled by such an uncharacteristic outburst from her normally docile daughter. She feels as I do, thought Sophia sadly, but there's nothing I can say to help her. I can't even find the words to comfort myself.

Martha could read her friend's unease, and offered constant encouragement.

"We both knew you couldn't remain here forever. I understand your fears, truly I do. It's no small thing to birth a baby in such circumstances. But you have a good man, Sophia, and Jane will help you. She's at a difficult age and unhappy with another change, but she will adjust quickly. And you'll have neighbours nearby, the MacLellans, of whom Hugh has spoken. I have prepared a small box of herbs for you; the ones to aid in childbirth are on top. Take these extra blankets too, for the baby. And remember, if you can't remain on your new land once winter comes again, come back to us. There will be a place for you here."

Sophia understood most of the words and even more of

Martha's tone. Relief and gratitude overwhelmed her, and tears rolled down her cheeks.

"I shall miss you like a sister, dear Martha," she said in Gaelic. "You have been so good to me."

Within four days of Hugh's return, the Fraser family was ready to begin their journey. Hiding her distress, Sophia said her farewells. At the cabin door, she clasped Martha's hands, then dropped them and turned away. She did not look back.

They made their way slowly along the forest trail. The track was icy much of the way, muddy in patches where the sun's rays broke through the trees. Their pace was very slow. Mary and Jane walked beside their mother, while Donald sat atop their belongings on the sled pulled by Hugh. Rubbing her lock of John's hair compulsively in one hand, Sophia told herself repeatedly that everything would be fine. But she could not shake a sense of foreboding.

On the second day, two Indians approached them on the trail. Sophia and the girls stopped immediately, panic immobilizing them.

Behind them, Hugh said quietly, "Be calm. I shall speak to them."

He left the sled and walked in front of his wife and daughters to meet the two strangers. He raised his hand in greeting, then smiled and nodded, as he had seen Samuel do.

The Indians stood still and studied him intently for what seemed a long, agonizing time.

Then the shorter, older one stepped forward and raised his hand. He held up one of the snared rabbits he was carrying and waved it at Hugh. He said a few words and then put his fingers to his mouth.

Hugh smiled and nodded. "I think he's offering it to us," he said, in relief, as he turned back to face the others. Sophia let out a long breath that she hadn't realized she had been holding.

But the Indians did more than that. They made a fire and skinned and cooked two of the rabbits, offering generous portions to the Frasers. Sophia was still nervous, but glad of the extended rest. As they sat around the fire eating the meal, Mary edged herself ever closer to the strangers. She seemed fascinated by their long hair and colourful, exotic clothing. Sitting beside the younger man, she reached out and touched the smooth animal skins that made up his leggings. He didn't seem to mind. He bent toward her to allow her to stroke the fur robe that covered his shoulders. Mary grinned up at him. "Soft!" she exclaimed. Both men laughed.

They finished the rest of the meal in silence. Despite the tension, Sophia enjoyed the succulent freshly cooked meat, so much tastier than the dry food packed for the journey.

Afterwards, instead of continuing on their way west, the younger Indian started to pull the sled, and the older man walked in front like a guide. It seemed their intention was to lead this white family on their chosen eastward path. Neither Indian said a word. Sophia could see that Hugh was concerned, yet unsure what to do. They were following the blazed trail toward Pictou, true enough, but where were these men ultimately leading them?

"Be calm," Hugh whispered to her. "We have no choice but to keep going. Remember, they have shown us only friendship."

At dusk, the Indians stopped and started to make a shelter, then a fire. Sophia marvelled at how quickly they erected a solid lean-to from the detritus of the forest floor.

The younger one patted the ground of the interior while looking at Sophia and, understanding, she went to the sled and took out a blanket which she arranged on the floor of the shelter. The young Indian smiled and nodded. The older one gestured to Sophia to enter and sit down. When she did so, he looked at Hugh and made a rocking motion with his arms. Hugh nodded to confirm, then said in English. "Thank you."

Both Indians nodded in comprehension. The older man raised an arm, and then both turned to go in their original westward direction. Impulsively Sophia called "Stop!" in Gaelic, which surprised not only her family but herself. The Indians halted.

She pulled a ribbon from her hair and held it out in offering. The older man came back, accepted the gift with a nod, then both turned and walked away.

"That was a fine gesture," Hugh said to Sophia, once the Indians were out of sight.

Sophia let out a sigh of relief. "It came to me all of a sudden. But Hugh, I am so very proud of you. I was terrified when they appeared, but you showed no fear!"

It was his turn to look pleased.

They slept exceptionally well that night, thanks to a solid shelter, a meal of fresh meat and the relief that came in the aftermath of their dramatic encounter.

It took them another three days to reach their land on McLellan's Brook. As they drew closer to Pictou, Hugh asked them all to look carefully for the blazed tree markings that John MacLellan had made to point their way toward the East River. It was Mary who spotted the first marking. Not long after they had turned off the Pictou track, it began to snow. This last part of the journey was the slowest and the most agonizing of all. It took them most of that day to reach Hugh's chosen site. It was becoming hard to see in the growing darkness; Sophia was exhausted and desperate for the trek to end. And finally they arrived, signalled by a cry of distress from Hugh.

"Oh, dear Lord!"

In the dim light, Sophia could see a partially collapsed mound. She stared at it in horror. How could they possibly survive in such a place?

Hugh moved quickly to fashion a temporary shelter using the sled and blankets, and helped Sophia and the children underneath.

She could hear him working to repair the lean-to. By the time he guided Sophia to the repaired shelter, he had a fire going at its entrance. He filled a bucket with water from the icy brook and then portioned out a meal of dried meat and bannocks. Despite's Hugh's coaxing, Sophia was too worn out to eat and fell into a deep sleep soon after.

Early the next morning she was awakened by agonizing pain. She felt Hugh at her side.

"Dearest, dearest, you have been moaning, what is it?"

"The babe's coming," she gasped. "Oh, dear Lord, not now! It can't be!"

"I will away to the MacLellan cabin for help," he said patting her hand. "Jane will be with you. I will be fast, my love, I promise." He kissed her hand and was gone.

Time passed in a blur. When bouts of pain subsided, anger and fear took over. How could she have ever agreed to leave Martha? To come to this godforsaken place? She would never forgive him.

After what seemed an eternity, Hugh's taut face came into view.

"My love, this is Jane MacLellan. She's here to help you."

Another voice cut in brusquely in Gaelic, "Mr. Fraser, get a fire going. You, lass, keep those wee ones out of my way."

Sophia felt capable hands adjusting her body gently, all the while reassuring her that all would be well.

"Breathe when I tell you and push when I say so. You are fine, lassie, I'm here." Her words were calming, and Sophia nodded in relief.

Only a few hours later, she gave birth to a son. Jane MacLellan wrapped the babe in a blanket and tucked him in beside Sophia.

"Mr. Fraser," she called, as she lifted a corner of the blanket, "you have a fine son. And a special one, at that, you understand, the first white manchild born on the East River." Jane paused. "What name for the lad?"

Hugh knelt in the snow at the entrance to the shelter. He looked from his new son to his wife and smiled hesitantly.

"My love," he began, taking her hand, "I would like to name him Alexander, after my grandfather."

Sophia pulled her hand away. "Oh, Hugh, call him what you like."

Then she turned her head toward Jane and managed a weak smile. "I can't thank you enough, Mrs. MacLellan. I am so relieved you were here."

"It's Jane to you, my dear. And you and the children will be coming to stay with me these next few days while you get your strength back." She looked about her and shook her head. "You can't stay here!"

Chapter Thirteen

Four days later, on a cool and sunny morning, Sophia and the children returned, accompanied by John MacLellan. Hugh watched them approach along the bank of the brook. He leaned on his axe, borrowed from Samuel, and studied the little group. John had something slung over one shoulder. At his side was Sophia, leaning on his free arm, while she cradled the newborn in the other. Jane followed, holding the hands of Mary and Donald. Hugh felt a flutter of happiness to see them again, yet he was uneasy about the reunion. Sophia's anger had been all too evident when they had left with Jane MacLellan. She blamed him, of course, for the sudden early birth of Alex. She blamed him, too, for taking her away from Martha when she needed her most.

As they came closer, he saw her eyes scanning the area. He hoped she would see the potential he had seen. Whatever else, she would see the shelter, a strange collection made up of boughs, bark, twigs, mud and cloth, with a fire pit at its entrance. She would see that it sat on a rise above the brook, a small clear patch surrounded by forest.

She would realize that it would take an insurmountable effort to turn this land into a farm, and he hoped she would notice the fertile strip down near the brook. Would Sophia admit, then, that he had chosen well?

He raised his arm and called out, "Welcome home!"

Mary broke away from Jane and, scampering towards him with arms outstretched, cried, "Father!"

John MacLellan echoed a greeting. As he neared the shelter, he tipped a large hunk of deer meat from his shoulder to the ground. Then he shook Hugh's hand warmly, promised to return the following week and took his leave. Sophia made no move to embrace Hugh. Instead she sat down silently on the log at the entrance to the shelter and began to suckle the baby.

Later the family sat by the fire to eat a substantial meal of cooked deer meat, bannocks, dried fruit and tea, prepared by Jane. All but Mary were unusually quiet. She filled the awkward silence by babbling on about their time with the MacLellans. Right after the meal, Hugh got up. "I must away back to work," he said, to no response.

And so their lives followed a routine. Every day Hugh attacked the trees with his axe. His first task was to clear enough land to plant potatoes. It was slow work on his own, with his limited experience. He burned the smaller branches and twigs among the stumps of the fallen trees, to make the soil more fertile. He left the larger logs where they fell, for future cabin construction. He stopped only for meals.

Sophia, meanwhile, was consumed by her own tasks. Cooking, washing and caring for Alex took up most of her time. The task of managing Mary and Donald fell to Jane.

Each afternoon, Sophia gathered her little group together, and they went foraging for berries and plants, as Martha had taught her. Hugh noticed they never strayed far; they were always within sight of the shelter. He heard Sophia warn the girls several times to stay close by.

It was as if Hugh and Sophia lived in separate worlds and came together only at mealtimes and to sleep in the same cramped shelter. Even then, their contact was limited and conversation almost non-existent. It pained him greatly, especially as he longed to hold his new son and talk to him. But Sophia made it clear she did not want him close, so he kept his distance. He felt sure that her anger and hurt would fade eventually. In the meantime, work would be his solace.

One night while his family slept, he eased himself carefully out of the shelter and sat on the log by the entrance. The fire smouldered. It was a still, clear night, and a full moon showcased the cleared patch he had worked so hard to create. It was like a tiny island in an immense sea of forest, but it was a start. From his jacket pocket, Hugh pulled out his pouch of Kiltarlity soil. He opened it and ran his fingers through home, his old home. He would treasure it always.

But he had a new home now, his own land. The thought made him smile, and he allowed himself a shiver of pride. He reached down and ran his fingers through the damp earth. This was the soil in which he would plant potatoes among the tree stumps and later, other crops. The soil of his new home. This was the land that John, Donald and Alex would inherit someday.

By week's end, however, his confidence was fading. He was beginning to doubt that on his own, he could ever clear enough land to plant the food they needed and to build a permanent home. All before winter arrived. He began to fear that his dream was in danger of failing.

Then John MacLellan returned, and Hugh was glad to see that Colin Mackenzie and Walter Murray were with him. To learn that his friends had indeed chosen land nearby, along the east bank of the East River, was the best possible news. Not only had they come to pay a social call, but they had an interesting proposal to present. Like Hugh, the others faced the same problem of clearing enough land before winter. John had a suggestion which would help them all.

"If we join together, we can hire experienced hewers from Truro to fell our trees. Not only will our land be cleared faster, but these men know how to hew the logs we need to build cabins."

"And the logs we don't require can be floated down the river to Pictou," added Colin. "Perhaps we can even earn money for that timber, once we have paid the hewers! What do you think?"

All were enthusiastic and endorsed John's plan without hesitation. John and Walter would journey to Truro within the week to make the arrangements.

Hugh felt like a new man. Now it could be done! They could stay. Perhaps even make a good start on a cabin. And perhaps make some income from the surplus timber. But the best part was knowing that he was not alone. After their departure, he attacked the trees with renewed vigour.

He told Sophia of their plans that night. She listened but made no comment. He was disappointed that she didn't share his excitement, but not surprised. After everything that had happened, she wouldn't be moved by talk alone. He could wait.

By early June, the weather was warmer and the hewers had arrived, but so had hordes of small biting insects. The children, especially, were covered with countless bites, as if they had a pox. Sophia suffered too, and she had the added challenge of coping with extra mouths to feed.

The hewers divided their time between the Fraser land and the MacLellans'. Before they moved on to the Murrays' and Mackenzies' properties, the woodsmen felled enough trees to produce some saleable timber. This allowed Hugh space to plant a potato crop, but not enough to clear the necessary land for a cabin. He would have to do that on his own.

As the summer progressed, he and Sophia continued to live their separate lives. But he noticed that she seemed more confident in her surroundings, as she was foraging farther away now.

Hugh hunted with his neighbours frequently and found that Indians would appear as if out of nowhere to join them.

The Highlanders were always happy to see them; they were far more successful when the Indians were with them.

Despite these developments, Hugh worried whether they would have enough food to last the entire winter. He longed to talk to Sophia about his fears, but knew the time was not yet right. So he waited patiently.

The moment presented itself after a bout of unrelenting rain. For five days, life in the shelter was pure misery as one leak after another soaked everything. Donald and Jane had developed coughs. Then it took another week to dry all their clothes and blankets. After that, Hugh slept out of doors, to give Sophia and the children more space in the cramped quarters. She had been abrupt and distant before; now he could see her agitation growing.

One night, once the children were asleep, instead of taking to her pallet as usual, she joined him where he sat at the shelter's entrance. She stood facing him.

"I have put up with this since we arrived here and said nothing," she began, her voice tight with controlled anger, "but I will not face a winter here. I can see with my own eyes that our cabin can't be completed before then. Living in this," she gestured at the shelter with disgust, "is misery enough now, but will be impossible once the snows come. We must return to Truro. You know we're welcome there." She paused, then looked directly at him. "I intend to go, Hugh Fraser, with or without you!"

Hugh was saddened by the disdain in her voice.

Of course she was right, but he had to admit that he had hoped for some recognition of his efforts, some faint words of praise. It sounded like a condemnation.

"You're right," he said wearily. "I can't construct a cabin in time. We'll return to the Blairs." But he thought, it will pain me to leave this land. And so help me, it will be the last time.

She nodded. "Good. I'm relieved that we're agreed. Now I'm off to my bed."

He sat staring into the fire for a long time before unfolding his own pallet and lying down.

In late August, Hugh and Walter Murray borrowed John MacLellan's canoe and journeyed down the East River to Pictou to buy supplies at the storehouse at Brown's Point. Robert Patterson would now allow them to use credit on future timber sales. When they arrived, he surprised Hugh by handing him a letter.

"It arrived on a supply ship that came in last month," Robert said.

Hugh expressed his thanks and shoved the letter in his pocket. Could this be news of John? Pray it was good news. Hugh was anxious to learn its contents, but there was only one man he trusted to read it.

He went to find John Patterson as soon as he and Walter had loaded the supplies into the canoe.

Hugh was not surprised to see that his friend's cabin was almost complete. John and a young lad were working on the roof as he approached.

"Hugh! It's so very good to see you," John called down in Gaelic. "Please bide awhile. I shall be with you presently."

After proudly showing Hugh the interior of his small cabin, he offered him a cup of buttermilk. They sat together on a log at the cabin's entrance, exchanging news of the past year. Patterson was soon laughing.

"For a man of few words, you have become a mighty talker!"

"My apologies, John. I've been starved of conversation of late. It's a comfort to speak with a good friend."

"No matter, Hugh. I am delighted to hear of your son's birth and of the land you've chosen. But I am sorry to hear you must leave once again at season's end."

Hugh nodded. "I hate to leave, but we've no choice."

Then he smiled, "But we'll return in the spring, put down permanent roots and never leave again!"

"I will drink to that," laughed Patterson and drained his cup.

"And, John, I'm so pleased to hear that you've wasted no time in turning your hand to the timber business. I know you'll be a great success!"

Then Hugh showed John the letter, telling him how it came to him. "I would be honoured if you would read this aloud to me."

John unfolded the paper and began, reading one English sentence at a time and translating it into Gaelic, before reading the next.

> "Dear Mother and Father,
>
> I am Well. I go to School. I learn to Read and Write and Speak English. I study Scripture, too. Granddad is not well. I look after him. At Christmas Service, Reverend Nicolson spoke of the *Hector* People and Blessed them all. He helped me Write these Words. He sends The Lord's Blessings to You, as I Do.
>
> Your Loving Son, John"

There was a stunned silence as Hugh stared at Patterson.

"Dear Lord, he's alive! He's well! And... and he can read and write in English! It's too much to take in." Hugh put his head in his hands and closed his eyes. He felt a friendly hand on his shoulder.

Then he looked up at Patterson. "It is true, is it not?"

"It is, my friend. Words cannot express how happy I am for you. This must be the best news you could hope for."

Hugh reached out for the letter with shaking hands and John gave it to him.

He traced a finger along the large graceful loops on the

paper, struggling to believe that these marks had been made by his son. Abruptly he stood up. "I must get back to Sophia!"

"If you would like it, I could pen a reply for you," said Patterson, softly, "when you are ready."

"Aye, I would that," said Hugh gratefully. "I'll speak with Sophia to consider our words, then return. Oh, thank you, John, thank you!"

"Of course."

All he could think of was what this small piece of paper would mean to Sophia.

"Sophia! Sophia!" cried Hugh excitedly as he approached the shelter. "Come! Quickly!" He sprinted the last few yards, arm outstretched, with the letter waving in his hand and almost knocked her over as she met him at the entrance.

"Look at this! Look! It's a letter from John! He's alive!" Hugh struggled to catch his breath. "Our prayers have been answered."

"No, it cannot be!" Sophia stared at him in disbelief. "I can't believe it... not after all this time." She searched Hugh's smiling face. "Oh, dear Lord... Hugh, is it true?"

"Aye, my love, it's true," he assured her as he guided Sophia to the log at the shelter's entrance. "Come. Sit. I'll tell you what it says."

Then he recited the letter's contents from memory, word for word. As he spoke John's words, her gaze shifted from his face to the paper in her hand. When he had finished, she clutched it to her chest, then sank to the ground soundlessly. Moments passed.

He hesitated, unsure what to do. Then she began crying in great shuddering sobs.

He motioned to the children to let her be. They all stood by awkwardly. Finally she stood up and started to laugh. She hugged Hugh and then each child in turn.

"My John's alive!" she cried. Then her face suddenly tightened. "It is true?" she cried desperately. "These are his words, you're sure?"

"Aye, my love, I'm sure, as is John Patterson, who read the letter to me."

"We must reply right away," she said briskly.

Together they composed a response. Hugh promised he would return to Brown's Point as soon as possible to dictate it to John Patterson.

> "Our Dearest John,
>
> We Praise the Lord that You are Well. We Send Our Love and Blessings to You and to Your Granddad. We pray he recovers soon. We are well. We have our own Land now and are working very hard so that You may join us soon. You have a new Brother, Alex, named for your Great-Grandfather Fraser. We are so very Proud of your Learning.
>
> Your Devoted Mother and Father"

For Hugh, John's letter was a priceless gift. Knowing that his son had not only survived but was prospering brought him tremendous relief. Finally he had the proof that his decision had been the right one.

But for Sophia, he could see it was life-changing. She became a different person. She talked and sang through her daily chores. Her joy spilled over into every look, every touch and every word. They all basked in it. But no one more than Hugh. He had been forgiven.

Hugh's new-found happiness, however, was tempered by

the certainty of their departure. It could be delayed no longer. Other families had already made the decision to leave for Truro before the first snowfall. Neither the small potato harvest, nor the meagre vegetable crop from the brook flats, would last them through the winter.

The construction of a cabin was barely begun. Reason told him he had no choice, but he knew that leaving would feel like losing a limb.

For Sophia, he knew it would be completely different. She would welcome a reunion with Martha, with her dear friend and mentor. She would feel confident of her children's well-being during a winter with the Blairs. And in Truro Alex could be baptized. Hugh could see that Sophia could not wait to go.

Chapter Fourteen

As they approached the Blairs' cabin, Mary caught sight of Andrew and Betsy and broke into a run, waving and yelling at her old playmates. The noise brought Martha to the door, and she waved. As they got closer, she hurried to meet them. With open arms she enfolded Sophia, who was carrying Alex.

"Welcome back, dear sister," Martha said and kissed Alex's cheek. "A fine boy," she murmured, as she looked up at Hugh. Then she embraced each of the children in turn, except Mary, who had already rushed off to the barn with Andrew and Betsy in tow.

"Mary!" Hugh called after her.

"Leave her be, Hugh," laughed Martha, "she needs to see her animals." Then she turned her attention to Jane.

"You, my dear, are becoming a well-favoured young woman."

Jane bowed her head and blushed, but not before Hugh saw her smile. With a start, he thought, Martha's right. Jane may be only twelve, but she's no longer a child. I had not seen it before.

"Come in, come in," Martha coaxed, "Samuel and the boys will be back soon."

It was a happy reunion, made even livelier by the Frasers' improving English.

Hugh sat back, said little and enjoyed listening to Sophia

recount the news of John's letter and then her wish to have Alex baptized as soon as possible. When Martha agreed to stand as witness at the ceremony, Hugh could see that Sophia's happiness was complete. He had not wished to leave his land, but Sophia's new-found joy made it seem worthwhile.

And he did appreciate how fortunate they were. None of the other *Hector* families had found such a generous and open-hearted reception in their winter lodgings. Hugh was determined to learn as much as he could from Samuel and to repay him by working tirelessly on his farm. This would be his last opportunity. He had promised himself that this would be their final winter there.

The awkwardness with which Hugh had tackled anything during his first winter fell away, and his confidence grew. He was most proud of his axe skills. His English was improving, although he still spoke Gaelic whenever possible, fearing to sound foolish in the new language.

Sophia's English was improving, too, and Martha's evening lessons with her and the children were helping her to read it and even write a few words. Unlike their mother, father and Jane, Mary and Donald were not self-conscious, so were picking up the new language quickly. Mary, especially, was chatting away naturally in English.

Sophia, too, tried to absorb as much as she could from her mentor. Martha's special talent was her understanding and use of healing plants.

Under her guidance, Sophia's knowledge of specific trees, plants and bushes was growing rapidly.

They all fitted easily back into the rhythm of life with the Blairs. Then one Sunday in February, Hugh heard some surprising news. After the Sabbath service in Truro, he met his old *Hector* friend, Hugh MacLeod, who had settled on the West River.

"Have you heard the news from Pictou?" he asked Hugh.

Hugh shook his head and MacLeod continued.

"You remember Donald Cameron, from the *Hector*? He's been given a government land grant on the East River."

"Wonderful news!" exclaimed Hugh. "Bodes well for all of us!"

Most settlers had applied for grants, but this was the first to be issued.

"Aye, and he's a Catholic too," laughed MacLeod, "so the rest of us should have an even better chance!"

When Hugh relayed the news to Sophia, he added, "I can't wait to return to our land. The sooner we build a permanent house, the sooner we get our grant."

"And the sooner John may return to us!" she exclaimed. His heart missed a beat. How times had changed! Even she was anxious to get back to McLellan's Brook.

By late March, Hugh's wish seemed about to come true. The snow was beginning to melt, and the ice on the river was cracking. Perhaps they would have an early spring and conditions for travel would be favourable. It had been a happy, productive winter for all of them, and Hugh's spirits rose as he considered the coming weeks. Sophia, too, seemed energized about the future. Then one day, everything changed.

It was a Sunday afternoon, when Jane told her mother that she wished to accompany young Samuel and Robert. They had to take their horse to the neighbour's farm. Their neighbour had asked to borrow the animal for a day or so.

"You know how much I love that horse," added Jane.

Hugh looked up surprised, and Sophia said, "Well, no, I didn't. It's Mary who is the animal lover."

Jane flushed and looked away, then murmured, "You know little of me."

Before Sophia could respond, Hugh waved Jane away, "Oh, go ahead Jane. You need a break from the wee ones."

Sophia glanced at him. "I may need her help this afternoon."

"She needs a break, Sophia," soothed Hugh. "Let her be with those closer to her own age for a change."

Sophia said no more.

And he thought no more about it, but an hour or so later, while he and Samuel were repairing the pigpen beside the barn, the sky began to darken. Then they heard faraway rumbles of thunder.

"A storm is coming," said Samuel. "We should get back to the cabin."

Hugh nodded. "I hope Jane and the boys are close to home, or have decided to remain at the neighbour's farm until the storm passes."

Once back in the cabin, the families waited tensely for the missing children. Rain and wind lashed the windows and door, and the cabin shuddered as the thunder rumbled overhead. Suddenly the door burst open and Robert stumbled in, his soaked clothes clinging to his body. Everyone froze, but Martha reacted first, throwing a blanket over her son and drawing him to the fire.

She rubbed him down vigorously, and when he had stopped shivering, he gasped, "The horse threw Jane! She was unhurt. But she and Sam ran after it. I lost them in the storm." He looked close to tears.

"Start at the beginning, lad," said Samuel gravely. Hugh could tell he was trying to remain calm, but his voice was worried. Hugh moved to put an arm around Sophia, but she did not seem to notice. She was staring dumbfounded at Robert.

"Jane was on the horse with Sam holding the bridle. The first crack of thunder spooked it. It reared, and Jane fell. Then it bolted. We all chased it. That's when I lost them. I yelled and yelled but they were gone. Then I ran back here."

Robert looked guilty and close to tears, as if they might blame him.

"You did the right thing, son," said Martha.

"What was Jane doing on the horse?" demanded Samuel.

Robert looked sheepish. "Sam's been teaching her to ride."

"Not with my permission!" Samuel's voice rose.

"What's important now is that they've taken shelter somewhere," said Hugh, gently. He did not want to dismiss Samuel's concerns, just keep an even perspective.

"As soon as the storm has died down, Hugh and I will go out to search," said Samuel, gruffly. "We can't do anything at the moment."

Hugh saw the worry on Sophia's face. In Gaelic he said, "Don't worry, my love. Sam's a smart lad, a strong one, too. He'll find shelter for them. They'll be fine." He hoped he sounded more reassuring than he felt.

She shook her head, then replied in Gaelic, "I told you I didn't want her to go!"

It seemed an eternity before the storm ended. When it did, Hugh and Samuel set out along with Robert.

It was dusk before they made it to the spot where Robert was sure that the horse had run off. The rain had washed away any traces of Sam and Jane. The men spent some time calling out for the two young people, then walked the short distance to the neighbour's farm where they expected to find them sheltering. They weren't there. Now Hugh was truly alarmed.

Images of Jane and Sam confronted by bears and wolves, while they huddled to stay warm and dry, terrified him. Samuel said nothing, but his body was tense. The neighbours promised that they would leave a candle in the window and search themselves at first light.

"Nothing more to be done this night," said Samuel wearily. "We must return home before the light is completely gone. They may already have found their way back." He paused and added, "And if they haven't, we'll resume our search at first light."

Hugh knew Samuel was right, but his fear drove him to consider staying out to keep looking, even in the darkness. Sophia would be distraught if he returned without them.

As if he could read Hugh's mind, Samuel said quietly, "I know you are heartsick, but hold fast to common sense, man. No sense in losing you, too. I have every faith in Sam."

And so they walked back slowly, stopping every so often to shout into the darkness.

Hugh didn't sleep at all that night. Sophia had refused to meet his eyes on their return. Her stricken face spoke for her. In the barn, she lay down with Mary and Donald, with Alex snuggled close to her, away from Hugh. He doubted that she slept much, either.

At dawn, after a silent, hurried breakfast, Hugh, Samuel and Robert set out again, carrying blankets, food and water. When they reached the place where the horse had bolted, Samuel pointed close to the river bank, where the trees were not as dense. "This way, I think."

They had walked less than an hour when they heard voices and, rounding a bend, saw two figures walking toward them. Sam had his arm around Jane supporting her and she was leaning against him. They broke apart instantly. Hugh caught a moment of guilt on both faces. Then Sam broke into a grin and called out, "Father! We're so happy to see you!"

Jane moved away from Sam unsteadily and went directly to her father. She said nothing, just hugged him tightly. With his heart pounding, Hugh hugged her wet body close and offered up a silent prayer of thanks. But his mind was racing. There was more going on between these two than a night lost in the woods.

"Give each of them a blanket, Robert," directed Samuel. "Once you two have had something to eat and drink, we'll return home." He held up his hand, as Sam opened his mouth. "No explanations now, son. Later."

With cries of relief, both families rushed out to meet the weary group once they neared the cabin. Samuel was glad to hear that the horse had made its own way back to them that morning, unharmed.

Then the family gathered in the cabin to hear what had happened. Sam described their chase after the horse and eventually his decision to make a shelter for the two of them to wait out the storm. Jane was silent throughout, but Hugh noticed the way she watched Sam with such obvious admiration. Afterwards, Samuel told young Sam to come to the barn with him to check on the horse. Hugh got his chance to speak to Samuel privately later in the afternoon, when Samuel invited him to walk by the river.

Samuel came straight to the point, once they were out of earshot of the cabin.

"Sam assures me that there was no unseemly behaviour," he began, "but he admits that the two of them have formed an attachment and wish to become betrothed."

Hugh was too astonished to reply immediately. Then he said slowly, "I suspected there was something more, a closeness, when we first saw them this morning, but didn't expect that."

"No, I'm as shocked as you are. And I'm fond of your Jane, mind, but they're far too young, of course. I have told young Samuel that this is out of the question and he must not be alone with her again. After all, you will be leaving soon..." Samuel let this thought linger in the air. Hugh knew what was expected of him.

"Yes. It's just as well that we'll be gone soon and won't return next winter."

"I knew I could count on your support in this. Thank you, Hugh."

They shook hands solemnly and then walked back in silence.

That night in the barn, Hugh told Sophia what he had seen, of his conversation with Samuel and their decision. Her shock seemed as complete as his had been.

"I'd no idea," she began in a daze, "I must talk to her, counsel her about being around young men."

"She's never said anything to you, never tried to confide?" asked Hugh gently.

Sophia looked up at him, bewildered. "No," she said softly, "how could I have possibly known?"

"No, of course you couldn't. Jane's always been a quiet

lass, keeping to herself, but I thought, perhaps, as a woman, you—"

Sophia cut him off. "As a woman, I've been too busy!" Her voice rose. "I've just learned that I'm expecting a baby again. And not happy about it. That's been heavy on my mind." Then she turned away from him. "But I'll speak to her. Have no worries of that."

Chapter Fifteen

Sophia managed to get Jane alone the next day after breakfast. They walked together to the barn for some privacy. Sophia started by warning her daughter about the unseemliness of allowing herself to be alone with a young man, even a lad like Sam, whom they knew so well. Jane was sullen and unresponsive and would not look at her mother. Sophia began to doubt she would get a word out of her. She finished by saying, "Your father and I know what's best for you, Jane. You must put aside any childish, selfish thoughts." Jane looked up then, and the fury on her face shook Sophia.

"Selfish!" she cried. "I've never been allowed a selfish moment in my life, never had a chance to have some time to myself! All I've ever done is look after the wee ones, done your bidding and worked hard every day! I've felt more like a servant than a daughter! No one has ever asked me what I want. I never wanted to leave Scotland. I never wanted to come here. Did you or Father know or care? But here, I found a person who does care. The only person who has ever bothered to take an interest in me. Sam is the only one who truly cares for me!" She burst into tears then and turned her back on Sophia.

Sophia was stunned. She stared at Jane as if she did not recognize her.

Then she reached out and put her arms around Jane.

"I'm sorry, Jane, I had no idea you felt this way. Your father and I have had so much to face since arriving here, we've had no time to think of anything else."

The two stood silently, Sophia holding Jane as her body shook, whispering in her ear as if she were an infant. Then Jane pulled away.

"We want to get married," she said firmly, "and Sam does not want to be a farmer. He wants to be a blacksmith." She smiled then, suddenly. It caught at Sophia's heart; so rarely did she see her daughter smile. "We both love horses. We know we can't be married till we're older, but we can wait, as long as we're betrothed." She looked pleadingly at her mother.

"Dearie," said Sophia, "you're too young to be betrothed." Then she held up her hand as Jane opened her mouth to protest, "When you're older, if you and Sam still wish to marry, we'll consider it." She hugged her eldest close. "I'm so happy you are safe. I thought I had lost you in the storm."

Sophia did not have an opportunity to talk to Hugh until that night in the barn. As she related what Jane had said, she tried to convey the resentment and bitterness Jane had been harbouring for so long, so that he, too, might understand.

"I had no idea that Jane was so unhappy," finished Sophia.

"Nor did I. What time has there been to think of feelings, ours or our children's? How could we have known?"

"But what are we to do about her and Sam?"

"There's no decision to be made," he replied, matter-of-factly. "We'll be leaving here soon, as planned. Jane's too young to be spoken for, as is Sam. And Sam is to be sent to Halifax to apprentice as a blacksmith."

Sophia looked up at him in surprise.

"I've spoken with Samuel today," he said. "He says it's the best solution for all. It's what the lad wants. It will help him accept the separation. After all, in a few years time, when they're both of age, and if they still feel the same, they may seek each other out."

"And Jane?" asked Sophia.

"I will speak to Jane, my love. You've enough concerns." He smiled, but Sophia did not share his optimism. This news will devastate her, she thought.

And Sophia was right. She was not present when Hugh talked to Jane, but he didn't hide from her Jane's distress and claim that she would never forgive her parents. Hugh believed that his daughter would forget soon enough, but Sophia doubted it. And she felt Jane's anger every day, despite no words being spoken. Everyone in the cabin felt the tension.

Not long after, young Sam left for Halifax, and within days the Frasers prepared to leave.

It was an awkward, subdued leave-taking, even amongst the children. Hugh and Samuel merely shook hands and nodded at each other. But Sophia and Martha embraced each other tightly.

"I shall miss you so," said Sophia.

"And I you," replied Martha.

As she stepped back, Martha pushed some stray hair back up into her bun. It was such a familiar gesture that Sophia felt a rush of grief. She wondered when she would see her friend again, if ever.

This time the journey to McLellan's Brook was easier for Sophia. Alex, almost a year old, was a sturdy baby who sat placidly on the sled. And the journey was uneventful. On arrival, however, they found that their shelter had fallen in under the weight of heavy snow. By evening, Hugh had rebuilt much of it and dug a new fire pit.

They soon fell back into the routine of the life they had known at the brook the previous year. Hugh set to work immediately felling more trees, helped by his neighbours and the hewers hired again from Truro. When they had extended the space begun the season before, they began to assemble the base for a one-room cabin by hoisting logs one on top of another, as the American settlers did.

With Jane's grudging help, Sophia planted potatoes in every cleared spot and vegetables on the brook flats. In the brook and up the river they fished for salmon which they smoked over the fire.

They collected plants and berries for food, drink and medicine. Over the course of the summer, this demanding routine was relieved only by a few gatherings with their nearest neighbours, the MacLellans, the Murrays and the Mackenzies.

But for Sophia, it seemed to be a harder season than the one before. Although she no longer had to deal with the demands of a newborn, she tired easily as she was expecting a baby again, and was uneasy about Jane's unhappiness. Both she and Hugh encouraged Jane to take some time for herself, but Jane remained withdrawn.

By summer's end, a basic cabin was almost finished. The stacked logs provided sturdy walls, but the roof was a jumble of boughs, twigs, bark, mud and clay, with a space just large enough to allow smoke from the fire below to escape. A fire pit had been dug in the dirt floor, and a large iron kettle was suspended over it. And a privy had been built well behind the cabin. Their furniture consisted of a table and two benches. Blankets spread over balsam fir boughs served as beds. Sophia worked on a quilt in the evenings. Their other quilt had been brought from Scotland, a gift from Hugh's mother.

Sophia went into labour during the first week of September. Once again it was a short labour, but Jane MacLellan and Christy Murray, wife of Walter, had time to attend her and help with the birth.

It was a girl this time, whom they named Margaret. Unlike Alex, however, she did not appear to be a sturdy infant. Sophia overheard Jane MacLellan whisper to Christy, "A wee, frail soul, this one."

Fear clutched Sophia's heart. She longed to hear

Martha's soothing reassurances more than anyone's. But it was not to be, so she kept silent.

Once she recovered from the birth there was little time for reflection, as the vegetables needed harvesting, and fish, fruit and plants had to be gathered and prepared as winter stores. Hugh dug pits beside the cabin to act as cold storage for meat once the snows came. He and his neighbours hunted together and worked hard to make their cabins as winter-proof as possible.

Sophia kept her worries to herself. She had little inclination to confide in Hugh. She was getting little sleep, as Margaret was a fretful baby who did not nurse well.

But a welcome piece of news raised everyone's spirits. Hugh returned from a late autumn trip to Pictou with another letter from John. Once again he recited from memory what John Patterson had read aloud to him.

> "Dear Father and Mother,
>
> Thank You for your Letter. Granddad and I are pleased to Learn of your Chosen Land. I am well. My Studies continue. I hold the Rank of Top Pupil.
>
> Granddad has recovered from his Illness of Last Winter, but feels the Pain and Weakness of Old Age. He says I am of Valued Help to him. Aunt Margaret cares for Him and cooks for Us. I trust that You are in Good Health, as are my Brothers and Sisters.
>
> I remain your Loving Son, John."

Once more John's words filled Sophia with happiness, as she dreamed again of their reunion. Together she and Hugh composed a reply, including news of Margaret's birth. Sophia insisted that they include a line promising John's return to them very soon.

Hugh said he did not want to raise the lad's hopes, that it

might take years to save enough for John's passage, but he included the promise for her sake.

In a more subdued tone she added, "My father's strength is fading. We must send him our love and prayers."

John's letter sustained Sophia for weeks. She had placed it reverently in a small wooden box made by Hugh. It rested there alongside John's first letter and the lock of his hair brought from Scotland. It helped her cope with a sickly infant, an unhappy daughter and the harsh winter that was soon upon them.

That winter was long and difficult, but the cabin protected them from the assault of snow, ice and wind. They had been able to stretch their food supplies to the limit.

By early spring, however, they had been reduced to eating nettle and herb soup a little too often. To everyone's relief, little Margaret not only survived the winter, she thrived. Sophia found herself facing each day with a lighter heart.

Although weak, the Frasers and their neighbours had no choice but to throw themselves back into the hectic work of clearing, planting, fishing, hunting and construction once the ground allowed it.

That year of 1776 brought new and unexpected complications. The Revolutionary War to the south affected their lives in many ways. With the interruption in trade, there were shortages of many household goods imported from Britain. But there were benefits as well. Many settlers, including Hugh, profited from the increased timber trade that a war-time Navy demanded.

A disturbing effect of the war was the souring of relations between the American settlers, who generally supported the rebellion, and the more recently arrived *Hector* Scots, who did not.

Hugh suspected that Samuel Blair would be sympathetic to the rebel cause. He believed that any hopes Jane may have had of a future with young Sam might be in jeopardy. Sophia was disheartened. Despite the year of separation, Jane had never wavered in her belief that she and Sam would eventually marry.

When a rumour surfaced some two years later that young Sam was betrothed to a girl in Halifax, Sophia was upset. If true, how on earth would she break such news to Jane? Once again, Hugh was determined to spare his wife. He would talk to Jane himself.

"It will come better from me, her father. She dare not rail at me."

But Sophia was equally determined that this time it was up to her. "She'll need a woman to talk to this time, Hugh. I know she's not opened up to me before, but now she must. Surely. It will be to her mother, if to anyone."

Jane did not believe Sophia when told of the rumour.

"No, it's a lie! You're saying that only to dissuade me from my course!"

She ran off then, and Sophia didn't see her for the rest of the day. By dusk, Sophia was openly fretting and Hugh went out to look for her.

It was then that Jane MacLellan appeared along the brook bank, arm in arm with Jane.

Sophia ran forward and embraced her daughter, but Jane pulled away.

"Go along inside, Jane," said Jane MacLellan. "Let me chat with your mother."

To Sophia's surprise, Jane dutifully walked away. Sophia stared after her.

"If you'll forgive the intrusion," began Jane MacLellan, as they stood by the brook's edge, "I've a suggestion. Our family is travelling to Truro next week. Perhaps we could speak with the Blairs ourselves, confirm the truth. It may be the only way to put Jane's mind at rest."

Sophia could not reply at first. There were too many thoughts swirling around in her head. Jane had confided in someone else, expressing all the feelings she had kept to herself for so long.

Sophia hesitated and then agreed to Jane MacLellan's plan. Surely it was best that Jane know the truth. Hugh agreed when she told him.

The MacLellans brought back the confirmation of Jane's worst fears. If Jane cried, Sophia didn't see it. Jane's silence and withdrawal were like a rebuke. Her daughter was suffering but would allow no one to comfort her, not even her mother.

Tension settled over the cabin. It was broken only a few weeks later when Hugh returned from a trip to Brown's Point. The unexpected smile on his face caught Sophia's attention and she allowed herself to be led to the chair by the fire.

Excitedly, Hugh gave her the news. John Patterson had offered to bring their John to Nova Scotia from Scotland by the end of the following summer. Sophia was speechless.

"I told him we had not yet saved enough money to pay for his passage," continued Hugh breathlessly, "but he said he would pay the rest! He says that as a clever and educated young man our John can be of use to him on the voyage, and here in Pictou. I find it hard to believe, too, but it's true."

Sophia nodded slowly. "Tell me again," she whispered, "so that I may believe it."

Hugh repeated himself, and Sophia looked up at him, watching his lips move and his face lit with joy.

She felt the tears streaming down her own face. This was what she had waited years to hear. She would see and hold and kiss her John again. Soon.

Part Two

1779 – 1815

Chapter Sixteen

John Fraser stood beside John Patterson at the railing as the ship entered Pictou Harbour. Even at twelve he stood as tall as the older man. It was a sunny late-summer morning and the air was filled with the scent of pine. Young John wanted to feel excited, but all he felt was unease. Patterson had described the settlement at Brown's Point and the growing number of farms along the Pictou rivers. They had spoken constantly during the voyage about life in Nova Scotia, but John was unprepared for this first sight of his new home. Patterson had warned him that it was nothing like the great port of Boston, which had been John's first experience of the Americas during their stopover. He was dismayed by the rough scene: a few log huts amidst the small cleared spaces near the shore, overshadowed and dominated by the mighty forest. But what he saw before him was worse than he had imagined.

"Where is the town?" he asked nervously.

"There is no town, lad, just a small settlement, a scattering of cabins and a storehouse."

They were speaking English. Patterson had encouraged it, telling John that he would have few opportunities to speak it once he rejoined his family. He turned to John now and laid his hand on the lad's shoulder.

"Oh, now I see that poor face," he said, reverting to Gaelic. "I know this is a hard land and hard to get used to.

But," and here he smiled, "this is the very best place for a smart, well-educated lad like yourself. You can make your mark here; there's naught to hold you back. You can be a success in this new land, far more easily than in the old country."

John felt the older man carefully studying his reaction.

Then Patterson added, "And I will be here to help you."

This last comment finally brought a smile to John's face. "I thank you for everything you have done for me, Mr. Patterson," he said, switching to English. "I'll be your faithful servant always."

"And I shall be your friend. You may count on me."

After Patterson had issued directions about the contents of the ship's hold, he and John took the first boat ashore.

"I shall send word to your father that you have arrived. You will stay with me until he is able to travel here."

John admired Patterson's cabin.

It was small but well-furnished. His skill as a carpenter was obvious in the well-crafted furniture: the table, the cupboard, the benches and chairs. But what impressed John most were the writing desk and the shelves of books. These marked Patterson as a man of learning.

After the hardships at sea, John's next two days were filled with comfort and plenty. He began to imagine what life could be like as the fortunate only son of a man of means. This was where he belonged.

His father arrived at Brown's Point on the third day. John was helping at the storehouse with an inventory of primers that Patterson had bought during their stop in Boston. When Hugh walked in, John looked at the tall bearded man. He was familiar, certainly, but different, greyer and much thinner than John remembered. And then he was being embraced by this man, the father he barely knew, as he stood stiffly, arms at his sides.

"John, my son," was all Hugh could manage.

After a moment, Hugh released him and looked expectantly into John's eyes.

"Hello, Father," he mumbled, glancing over at Patterson.

"The Lord has answered our prayers," said Hugh. "I've waited for this day for so long, my son. And you've become a fair, fine-looking young man." Then he hugged John again and said, "Your mother can't wait to see you. We must away quickly."

John looked nervously at Patterson, who nodded and said, "Aye, you have kept your parents waiting long enough. Away to my cabin and gather your bag, so you may be off with your father."

John felt a moment of panic. He didn't want to go! His face must have given him away, because Patterson added, "I trust you can come back soon to help me and continue your studies, as we discussed."

He opened the door, waved John through and closed it. John hesitated on the other side, then turned and listened at the closed door.

He heard Patterson clear his throat and say, "With your blessing, Hugh, I would like to help the lad in his advancement. If you could spare him a few days each month, in fair weather, he could work here with me, learn from me. I believe he could be a leader in this community. He's a bright lad."

There was silence. On the other side of the door, John shifted nervously from foot to foot, waiting for his father's response.

Finally Hugh replied. "A kind offer, John. I'll talk it over with Sophia first, with your leave."

"Of course, Hugh, of course," Patterson agreed. There was a pause and then he added, "My greetings to Sophia, and safe journey home."

At that point, John bolted from the door, racing all the way to Patterson's cabin, and returned with his bag. After their farewells to Patterson, Hugh led his son down to the shore and placed John's bag in a long shallow craft beached at the water's edge.

John's face blanched. Surely he was not expected to clamber into a hollowed-out log for the journey.

"Climb aboard, son," encouraged Hugh. "It will feel a little tippy at first, but you'll quickly get used to it."

And so they set off. Hugh paddled down along the shore of the harbour to the mouth of a river and from there south. John sat in the bow, gripping the sides of the canoe tightly, fearful of the strange motion. He was uncomfortable, too, in his father's presence, for this man was a stranger. The journey passed in silence.

Eventually they turned into a narrower waterway, and Hugh said, "This is McLellan's Brook, John. We're almost home." Then a little later, Hugh lifted his paddle and let the canoe glide toward the bank.

"We're here," he said proudly.

John saw a small log cabin on a rise above the brook, with an area of planted crops amongst many tree stumps, a small open space surrounded by forest.

Hugh beached the canoe, climbed out and called, "Sophia." As he helped John out, a cry came from the back of the cabin. A girl came racing down to meet them, followed by a boy and then a much older girl, walking slowly and holding the hands of two small children. Hugh intercepted the red-haired racer before she could bowl John over.

"You remember Mary," began Hugh, "and Jane...? And this is wee Donald, who was only a babe when we left, and here are Alex and Margaret."

Then John heard a cry from the cabin. A thin woman, carrying a baby in her arms, emerged and moved toward John as quickly as she could. With tears streaming down her face, she handed the baby to Jane and embraced him.

"Oh, my dearest son, I've waited for this day for so long. I never wanted to leave you and I've prayed every day for your safe return." She was trembling as she clutched him tightly.

John didn't know what to say or do. He was overwhelmed by all of them. And this woman did not resemble the mother he remembered. She had been a beautiful, soft angel, not this bony stranger.

When Sophia released him, she wiped her tears and studied him closely. "You're even taller than I imagined you might be and very handsome." He blushed, but he could tell that she was pleased by his reaction.

"Come away to the cabin now. You've so much to see and learn."

His new home was yet another disappointment. It was smaller than Granddad's in Kiltarlity and, with little furniture, meaner and sparer than he was used to. Mr. Patterson's cabin was small, too, but had much more furniture. There was no writing desk here and there were no books. This was no better than Kiltarlity! He didn't belong here. And there were more disappointments to come.

There was little space and privacy in the cabin. After sharing with just Granddad and Aunt Margaret, John found daily life suffocating here amongst eight others. The noisy antics of the younger children irritated him.

And much of the work was unfamiliar and much harder than he was used to. Cutting trees, clearing and preparing the ground for planting were back-breaking tasks. Hunting strange animals was terrifying. And most unbearable of all was the lack of schooling; he missed his studies terribly. Although he was at an age when most in Scotland had finished their education, he had cherished the hope of further education, perhaps of even becoming a minister.

The only respite he found was reading in the evenings. Thank the Lord, Mr. Patterson had lent him some books. He was pleasantly surprised to learn that his family could speak some English and that Mary was almost fluent, even though her constant chatter annoyed him.

As the days and weeks passed, John was dutiful but aloof, anxiously waiting for permission to visit Mr. Patterson. Eventually he approached his father one evening.

"When will I be able to visit Mr. Patterson?" he asked, then added quickly, looking down, "To work with him, as he suggested."

His father said nothing, while John fidgeted in the awkward silence.

Finally his father spoke. "You've only just arrived, after so many years apart. Your mother has missed you terribly, and you've hardly come to know your brothers and sisters." He hesitated then asked, "Are you unhappy here, lad?"

John felt his face redden and he stumbled in his reply. "Of course I'm happy to be here, Father, but... I... it is... it's only from Mr. Patterson that I may borrow more books. And he has promised to teach me about business... for my future success, you know?"

In silence, Hugh studied his son thoughtfully. Then he sighed, "I'll talk to your mother about this, lad."

That night, he heard his parents speaking quietly together by the fire, as he lay on his pallet, surrounded by his sleeping brothers and sisters.

"He's been so quiet, like a stranger. He hardly says a word," his mother said softly. "He's not at all like the John I remember."

"It's been hard for him, after all these years," said his father. "Six years, mind. He's lived a different life and been schooled."

"It was so wonderful to have him back, but now I feel he's lost to us. We lost him all those years ago and I feel we'll never get him back." Her voice was close to breaking.

"He's not lost, my love. It'll just take time. We must be patient while he adjusts to life here and to us." After a pause, Hugh continued, "I think we should allow these visits. It will be hard to let him go, even for a few days each month, but it's very important to him. And he can learn a great deal from Patterson."

"You're right," said Sophia reluctantly, "although it pains me to let him go at all."

In the darkness, John grinned broadly as he heard these final words. He could go!

Chapter Seventeen

John's monthly visits to Brown's Point became his lifeline. He spent three or four days each month with Patterson. He learned carpentry from his mentor, as well as an introduction to the export timber business. The two spent evenings in the quiet cabin reading and then discussing what they had read.

It was a calm, well-ordered life of ideas, so different from his life at McLellan's Brook. John revelled in it. After that very first visit, he was reluctant to return home. Patterson must have sensed his unhappiness, for as John was leaving, he told him he had some words of advice.

"I can see that your present circumstances chafe you. But your mother and father are very fine people whom I admire greatly. Your father has worked hard to create a farm out of an unforgiving forest. He is the master of his own land. He left the old country to make a better life for all of you. Respect him. Learn from him, as you learn from me, and you will have a prosperous future."

All the way home, as John stroked the supple leather cover of his newest borrowed book, he thought about Patterson's words. If Mr. Patterson directed him to make a greater effort with his parents, especially his father, then he would do so. He would talk to his parents more often. But he didn't believe there was much point in doing so with his brothers and sisters.

After all, their education would never match his, and he would have little in common with them as they grew older. But to please Mother and Father, he would teach his brothers and sisters a little reading. John could accept his current circumstances more easily now; Mr. Patterson had reminded him that they were only temporary.

Almost immediately, John could tell that his parents were pleased with his efforts. His mother especially was delighted. Her mood brightened considerably, and she sang often as she worked.

But he noticed that the other children were unmoved. It was obvious that his mother favoured him and just as obvious that they resented it. But their feelings did not concern him. His focus was on the future. His circumstances would change. Mr. Patterson had promised that. All he had to do was bide his time.

Three years after John's return, twins Sophia and Ann were born. Sophia had no energy to suckle two babies, so Hugh had to travel to Truro to find a wet nurse. Eleanor arrived to live with them, to John's great irritation. Another person to take up space in the cabin.

At thirty-nine, his mother seemed worn out. For the first time John felt a stab of fear. He had come to care deeply for her, as he had as a child in Scotland.

He felt a bond with his mother that he felt with no one else in the family. And, thanks to Mr. Patterson, he felt a new respect and appreciation for his father.

Circumstances did begin to change for John and the Fraser family just two years later. On a sunny August afternoon in 1783, John burst into the cabin. "Father! Mother! I've wonderful news! All at the harbour are speaking of it!" Pleased to see the look of anticipation on their faces, he continued, "The government is going to give thirty-five *Hector* families title to the land they occupy. And we are among those families!"

Hugh had jumped to his feet but was silent, staring at John in disbelief.

"How has this happened?" asked Sophia.

"It seems the government wishes to reward those who remained loyal during the war," said John.

"This is what we have wanted for so long!" cried Sophia and she hugged her still-silent husband, then John.

John watched as his father sank into his chair. He had to lean forward to catch Hugh's almost inaudible words. "Finally. We have our own land."

More change followed with an influx of new settlers to the area, due to the American war. Disbanded soldiers arrived, mostly Scots, having been granted land as payment for their services.

To John, now seventeen, Patterson described the newcomers as a mixture of types, some sober, hardworking men, others drunken profligates. To effervescent Mary, all these new men meant an endless round of fun and flirting.

John had heard Hugh caution Mary, but he didn't believe his father had gone far enough. He was angered by her unseemly behaviour.

He discussed the issue with Patterson, despite knowing that his father would not approve.

"She will bring disgrace to us all," he moaned on several occasions.

"Aye, it is unwise behaviour, lad," agreed Patterson.

John's relations with Mary worsened as he decided to act. He watched her constantly and reprimanded her whenever he saw her with any man. She was furious. Their arguments often ended in shouting matches in the cabin, when their father was not present. John regretted the distress these rows were causing his mother, but he could not help it. Someone had to do something.

One morning, John confronted Mary in the barn. "Think

of our family, girl! Mr. Patterson agrees with me that your actions taint us all!" Mary simply stamped her foot and strode off.

"John!" cried a voice behind him. John turned quickly and came face to face with his father.

"You have discussed our family business with Mr. Patterson?" He heard the hurt in his father's voice, even as he saw the anger on his face.

Momentarily tongue-tied, John mumbled, "Her behaviour is no secret."

"That is not what I asked." His father's voice was quiet now. Somehow that was worse.

"We may not be as fine or as learned as Mr. Patterson, but we deserve our privacy. You will never again discuss family business with anyone else. Do you hear me, lad?"

John was indignant. His father made no mention of the subject again, even as John kept his eye on Mary. Mary, for her part, was either heeding his advice or becoming more cautious.

At their next meeting, Patterson had some good news for John.

"A young man of twenty-seven, the Reverend James MacGregor, has been appointed to the post of Presbyterian Minister of Pictou. A permanent clergyman to shape and guide the moral tone of this community!"

Patterson enthusiastically recounted his meeting with MacGregor, on a visit to Scotland. "You will like him, John. He's a scholarly man, of considerable energy and commitment. This will be his first post."

MacGregor arrived from Scotland the following summer and preached his first Sabbath service in Robert Patterson's barn. It was well attended, and the Frasers were there.

As he listened to MacGregor's sermon, with its emphasis on a strong work ethic and commitment to education, John's excitement grew. Here was a kindred spirit. He sought him out after the service. MacGregor was a tall imposing figure.

He seemed impressed with John's excellent English, his scholarship and his sober outlook, and told John he looked forward to working with him. John was elated.

People were so pleased with their new minister that they promised to build him not one, but two, log churches. The first was built near the harbour. The second, completed soon after that, was situated on the East River, not far from the Frasers. One of the first celebrations in the new East River Church was the marriage of leading citizen John Patterson.

Now twenty-one, John Fraser believed that the future he had imagined for so long was on the horizon.

His work with Patterson and his relationship with James MacGregor kept him occupied and stimulated, even as they distanced him more and more from the daily life of his family.

Chapter Eighteen

Although it was John's practice to attend English services only, to please his mother he accompanied the family to a special Gaelic Sunday service to mark the first anniversary of the East River Church. Many had come from a great distance, including the Murrays, old friends of the Frasers.

They had moved from the East River to Merigomish, on Pictou Harbour and Hugh and Sophia had seen Walter and Christy seldom since then.

It was a noisy reunion of the two families, with the exception of John who stood a few feet distant, uncomfortable with the fuss. When he felt eyes on him, he looked up to see one of the Murray daughters staring directly at him. He blushed and looked away, but not before he had taken a good look at her: a dainty young woman with a vivacious smile. He studied her all through the service, but was careful to do so in a way that would not draw attention. Or so he thought. After the service, she approached him and spoke first.

"My name is Jannet, and I know you are John. I'm very pleased to meet you. I'll be at the harbour church next Sabbath. Maybe I'll see you then."

With a smile, she put out her hand, and he took it tentatively. He mumbled a few words in reply, then looked away. He may have been much older, but he felt as if he were the pupil and she the master.

He was in his twenty-second year and she was only fifteen; she spoke no English and had had little schooling. He told himself that such an uneducated girl held no interest for him. But he went to the Sabbath service at the harbour church the following Sunday, hoping to see her. And when he saw her, he was captivated.

She had large hazel eyes which were luminous. Her brown curls framed her delicate face perfectly. And her smile was infectious. She spoke to him effortlessly, in a voice that bubbled with excitement. He was content to simply listen to her. What she said didn't matter. He could speak to older men like John Patterson or James MacGregor, but was awkward around those of his own age. With Jannet, however, he felt completely at ease.

When John asked Walter Murray's permission to court his daughter, Walter's approval was immediate. John was more than suitable: tall, handsome, well educated and the first-born son. And his parents were friends.

After that, the young couple's pattern was to meet as often as possible on Sundays. If the weather was fine, they would walk together along the riverbank or by the harbour. Jannet would speak of her family, or of needlework, or of the warmth of the sun that day, then stop to gather flowers. She seemed to find promise in everything. John was content to be silent, letting her happy conversation wash over him.

After several such meetings, John was invited to Merigomish to share a Sunday dinner with her family. He would return the following day. His mother encouraged him to accept when she saw his reluctance.

"It would be a slight to refuse," she said. "I know your interest is in Jannet alone, but it's important that you make an effort with her family."

John accepted. He found much of the conversation at the dinner table tiresome. But when Mr. Murray asked him about his work with John Patterson, he became animated.

He glanced at Jannet afterwards and noticed that she was beaming at him. He was glad he had come.

The following morning, he thanked his hosts, then went to the barn to saddle his horse. A hand on his back startled him and he spun around.

"Oh, Jannet, I was coming back to the house to say goodbye."

"I know that, John. But I wished a word in private."

She took his hand and said in a rush, "I care for you very much. I hope you feel the same."

He was taken aback. Did he care for her? He must. How else could he account for this strange exhilarating feeling whenever he was with her?

She was looking up at him, waiting. What should he say?

"I... care for you, too, but..." he stumbled, as he saw her face fall. "Jannet, I..." But she had already rushed away.

As he rode to Pictou for his weekly meeting with John Patterson, he cursed himself for his blundering. How could he have been so foolish?

"I hope I haven't hurt her feelings."

"It will be easy to make amends, I wager," said Patterson. "When you are away from her, do you think of her, wish to be with her?"

"I do."

"Then I believe you have your answer, my friend. You do love her. Tell her, and all will be forgiven."

"But... she has no schooling, no English."

"That can be easily remedied," laughed Patterson.

On the following Sunday, John attended the service at the harbour church in the hope of seeing Jannet. And she was there. As she was coming out of the church, John stopped her when she tried to move past him. "Jannet, please listen." He took her hand gently and said, "Jannet, I do love you. Please accept my proposal."

When she saw the love in his eyes, she knew it was true.

"Oh, John! I love you too! I'm so happy!"

He led her away from the church and took her in his arms.

Gently, he pulled her to him, tilted her face up toward his and smiled into her shining eyes. "I love you so much, Jannet," he breathed, and kissed her. Of course he loved her.

Hugh and Sophia were delighted by John's proposal, as were the Murrays. But they insisted that their daughter wait until she was sixteen to marry.

Jannet was upset and complained to John, but he persuaded her to honour her parent's wishes with grace. Duty was all-important. He told her they would have all the time in the world once they were married.

Unexpectedly, his older sister married before him. John, like the rest of the family, had doubted that serious Jane would ever marry, especially now that she was twenty-five.

He had thought little of her, other than as a welcome contrast to Mary, and as the dutiful daughter who spared Sophia the most demanding household chores. He had doubted that Jane had the capacity to attract a suitor, let alone show interest in one.

But she had met John Fraser, an ex-soldier of the 82nd Regiment, who had been granted two hundred acres of land near Merigomish. He approached Hugh and asked for permission to court Jane.

John was surprised at his parents' relief and delight.

"Poor Jane has pined after her first love for years now, and I have always felt so sorry for her," said Sophia. Then she recounted the story of Jane and Sam.

"When news came that Sam was betrothed to another, I think it broke Jane's heart," Sophia said sadly, and John put his arm around her thin shoulders.

"I'm sure she will be happy now," he said softly, "All that hurt is in the past."

John looked at his sister differently now. Like me, she's in love, he thought. He offered her heartfelt good wishes and when Jane responded with a radiant smile, John was surprised. He had never seen her so happy.

Jane and her John were married at the Fraser cabin. For the first time John felt part of a family gathering. With Jannet at his side, he felt as if he finally belonged among them.

After the wedding, Sophia pulled him aside and said, "John, I have never felt more blessed. Not only has my Jane found happiness at last, but I feel my son is now truly a part of this family."

Later that same year, the wedding of John and Jannet took place at the Murray farm in Merigomish, with James MacGregor officiating.

Wedding guest John Patterson offered congratulations and some words of advice for John.

"I don't expect to see you at Brown's Point for a time," he said. "You will be busy building your own home and seeing to your wife, as it should be."

John couldn't hide his surprise. "I had hoped to continue, perhaps not as often, but I'd intended to keep working as your assistant. I still have much to learn from you."

"You will be occupied clearing your land, and your wife will need you. They must be your priorities now."

"She wishes to learn to speak English," said John proudly, "and to read and write it. I believe she has a quick mind."

"Yes, and you can teach her. At home," Patterson added pointedly, with a smile.

After the wedding, Jannet and John moved in with his parents while their own log cabin was constructed on Fraser land. Hugh had added other rooms to the original one-room cabin, and they took one as their own.

As Patterson had predicted, John had time for nothing more than the clearing of his own section of Fraser land, the construction of his cabin and later preparing the land for planting and setting up a household. Within months, Jannet was expecting a child and was sick much of the time. John's intention of teaching her English would have to wait.

His new priority became furnishing his house, including a writing desk and bookshelves. His home would be just like Patterson's.

Chapter Nineteen

Almost a year to the day of their wedding, Jannet went into labour with Sophia at her side. Elizabeth, Jannet's older sister, was sent for as planned and arrived the next day. Even though he was kept from the chamber, John could sense that it was a difficult labour. Despite her strength and determination, Jannet became worn down by its length and severity.

Sophia reassured John that she was using herbs to treat the pain and her considerable skill to try to ease the baby out of the womb. But, she said, it was as if the baby were trapped inside Jannet's tiny, fine-boned body.

Finally, on the morning of the third day, the baby was born.

"A healthy wee boy," declared Sophia proudly when she emerged from the chamber to present John with his newborn. John held his son briefly, then asked to see Jannet.

"She's very weak after such a birth," warned Sophia.

When John entered the room, Jannet struggled to raise herself, smiled weakly at him and sank back immediately onto the bed. He was appalled by her appearance.

Elizabeth bundled the baby and laid him on Jannet's chest, but she had no strength to hold him.

John did not miss the look of concern that passed between his mother and Elizabeth. He named the newborn

Hugh, but declined to hold him again. His concern was solely for Jannet.

His father tried to comfort him. "It takes time for a new mother to recover, lad. Don't worry, she's in good hands."

But Jannet did not regain her strength and was too weak to feed the baby, so a wet nurse was found. John didn't want to leave his wife's side, but was finally persuaded by Hugh.

"Leave her to the care of the women, lad. Come away with me to work on your cabin and land. You can sit with her this evening."

It was good advice. In the physical work John found a release from some of his frustration and fear. Although father and son shared little conversation while they worked, John found Hugh's presence comforting.

Exhausted, John slept well each night, holding Jannet's frail body close to his, as if he might transfer some of his strength and warmth to her.

Walter, Christy and Elizabeth visited often, and Sophia welcomed them. Jannet seemed to rally with the New Year. Her appetite improved and she was able to sit up and hold her baby. John was ecstatic and believed she was on the road to recovery. They all did.

But one day in early February, everything changed. Jannet awoke with an aching body and high fever.

"John, love," she began, "I think I wish to sleep a little longer. I'm very tired and so hot." Her teeth began to chatter.

John caught his breath. Jannet was ghostly pale, and her breathing was shallow and raspy. Oh, dear Lord, he thought, panic-stricken. But he swallowed his fears and gently took her hand. "Don't worry, love, I'll get my mother. She'll know how to help you."

Within minutes, Sophia was at the bedside. She prepared an herbal tea to treat the fever, coaxing Jannet to take small sips. John, meanwhile, bathed Jannet's face and limbs with cool cloths. Nothing helped.

Jannet slept much of the day but as the shadows lengthened into evening, she seemed to rally. "Where's my babe? Please, John, bring me our son. I want to see him."

John slipped from the room and returned with the sleeping baby. "Here he is, my dearest," he whispered, as he gently placed the baby by her side.

Jannet smiled tenderly at her son. "Now I can rest. Thank you, John."

By early morning Jannet was gone. It was February 7, 1792. She was seventeen.

John was grief-stricken. He continued to hold her lifeless hand as the first rays of light penetrated the cabin. How could she possibly be gone?

Sophia appeared at his side. She hovered over Jannet for a time, touching, listening, then turned to him. Tears were streaming down her face.

"I'm so, so sorry, John."

His father came and tried to pull him away gently. "It's over, lad. She's at peace now. Come away."

But John pushed his father away. "She's not dead!" he shouted. "She can't be dead! Dear Lord, she can't be!"

The noise had woken his younger sisters, Margaret, Ann and Sophia. Their anxious faces appeared in the doorway of the chamber.

All eyes seemed to be on him. He stood up. He had to get away, to escape the staring faces. He pushed past everyone and rushed out of the cabin into a clear, bitter winter morning and ran along the snow-covered path to his almost-completed cabin.

Inside he paced back and forth compulsively, until finally, worn out, he collapsed onto a blanket on the floor and slept. He woke in the night and resumed his pacing. To remain still and think was agony.

When he returned to his parent's cabin the next morning, much of his agitation had spent itself. He felt numb.

In his absence, Sophia had washed Jannet's body and dressed her in the blue wedding dress the young mother had worn such a short time ago. Jannet was laid out in the main room of the cabin.

In a daze, John sat down beside her. He took one of her cold hands, but did not look at her. He refused to talk to any of them. And he refused to hold his son.

The following day, the Murrays, along with Jane and John Fraser, arrived from Merigomish. Neighbours called in and brought food.

John ignored them all, including Patterson. He sat silent and aloof as family members took turns sitting by Jannet's coffin in a solemn vigil, day and night, keeping company with her soul.

He remembered nothing of the brief service the following day. MacGregor's words were meaningless anyway. God had abandoned him.

John helped carry the coffin outdoors to the back of the cabin. The men covered it in snow, topping the mound with spruce boughs. There it would lie protected until it could be buried properly in the spring. That evening he sat apart, as Christy spoke of her daughter's childhood, and his mother and sisters sang laments.

The next day, the Murrays, and Jane and John Fraser prepared for their journey back to Merigomish. Before leaving, Christy took her sleeping grandson in her arms and approached John.

"This boy is my Jannet's," she said. "He's all we have left of her. You do no honour to her or to us by ignoring him. It's not his fault she died."

She held out the baby to him. Then in a pleading voice she cried, "Please John, if you love Jannet, love this child, be his father!"

John stared at Christy. They stood facing each other for several moments. Then Christy placed the baby in John's arms.

He looked down at his son. There was silence, as if everyone in the cabin were holding a single breath.

Suddenly John buried his face in the little body and wept. When the worst had passed, he looked up at Christy and nodded. He would do his duty. He would raise his son for Jannet's sake. And hope that one day his heart would thaw and allow him to do it with love.

Chapter Twenty

The months following Jannet's death passed in a blur. During the day, John drove himself hard working on his cabin. In the evenings, he returned to his father's home to share the evening meal with the family and to sleep.

Baby Hugh was not with them. John had allowed his mother-in-law to take his son to Merigomish to bide for a time with the Murrays. He had yielded to her pleas more to put an end to them than due to any feelings he had on the subject. Sophia had urged him to reconsider. John had looked into her distraught face and shaken his head.

"Please Mother, let me be. I don't wish to talk about this. I just want to be left alone."

"But John, by the time you're ready, your son may be lost to you forever. Don't do what I had to do. I had to give you up and come here. I believe I never truly got you back."

The pleading in her voice and the tears in her eyes irritated him. He felt a tinge of guilt, but turned from her and walked away. He couldn't wait for the day when he could move into his own cabin and escape all of them.

That day came in early spring. And the relief he found in solitude did bring some peace.

When, a month later, he heard the sound of a horse approaching, he found himself intrigued rather than annoyed. At last, he felt ready to welcome a visitor. It was James MacGregor.

The day was sunny and warm, so John suggested they sit on the bench by the door.

"You've built a fine cabin here," began MacGregor. Then he paused and continued in a more serious tone. "I've been thinking of you a great deal, my friend. I know what a blow it was to lose your Jannet, but with a son to consider, I'm very glad to see you settled on your own land."

John said nothing.

"But," MacGregor continued, "this is not a bachelor's home you've built here. It's for your family, and your son is not an orphan; he needs to be here, in his own home. Would Jannet wish him to be without his father?"

MacGregor reached out and put a hand on John's shoulder. "You must do this," he said gently. "It's the Lord's will and your duty, and you cannot argue with that. Your home is ready for your child. Time to fetch him."

They stared at each other for a few moments. Then John turned his gaze to the forest. MacGregor waited patiently. Finally John looked at his friend and sighed, "I know you are right."

Shortly after his meeting with MacGregor, John moved his son into the home he had planned to share with Jannet. At Sophia's suggestion, his younger sister Margaret came to live with them to care for the baby.

Baby Hugh was fussy at first, adjusting to another change, but after a few weeks he settled down. John could see that Margaret was a good choice. She was enthusiastic about her role and, at fifteen, seemed to relish her position as lady of the house. Although he still felt no attachment to the baby, he did believe that the decision was the right one. Facing his mother for the first time in months, he thanked her for her help and counsel. His words felt inadequate to his own ears, but he saw the delight on her face.

In mid-summer, Patterson paid him a visit. They had not seen each other since the funeral, when John had avoided him. But John was glad to see him now. He knew that his friend had stayed away all this time to respect his privacy, and for that he was grateful.

First, Patterson briefed John on the progress of their shared business interests, which he had managed in John's absence. Then Patterson got to the point of his visit.

"The Court of Sessions of our new District of Pictou," he began, "has licensed Peter Grant of Brown's Point to open a school within the year. I hoped you might assist him in designing a course of study. I suggested that to the Court, and they are in favour."

John was silent for a time, then said, "I would be honoured. Truth be told, I think a challenge might be what I need."

"Good man!" Patterson shook his hand vigorously. "Come to Pictou and bide with me. Soon. So you may meet Mr. Grant."

John was there three days later. He met Peter Grant at Patterson's cabin. In Grant he recognized a similar love of scholarship, dedication to hard work and a belief in education for the young. Peter was only a few years younger, having just completed his studies in Halifax. They compared notes about their respective early schooling, John's in the Old World and Peter's in the New. Then they made a start in designing the course of study.

John returned home with a newly awakened interest in the future. Although there would be no schoolhouse built as yet, children in the area would have the chance of an education.

As his interest and work in the project increased, he could feel his reserve thawing. He found he looked forward to holding his son at the evening meal, to watch the light of recognition in the baby's eyes when he saw his father, and to hear him babble a greeting.

One day, as he found himself talking to the baby about his future school days, he heard Margaret laugh behind him, and soon he was laughing, too. He was beginning to act like a father and had come to love his little son. Finally.

After one Sabbath service, as the Frasers left the church, Sophia touched John's arm and pointed to a young woman nearby with several children grouped about her.

"That's Catherine Ross," she said. He looked over to see a tall, striking woman.

"She's a widow," continued Sophia, "with four children. Even so, she's still young, only twenty-three. She and her parents were on the *Hector* with us."

John looked down at his mother suspiciously. "Why are you telling me this?"

Sophia glanced over at Hugh as if for support, then said quickly, "She's in the same position you are, my son. She must marry again to provide for herself and her children."

John turned shocked eyes on his mother. "Marry again! My Jannet has not been gone a year!"

He turned away angrily and motioned to Margaret, who was holding baby Hugh. She hurried after him as he strode away from his mother. He was seething. How could she? Did she know him at all?

A few days later, early one morning before John had left the cabin, his father arrived at the door. John scowled. "I must away. I'm off to Pictou on business."

"I have only a few words to say. Then I'll be gone." His father's hard tone was unusual. Hugh stood in the doorway, obviously not prepared to move out of the way.

John shrugged, turned back into the room and gestured at his own chair by the fire. Hugh sat down, but John remained standing, arms folded.

"Your mother is thinking only of you and your son. For

that love you have shown her contempt." Hugh paused, as if struggling to control his anger. Then he continued in a calmer tone.

"Your lad needs a mother. You can't expect Margaret to live here forever. She'll want a life of her own soon enough and at some time a husband and children. And without a wife you can't have more children. You have no choice but to marry again."

With that, Hugh stood, nodded to Margaret and strode out the door.

John clenched his fists. If only they would let him be!

He brooded on his father's words all the way to Pictou. If his mother, who had loved and supported him always, had been hurt by his words, then, yes, he did feel regret. That evening he stayed over at Patterson's cabin.

Once Patterson's wife had withdrawn to leave the men on their own, John complained of the pressure he felt from his parents on the subject of remarriage.

Patterson smiled. "I think you are upset because you know that they are right. You do no dishonour to Jannet by providing her son with a new mother. You may never feel the same love for another, but marriage to a good woman such as Catherine Ross would be a wise move."

"But I am in no way attracted to her. She is nothing like Jannet!"

"That's not the point. This is a practical matter. She needs a husband, and you need a wife and a mother for your son. She is a handsome, capable woman. You could do much worse!"

John knew when he was beaten. He would seek an introduction to the widow through James MacGregor. And he would return to thank his parents for their advice and apologize for his first hasty reaction.

Catherine seemed to accept his courtship in a reserved, cool manner. She was quiet, letting him carry the conversation. She was serious where Jannet had been flirtatious. She was practical about the future, where Jannet had been impulsive. With Jannet, there had seemed little work on his part during courtship. Courting this woman seemed an effort.

She told him that her dead husband, Alex, was an only child, and that his parents wished to bring up his four children themselves if she were to remarry.

It surprised John when she told him that this arrangement might be for the best. Surely this was an unnatural thing for a woman to choose? But Catherine was an unusual woman; she could speak, read and write English.

John was not surprised when she accepted his proposal. He knew he was a worthy suitor. He felt no emotion himself and was unprepared for her reaction when he took her hand in his. It was trembling, and in her face he read an attempt to control some strong feeling. This was not the calm, cool Catherine he had come to know.

Quickly, she pulled her hand from his and turned away. "Thank you, John," she mumbled, "but I must away now."

John watched her walk away with a sinking heart. Not a warm woman at all, not like my Jannet, he thought.

Chapter Twenty-One

The wedding of John and Catherine took place in early April of 1793, with James MacGregor officiating.

The start of the marriage was difficult for John. He knew he must get used to a wife who was very different from Jannet, who had been warm and bubbly. But he could sense Catherine's difficulties, too. She had given up her children, after all. He was secretly relieved that he had escaped responsibility for another man's children. And young Hugh was not responding to Catherine and was fussy much of the time.

Catherine was certainly trying very hard in her new role. John could see that she was efficient and capable. Yet with each passing day she seemed more withdrawn. It was not a happy household.

He was surprised when she told him she was with child. He had not considered the possibility so soon and in such trying circumstances. She looked at him pleadingly, as if needing reassurance. John stepped forward to embrace her, then stopped himself, fearing she might not welcome it. Instead he smiled and said, "That is very good news, Catherine. I am happy to see our family grow."

She smiled nervously.

But expecting a child seemed to agree with her. Her mood lightened, and she became more open and a little more talkative. Even baby Hugh sensed the change and became more content.

John was happy to leave household matters to Catherine; he was preoccupied with business interests. His brother Donald proposed building grist and sawmills for the expanding community on McLellan's Brook. With plans for the school set, John welcomed this new challenge.

Before Christmas, nine months to the day since the wedding, Catherine went into labour. Sophia attended her, as did young Margaret. It was a very difficult labour, and Catherine suffered greatly. John, too, found the process traumatic, reliving Hugh's birth which, only months later, had ended so tragically. But this time he was presented with the opposite situation: a healthy mother but sickly babies. For Catherine had delivered a set of twins, tiny, frail little girls.

"We will do our best and, Lord willing, they will survive," Sophia told him. "Now go to your wife. Comfort her."

John knelt beside Catherine's bed and took her hand. Her eyes were closed. "Catherine," he said softly. She opened her eyes and then burst into tears. John was taken aback. He had never seen her express any strong emotion, let alone cry.

"I'm so very sorry, John. I wanted to give you strong children, sons. I have let you down."

John shook his head. "No, no, it's not your fault. It's the Lord's will. No more words. Rest now."

She clutched his hand even tighter. "I love you so!" she said desperately.

John was stunned. Was this his composed, cool Catherine? But he recovered quickly.

He smiled. "I'm very happy to hear that. But now you must rest and be strong for the babies, for all of us." He kissed her forehead.

She lay back, content.

They named the girls Marran and Sophia, and they did

survive. Although tiny, the twins gained strength each day. And with their survival, Catherine's confidence grew. She began to show a warmth and depth of feeling that surprised everyone, especially John.

There was a new ease in their marriage, but John was sure he could never feel the same passion for Catherine, as he had for Jannet.

Sophia was delighted to have a baby named after her. She admitted to John, what she could no longer deny even to herself, her special feeling for him. Of all of her grandchildren, she said, she could not help doting on John's most of all.

As Marran and Sophia thrived, and little Hugh became a hardy toddler, Sophia seemed to regain some of her energy. She was a frequent visitor, and Catherine seemed happy to have her help and company.

A year and a half after the twins' birth, Sophia arrived at the cabin one day in a terrible state. John was there and was shocked by her grim, tear-streaked face.

"What ails you, Mother?"

"Oh, my dear John, I can't speak to your father. It would hurt him so."

Now John was really concerned. "What is it?"

"Mary is with child."

John bit his lip and then could not help expressing his first thought.

"I would not have been surprised if this were ten years ago, but I am now. I thought Mary had more sense at twenty-six. She seemed to have become a more sober adult."

Sophia nodded.

"Do you know who is the father?" demanded John.

"Duncan Cameron."

This was another surprise. Duncan was a respected farmer from Merigomish. Mary's taste in men had indeed improved over the years. This was fortunate.

"I shall speak to him right away. He'll have to marry Mary as soon as possible. Have no worries, I'll see to it."

"Oh thank you, thank you, John." Sophia squeezed his hand. Then added, "But mind, no word of this to your father."

John was as good as his word, taking Duncan aside after the very next Sabbath service. He felt a little sorry for him. Duncan was a good man and startled when he learned the news. Mary had not told him. He agreed to the marriage immediately, saying that he had already asked her to marry him, but had received no response. I wonder if the poor man realizes what he will face, thought John.

When John approached Mary, she was defiant. "It's my concern, not yours! Perhaps I don't wish to marry him."

Angry now, John raised his voice. "You have no choice. You will do what you must or disgrace the family!"

When Mary continued to stare at him petulantly, he added, "It's hurting our mother terribly. She has wept countless tears over you."

With that, Mary's face crumpled. She was devoted to Sophia.

"If it's the wish of my mother, I shall do so," she agreed, but added in a hiss, "but not for you!"

Mary married Duncan, and their son was born five months later.

That following year a son, David, was born to Catherine and John. Catherine's pride and delight in presenting her husband with a healthy son were obvious. John knew he and Catherine worked well together.

Their household had become a happy one, and the farm prospered. John's businesses continued to expand and diversify, in partnership with his long-time mentor, Patterson. He was building log cabins for new arrivals, in addition to exporting timber to Britain. The following year he and his brother Donald opened their saw and grist mills.

The next year Catherine was with child again. John began making plans for a larger home. His father offered him a large plot of his own land overlooking the brook. John was happy to accept.

While overseeing work on his new house, John made a habit of stopping in often to see his parents.

He could little afford the time, but he found he had a need to do so. His own family was growing and, as it did, John found himself thinking more about his own childhood. And Sophia encouraged him to talk of their time apart, to describe the years with her father. Gradually John's innate reserve lessened as he spoke of his life with Granddad and Aunt Margaret. He admitted how difficult it had been to arrive in Nova Scotia and become one of many, after living the life of an only child, doted upon by two adults.

But John learned just as much from his mother.

With adult perspective, he learned how terrifying it had been for her to leave him, and how painful and hungry those first few years had been.

As a husband and father now, he came to appreciate his mother's strength and dedication to her family. And through her, a clearer picture emerged of the quiet, solid bedrock that was his father.

Chapter Twenty-Two

The new century arrived with every indication that prosperity for the Frasers would continue. That year saw the family prepare to celebrate the birth of John's sixth child and the marriage of his brother Alex.

The baby's birth was perhaps a month away when John arrived at his parent's cabin on a sunny October day.

Sophia's face lit up when she saw him, as it always did.

"Your mother is very tired today," Hugh cautioned, "Don't let her talk too long."

"I won't allow her to do any talking. She will listen to me this time," John said with a smile before sitting down.

But she was eager to talk.

"You are so much like my father, your Granddad, John."

"And I'm happy to hear that. He was so good to me. I've tried to be like him, you know."

Tears came to her eyes. "It means so much to hear you honour him so." She grasped his hand and said urgently, "Please! Forgive me for ever leaving you. Please, John!"

This was a familiar refrain, but today the level of her distress surprised him. He bent down to kiss her cheek. "There is naught to forgive," he whispered softly. "I love you, Mother."

With that, she seemed to relax.

"I'll return tomorrow," he promised.

She lay back and closed her eyes. Once she was asleep, John nodded to his father and left quietly.

The following day, John's sister Ann arrived at his door just after dawn with a blunt message, "Our mother is dead."

John's immediate reaction was to remember the words of love he had spoken to her only the day before. It brought a rush of overwhelming relief.

Then he reeled as if someone had struck him. His mother was gone. He felt Catherine at his side, steadying his arm. She sat him down, pressing his head to her chest, and held him quietly until he felt composed enough to stand. "We must go," he said to her.

She nodded and, together with the children and Ann, they made their way silently to the Fraser cabin.

Hugh sat slumped in his chair by the fire, while young Sophia prepared her mother's body. John could not bring himself to look at his mother. Instead, he touched his father's shoulder, but Hugh did not respond.

John bent forward and whispered, "Father, tell me what you wish me to do."

There was a long silence. Hugh continued to stare at the floor. Finally he looked up and John had to control the urge to look away. The grief on his father's face had changed it. It was like looking at a hollowed-out version of his father.

"Do what you must, my son."

And John did.

The other Fraser children and their families arrived over the next few days and took turns keeping vigil by Sophia's side. Once everyone had arrived, James MacGregor conducted the funeral service.

Afterwards, Hugh approached John and pressed a frayed piece of cloth into his hands. John opened it and saw a lock of fine, fair hair.

"Your hair, lad," whispered his father. "She clipped it from your head as you lay ailing with the smallpox, before we left Scotland. It has been her comfort and talisman all these years. Keep it now, for her sake."

John's eyes filled with tears as his hand closed around it. He nodded at his father.

"I will."

For John, Sophia's death was a sadness that refused to go away.

It was not like the traumatic aftermath of Jannet's death, but it brought a pervasive sense of guilt and an emptiness that he could not shake. His mother had been true to him always, but he had judged her and found her wanting when he first arrived in Nova Scotia. He had never fully appreciated her while she lived.

In other ways, the beginning of the new century was kind to John. His success was a reflection of the success of the whole Pictou community, from the harbour down along the three rivers. The grist and sawmills that he and Donald operated were doing well. John's business ventures had expanded substantially and he was trading in milled timber, not only with Britain, but with the West Indies, too. And he was profiting from the import of rum, sugar and molasses from Jamaica. Thanks to the Highland Clearances, a stream of poor Scottish immigrants was arriving in the area to create an even larger market for the log cabins he was building. John moved his family to their new home, a frame house with two rooms, a stone fireplace and a sleeping loft.

His family life was harmonious, too. He appreciated Catherine's efficiency in running his household and her firm but loving hand with the children. But most of all, he valued the compassion she had shown him after Sophia's death. She had encouraged him to talk about his mother often, and that had brought him some peace.

And one night he managed to open his heart to his wife. “Thank you for the love and understanding you have shown me since my mother’s death... and always... I do love you.”

Catherine was silent for a moment, studying her hands. Then she lifted her face to his. “You are everything to me, John Fraser. I have loved you always.”

John had not seen his father for some time, and they had spent no time together since Sophia’s death. Hugh beamed as he opened the door to his eldest son one cool November morning. “John, I’m so happy to see you. Come away in and sit by the fire.”

They exchanged news of the family and John’s businesses. Then John spoke of the new road being built from the harbour along the East River as far as Hugh’s farm. John agreed to stay the night and could tell his father was delighted.

They went to bed early that evening. It was clear and still, but during the night a series of loud booms woke them and sent them outside. An orangey-red glow could be seen above the tree line far to the north.

“What in the Lord’s name—” gasped John. “Those are explosions! What could they be?”

“From the harbour, I fear,” said Hugh. “No doubt ships or storehouses on fire.”

He turned to John. “But there is naught we can do this night. Come away in.”

“I must leave at first light,” was John’s terse reply.

He was anxious by the time he arrived in Pictou the following morning; the destruction was far worse than he had imagined. A fire at the Pictou shipyard had destroyed several buildings adjacent to the wharf. Fortunately no one had been injured. For John, the worst blow was the gutting of a large storehouse which had held his timber ready for shipment to England, and a winter's supply of rum, sugar and molasses newly arrived from Jamaica. The thunderous booms that they had heard the night before were the rum barrels exploding. Everything had been destroyed. His business losses would be huge.

Chapter Twenty-Three

The disaster at the shipyard was yet another blow for John. The sadness he had experienced after the deaths of Jannet and Sophia returned and he became anxious. He took no solace in Catherine's support this time. He had welcomed her help in coping with Sophia's death, but now her attempts at comfort irritated him and he rebuffed her. After all, this was business. What did his wife know of that? Eventually Catherine gave up trying and let him be.

John was preoccupied with rebuilding, and unaware that Catherine was unwell, suffering from extreme fatigue as she awaited the birth of another child. But as February approached, he felt a familiar sense of foreboding. His beautiful Jannet had died that month. When Catherine gave birth to another healthy son, Edward Smith Fraser, on February 3, 1806, both parents were relieved.

Another son, John McPherson Fraser, was born two years later and John moved his family north and east to Merigomish. With nine children now, ranging in age from one to eighteen years, he built an even bigger house there.

Prosperity was at its peak in the area, but John sensed a decline coming and was proven right. The first sign was the drop in the timber trade. Much of the settlers' lands had been cleared of trees by then and many farms had been subdivided many times over.

Young people were forced to look for work elsewhere, many going to New England and some to Australia, as servants or homesteaders. The economic health of the whole area was on everyone's mind.

"I cannot help but be concerned about the future of our sons here," said Catherine one evening as they sat alone by the fire.

"Don't worry," said John. "There will be room in my businesses for all of them."

"Your father has concerns, too," she added. "He says that all business will drop off, even yours. Donald agrees."

John bristled. His father and brother had no right to sow seeds of doubt in his wife, and she should not be throwing their words back at him.

"Don't listen to them," he insisted.

But John felt anger welling up inside him and could not leave it at that. "Let me take care of business matters. They are not your concern. Your responsibilities are the household and the children."

Catherine averted her eyes, but not before he saw the hurt in them. Even as his hands trembled with anger, he felt regret. Once again his words and tone had been more hurtful than he had intended.

Catherine did not bring up the subject of the children again. Instead, it was he who raised the subject when next they spoke.

John had taken three of his youngest for a rare father and sons outing. For nine-year-old Edward, it was his first hunting trip, along with two of his older brothers. Despite his father's warnings, young Edward had wandered off from the small group not once but twice.

John's angry voice preceded him through the door. He threw an empty sack to the floor in front of a startled Catherine.

"Nothing to show for the morning! I will not take that boy hunting again! Edward was a danger to us all. What's wrong with him? A brainless sheep would have been more help!"

"Hush, John. He will hear you," said Catherine.

"I hope he does," said John wearily and sat down.

"It's true," said Catherine gently, "he frustrates me, too." She was silent for a moment and then took a deep breath.

"John, I have wanted to talk to you for some time about Edward."

He looked up at her. "What is it?"

She clutched the back of a chair and spoke quickly, in a rush. "He's not like our other children. Of course they are all different, but he's a dreamer. He just can't seem to attend to any task, to see it through."

"What do you mean?"

"I'll send him for water and he'll forget, or not return until much later. I'll tell him to get some eggs from the barn, and he'll come back with a bucket of milk instead."

John waved a hand in the air. "That's easy enough to remedy. I'll drill some sense into his head."

"Please do not be too harsh with him, John. In all other ways he's a lovely boy. He has a warm heart and a wonderful imagination. He reminds me of your mother. He has her gift of storytelling, too." He heard the pleading in her voice.

"You try to soften me, Catherine, by comparing him to my mother. Storytelling is a pastime for the evening fireside, not for the day's work. My mother knew the difference. That boy needs to learn the difference, too!"

Then he slammed his fist on the table, and Catherine jumped back. "I shall fix what is wrong with that boy!"

Neither of them knew that Edward was on the other side of the door. He had heard every word. It was true that Father was hard on all of them, but it was shocking and hurtful to hear such anger directed at him.

He ran.

Part Three

1815 – 1848

Chapter Twenty-Four

Edward wanted to run as far away as his legs could carry him, but he knew he could not go far. If he was called for, he must be close by. His father was angry enough already. So he ran back to the barn and climbed into the loft. There he fell back into the straw, clenching his fists, squeezing his eyes tightly and refusing to let the tears come.

Edward could not understand why his father was so upset. He minded his father, he helped his mother and he watched out for his younger brother, John. He did whatever his older brothers, Walter and Alex, asked him to. He wanted above all for his father to be proud of him.

When he heard his mother calling, he climbed down out of the loft and walked back to the house warily, hoping to avoid his father. His mother stood alone at the door. She opened her arms to him.

"Come here," she said softly. "You heard, didn't you?"

Edward nodded.

"You're a good, kind lad with a lively imagination, but too much the dreamer."

"Is that bad?" asked Edward.

"No, but you must learn that there is a time to dream and a time to work. Sadly, working time must be the biggest part of our lives. Now come inside."

When they were seated by the fire, she continued, "All of

us must work hard in this life, no matter who we are or what gifts we have. You must put your mind to every task, here at home or in the school room. Most of all you must listen to your father. For your sake and mine. That will earn his respect." She looked into his eyes. "Now find your brother and move the animals into the barn before our meal." Then she smiled, "And no dreaming while you do it!"

Edward worked hard to tame his mind, but it was a constant struggle. His mother, Walter and Alex did their best to coax and encourage him, and with their help, he was often successful. At home. But he could not rely on them in the school room, and his studies suffered despite his best efforts.

When Edward turned twelve, he summoned the courage to approach his father and ask permission to leave school.

But as he pled his case, he watched his father's face redden. "You will take your schooling seriously!" John snapped. "No son of mine will leave before his studies are complete. And you, especially, have much more to learn."

"But Father, I'm not suited to it. I'm not like Alex and Walter, who have a talent for figures and writing. Let me work instead. Please! I'll make you proud of me!"

"No!" thundered his father. "Education made me the man I am. This family has a good life because of it! To find success in this life, you need a good education and the ambition to work hard! It's very simple. You need to pay more attention, at school and at home!"

Edward opened his mouth, but his father held up a warning hand.

"We will discuss it no more," he said brusquely, and walked away.

Edward was shaking with rage. His father was cruel and unjust. He hated him!

As he saw his mother approach, he shook his head at her and walked away. There was nothing to say.

Edward remained at school, but even more unhappily than before. His attempts at disciplining his mind became half-hearted. Instead, he dreamed of sailing to far-off places, India or Australia. Or Jamaica perhaps, a tropical island, not quite so far away. Or he could even become a great explorer, like Captain Cook, discovering new worlds. But his father would never allow him to do what he truly wanted!

His brother Alex tried to convince him to pray for guidance.

An adult now, Alex was establishing himself as a tailor and merchant, but his passion was the church. He coached Edward to pray to the Lord to discipline his mind so that his true calling might be revealed. But it didn't work. Edward received no divine revelations about his future direction, no matter how hard he prayed.

And his academic results continued to be poor. The tense stand-off with his father cast a chill over the entire household.

Finally, on his fourteenth birthday, Edward received the gift he had longed for. His frustrated father told him he could put aside his studies.

"I can only hope," said John wearily, "that you develop an aptitude in one of my businesses. I pray that somewhere, in the mills, in the timber yards or shipyards, you will find your calling."

"I know I shall," promised Edward enthusiastically. "I'll make you proud of me, Father."

John said nothing, just shrugged his shoulders and turned away.

His mother grasped Edward's hand.

"This is your chance, my son," she said softly. "Take it and make him proud."

"I will. You know I will."

And he did try. At the wharves and warehouses of Merigomish and Pictou he felt most alive.

He was enthralled by the foreign men he met at the harbours. He wanted to learn about their lives in distant places. And so he spent more time talking to sailors and traders about their travels than he did focusing on his job. As a result, when Edward was on duty, mistakes and oversights happened with increasing frequency.

John became enraged when he found goods unaccounted for on Edward's watch. He grew tired of reprimanding Edward for his many errors and told him to report only to his elder brothers. John had no wish to deal with Edward anymore.

Catherine, meanwhile, became concerned about the many accidents that befell her inattentive son at the docks: the cuts, bruises and even a harbour dunking.

As the tension rose at work, so it became much worse at home. Edward spent more time at McLellan's Brook, where he found a sympathetic ear, as he always had. Granddad Fraser had always listened without judgment. Ever since he was a little boy, Edward had loved listening to his grandfather's tales of his voyage across the ocean and the struggle to make a better life in a new land. To the other grandchildren, these stories were merely diverting tales. But to Edward they were a blueprint. He wanted to follow in his grandfather's footsteps, to travel across the sea to find a different future. Granddad had done it. Granddad surely understood his grandson's dreams.

After Edward recounted his latest row with his father, he noticed his grandfather smiling. "How can you make light of this?" he asked in a wounded voice.

Hugh shook his head. "No, lad, trust me, I don't find it amusing." He spoke in English, an effort he made with all of his grandchildren. "But I smile because I see you are more like your father than you know."

At that, Edward flushed angrily, but Granddad continued, "Let me explain. As a lad, your father, too, felt like an outsider. He had led a very different life in Scotland and then was cast into a new one when he came here. He felt he didn't belong in this family, and it took him a very long time to find his place."

"Then he of all people should understand how I feel!" cried Edward.

Granddad was thoughtful, then added quietly, as if to himself. "Perhaps, but I fear that people often don't see what is right in front of them."

Edward continued to confide in his mother, too. Her compassion for him and attempts to encourage him never wavered. He had noticed her waning energy and strength and tried to minimize her stress by staying out of his father's way. His father seemed content to ignore him, and so a tenuous peace was established.

The death of his mother, the following year, struck like a thunderbolt. It changed Edward's life forever.

Her heart attack, at fifty-seven, shattered his father. He heard his father rail that another February death had stalked him and claimed a life dear to him. Grief paralysed him. Edward's eldest brothers, Hugh and David, took charge.

Catherine was laid out in the front room, and the family gathered. It was only when Edward approached his mother's body that John was roused from his stupor. Rising from his chair, he wagged a finger angrily at Edward.

"Her concern over you brought her low!" he cried. "You gave her endless worries, and now she's gone, lost to all of us!" He slumped back into his chair and in a softer voice said, "Over you, your mother and I drifted apart, and now there is no chance to right the wrongs."

Marran put her arms around her father to comfort him, while Alex and Walter drew a stunned Edward away.

"Don't listen to him," whispered Alex. "It's grief talking, no more. The Lord has taken her to Him, to give her a much-needed rest."

Walter added softly, "Father is aggrieved by his own guilt."

Their words were soothing, but still his mind was in turmoil. He had lost his beloved mother. Was it possible that his father was right, that she had been worn down by worry over him? He had no future in this family. With sudden clarity, he knew what he had to do.

Chapter Twenty-Five

"With my mother gone, there's nothing left for me here," began Edward, "my future lies elsewhere, like it did for you."

He was sitting opposite his grandfather by the fire, in the quiet front room at McLellan's Brook. Outside, a February snowstorm raged, rattling the shutters.

"But remember, lad, I had no choice," said Granddad. "Desperate times drove me to leave Scotland."

"It's the same for me!" protested Edward. "My situation is desperate too. My father hates me. He says I am the cause of my mother's death. I'll never be like my brothers, no matter what I do. There's nothing here for me."

"Lad, your father is grieving. He does not mean what he says. Give him time." He reached over to touch Edward's knee. "Seventeen is too young to be speaking of leaving, lad. I beg you to think on it for a time, for my sake. And while you do, you could come to live with me." He smiled. "It will help an old man to have a brawny lad like you around!"

Hugh began to cough, and it shook his whole body. Edward was alarmed. "Are you ill, Granddad?"

"No, no, lad, it's simply old age. Will you promise to wait a few more years, before you consider leaving?"

Edward was torn, but finally he nodded. He would stay. For the present. For Granddad's sake. And, it would be a relief to leave his father's house.

And so Edward waited. Determined to honour his mother's memory and keep his promise to Granddad, he took direction from his older brothers and tried to focus on his immediate surroundings. He still longed for another life, but did his part in keeping peace within the family, mainly by avoiding his father.

John gradually shook off his lethargy. Once again business challenges brought him back to life. John's announcement the following year that he was remarrying felt like a betrayal to Edward. After all of his efforts to bury his own feelings, to appease his father, it felt like a slap in the face.

Now eighteen, he wisely resisted the urge to confront his father. But he could not hide his feelings from Granddad.

"How can he do this? My mother hasn't been gone a year!" Clenching his fists, he dared his grandfather to justify it.

"It has been fifteen months," began Hugh, "It's no disrespect to your mother, lad."

"But it is!" exclaimed Edward. "I won't forgive him for this! I've set my mind on leaving. I wish to be gone!" He took a breath and calmed himself. "Forgive me, Granddad. I'm not angry with you."

"I know. Now, sit down. Keep silence for a time. Let your anger drain away."

They sat quietly for a few minutes.

Edward broke the silence first. "Thank you." He smiled. "But I'm determined to go. For years I've wanted to leave. You can't dissuade me this time, Granddad."

Hugh nodded slowly, then asked, "Where will you go?"

"To Jamaica," declared Edward, without hesitation.

Hugh was surprised by the confidence in his grandson's voice. Edward went on. "I've thought about it for a very long while. Many have gone to the plantations there. I've listened on the docks. It's another world: the land, the sun, the people. I seek a life that is different from my father and brothers. I know I'll find my calling there."

A bout of coughing delayed Hugh's reply.

"Have you spoken of this to anyone else?"

"To Alex," said Edward. "He's considered going there himself to minister to the slaves. We've spoken about the conditions on the plantations at length, of the terrible plight of the Africans. Alex believes I could be of some use there," said Edward proudly, "to help the abolitionists' cause." Edward looked at his grandfather expectantly, wanting him to share his enthusiasm.

"You've put much thought into this, I see now," said Hugh. Then he added, almost to himself, "Emigration made me. It gave my family a better life."

"You will support me, then!" cried Edward.

"Yes, but I'll be sad to see you go."

Edward was thrilled to have his grandfather's support. He could not remember a time when he had been as happy. He had lived with tension for so long that now the world seemed suddenly bright and alive. He could not wait to approach his father, with Granddad at his side.

But his father would not listen to arguments from either of them. Instead, the discussion deteriorated into a shouting match between father and son.

"I will never agree to such a plan! You are a coward for wanting to run away from family responsibilities. To Jamaica, of all places."

"I thought you would be happy to be rid of me!" Edward countered. "You've always despised me, never accepted me as I am!"

As he stomped out of his father's house, Edward turned back to glimpse his distraught grandfather trying to calm his father. He determined then and there to lay plans to take passage to Jamaica, despite his father, and no matter how long it took him to arrange it. His only regret over the confrontation was the suffering it was causing Granddad.

For a time a truce existed. John and his new wife, Elizabeth Matheson, settled into their life together. Edward avoided all family gatherings.

A year later, however, a family tragedy changed everything. Walter, twenty-four, married only three years, died in a milling accident. His death devastated everyone in the family. Edward and his father found common ground at last in their shared grief. At the funeral, they embraced wordlessly, while Hugh looked on.

For Edward, now nineteen, the loss of yet another of the few people close to him was proof, finally, that the time had come. For John, the tragic loss of his son brought on a bout of soul-searching. Worn down by grief and anxious to put an end to the strife, John gave in. He told Edward that he would make the necessary arrangements to book his passage to Jamaica.

Edward was stunned, but felt no rush of pleasure at the news, just relief. Walter's death had erased any enthusiasm he might have felt.

"I will contact my agent in Jamaica. He will arrange work for you on Stony Gut Estate," John told his son. "It's a small plantation on the east side of the island, so you must be prepared to take on a variety of tasks."

Edward bowed his head and said quietly, "Thank you, Father, you won't be sorry. I promise you." He didn't ask what his responsibilities there might be. He just wanted to go.

Edward went to see Granddad immediately to share the news. But his grandfather's reaction was a surprise. "Granddad, you look sad. Is this not the day we have both longed for?"

"I'm happy for you, my dear Edward, but now that the time has come, I fear I will not see you again..." He paused and stood up slowly, shaking his head. "Oh, don't listen to an old man." He smiled broadly at Edward. "There's something I've always wanted you to have."

When he returned from his bed chamber, he carried a small leather sack. He held it out to his grandson. "This pouch holds some soil from my farm in Kiltarlity. Foxhole Farm it was called. I have nothing else of value to give you.

But in here is your family's past, Edward. Take it with you, to remember who you are."

Edward hesitated. He realized the value of such a gift. "Granddad, are you sure you want *me* to have this?"

"I am. Go with my blessing."

Edward's passage was booked on a trading ship bound for Jamaica, via Boston, due to leave Pictou on December 22, 1825.

As the time drew near, Edward's excitement grew, but so did his doubts. He hoped he could face bravely an unknown future as Granddad had and not prove himself a coward as his father had once suggested.

And Granddad? He worried that he was leaving the man who had given him so much, at a time when the old man seemed to be fading away.

It would be easier to leave Alex, as the brothers had made a plan to keep in close touch. And Father? He would be leaving him just as they were making a peace, of sorts.

The morning of Edward's departure was very cold, but clear, and the wind was fair for departure. He stowed his belongings aboard, then came down the gangplank to the dock, where his father and grandfather waited. Granddad, wrapped in a thick woollen cloak, shuddered as he coughed.

Edward gripped him hard and said, "Take care, dear Granddad. I will never forget what you have done for me. I'll miss you."

Hugh smiled. In a hoarse voice he said in Gaelic, "My love and my prayers go with you."

Edward turned to his father.

"Father, I'm sorry for so much I have said in anger. I'll make it up to you. I'll make you proud of me, I promise."

John pulled him close and whispered, "My son, may the Lord protect you always." He squeezed Edward's shoulders once, then released him.

Once back on board, Edward stood by the railing as the ship cast off. He remained there until the two figures on the dock became smudges in the distance. He gave one final wave to his homeland and went below. It was then that a jolt of excitement gripped him. He was off to Jamaica at last!

Chapter Twenty-Six

The first few days at sea were ones of excited anticipation for Edward. The weather was fair, and so were his spirits. Despite numbing cold on the open deck, he spent endless hours alternately pacing it and standing by the railing, gazing at the vastness of the ocean. His daydreams roamed freely. He saw himself as a great success in Jamaica, although he could form no image of what precisely he was doing there. He imagined the pride of his grandfather, father and Alex, as they considered his accomplishments. He pictured his mother, too, with a smile on her face, nodding approval.

He met another passenger by the railing on the second day. There were few of them, all men, and most were reserved. But Matthew Macfarlane, from Truro, introduced himself to Edward. He seemed nervous and eager to talk. His family had fallen on hard times, he said. His father's farm was no longer able to support all of them, so most of his brothers and sisters had hired themselves out in the area. But Matthew, the youngest, had decided to indenture himself to a business in Kingston, Jamaica. Like Edward, he was seeking adventure and change, but now was beset by doubt.

"I wanted to escape, but now wonder if it was the right decision. I don't know what I will face."

“What are the terms?” asked Edward.

“I must work for seven years for my employer,” began Matthew, “in return for room and board, in addition to my free passage, of course. When my term is over, I’ll receive a lump sum or a piece of land.”

“A fair bargain, then,” said Edward.

“But I’ll be at the mercy of my employer. What if he’s cruel? What if I must work day and night? I could be treated as a slave.”

“Surely not,” said Edward.

“I hope you’re right. As low in society as I’ll be, at least I will rank above the Africans,” concluded Matthew. “And the place is full of them, I hear. But my employer does not wish a black or coloured to act as his manservant or driver. He wants a white man.”

“What’s a coloured?” asked Edward.

“Not all of the slaves are as black as night. Some are varying shades of brown. Those are the coloureds.”

“There is much I have to learn,” sighed Edward.

The weather changed after their stop in Boston. The seas were rough, and most passengers, including Edward, took to their bunks with seasickness. The odour in the hold and the constant moaning of the afflicted drove Edward on deck the very next day, although it took all his strength to get there.

Once in the fresh air he felt better, even though his stomach remained unsettled. Like the fair weather, his earlier enthusiasm had deserted him.

Perhaps it was his conversation with Matthew, perhaps it was his seasickness, but now he felt doubt. Had he made the right decision? Was Jamaica truly his path to the future, his chance to prove himself, to make his family proud?

Fair weather returned by the second week, and as they sailed south, each day brought ever-warmer sea breezes along with calmer waters. Edward’s spirits improved once his stomach settled, but doubts still troubled him. He scanned the horizon now, fearing that he might see Jamaica at any moment and be forced to confront his future.

Three weeks to the day since the ship's departure, it reached its destination. Edward had been on deck since dawn, nervously peering into the semi-darkness. Matthew joined him soon after. Together they watched the dark hues of a forested, mountainous land emerge from the sea as the ship drew closer. As the sun rose, the hues came into sharper focus: the distant mountains becoming a deep blue and the forests turning a vibrant green. The sea that ringed the base was a brilliant aquamarine.

The vivid colours seemed to dance in the brightening light, and Edward had to look away. Then he squinted through half-closed eyes as the town of Kingston came into view. Great white mansions dotted the hillsides above the town. Below them were clusters of ornate buildings flying colourful flags, alongside many smaller structures.

On the docks, figures swarmed among rows of warehouses and leaning shanties. Both men stared, mesmerized and silent.

On disembarkation, the passengers were taken to a large shed, where they waited for their travel documents to be checked and their baggage to be unloaded. Although much relieved to be on dry land and out of the sun, Edward and Matthew were dry-mouthed with anxiety. Perspiration rolled off them. Neither acknowledged the other. At last, they had to face their long-anticipated futures.

A loud voice boomed. "I seek Edward Fraser and Matthew Macfarlane. Are they within?"

Edward turned toward the far end of the shed where two men, shadows in a doorway, stood with their backs to the sun outside. One was tall, well built, with a wide-brimmed hat, the other much shorter and slight. Edward raised his arm and called "Here" but it came out as a squeak. He repeated himself, louder this time, and moved toward the two men. Matthew followed.

“I am Richard Lane, overseer of Stony Gut Estate,” said the taller man, “and this is Daniel Cowall, Mr. Graham’s man. Which of you is Matthew Macfarlane?”

When Matthew stepped forward, Richard Lane said briskly, “You have your man now, Cowall. Give my regards to Mr. Graham.” Without a word, Matthew followed Daniel Cowall out of the shed.

Lane looked at Edward. “You must be Fraser. Come, we must be away now. I wish to be back before dark.” He turned to go.

“But sir,” said Edward, holding a letter in his hand, “I have a letter of introduction for Mr. George William Hamilton.”

“I know,” said Lane, “I’ll take it.”

“But—” began Edward.

Lane interrupted him. “Young man, you were hired as a bookkeeper for the Stony Gut Estate. I run the estate. You take orders from me. Mr. Hamilton, the estate’s attorney, lives in Kingston. He visits the estate from time to time. You will seldom see him. Now bring your trunk. The wagon is outside.”

In a daze, Edward picked up his trunk and staggered into the bright sunshine. It was like stepping into chaos, a world of strange noises, colours and movement. Humans, animals and birds called, cried and screeched. Fruit sellers and peddlers lined the road’s edge. There were swarms of people of every skin shade, from darkest black to lightest honey to lily white. And they flowed in all directions, dodging carts, wagons and carriages pulled by mules or oxen or horses. The sweet scent of flowers and fruit mingled with the smell of sweat and dung. The air itself was a moist, heavy blanket poised to suffocate him. The blinding sun beat down on his head.

Edward felt a wave of nausea and stumbled. Black hands steadied him. Those hands, along with Lane’s, pushed and lifted him up onto the wagon’s front bench. Lane climbed up beside him.

“Be off, James,” he said to the black driver, now sitting to Edward’s left. “We must get back before sundown.”

"Yuh, sah," said James, as he flicked the reins and clucked at the two horses.

"And give this man your hat. He may die before we get back without it."

James removed his hat and offered it to Edward, who took it numbly.

"Thank you," he said to James.

James grinned, showing just a few teeth. "Mah pleasure, sah."

The wagon moved through the throng, with Edward conscious only of a blur of movement from under the frayed brim of the straw hat.

Only after they had pulled away from the crowded town and were following a road along the coast, did Edward recover enough to notice anything of his surroundings. His headache persisted, but the breeze off the sea helped. The road was busy with wagon traffic in both directions. Swampy land bordered the road on the coast side, dense green jungle on the other.

James hummed as he stared ahead. He was small and wiry, with tight grey curls at the top of his head. Edward found he was staring at the coal-black skin of his arm. Embarrassed, he looked away to study the man on his right, his boss, Richard Lane. He was taller and broader than Edward and probably his senior by a decade at least. A nasty, lumpy scar ran the length of his clean-shaven left cheek from just under his eye to his jaw.

"A slave's machete blow," he said, not looking at Edward. "A constant reminder of the need for vigilance and discipline... stop the wagon!"

The wagon came to an abrupt halt, and the jolting ceased. "Get him some water, James; he looks as if he might expire." The black man jumped off the bench and went to the back of the wagon. He returned with a tin cup of water.

"Drink up," said Lane. "You're not seasoned yet and will need more water than you know. This place is a graveyard for white men. Within three months half of all newcomers are dead, mainly from fever. I plan to protect our investment."

This news shocked Edward, but the pounding in his head did lessen after he drank the water.

"What is seasoning?" he asked.

"When Africans first arrive, they must be conditioned to the heat and the work here. Even with seasoning, a third of them die within a few years. Now that has all changed, of course."

"Why?"

"Parliament has halted the Atlantic slave trade. Now we can get new slaves only from other plantations or islands. Or ones we can breed ourselves. No seasoning needed."

"But that is a good thing, surely?" said Edward. "Slavery is evil. The Negroes should be working for us, not owned by us."

Lane laughed. "You have much to learn, young man. Slavery is a necessary evil. We can't run our plantations without it. And these Africans aren't like us. They are simpletons: lazy children who need constant discipline. You'll see."

Edward glanced at James, embarrassed for him to hear these words. But James seemed oblivious.

"James is no longer a slave," explained Lane. "He's a free man; he bought his freedom a few years ago. He agrees with me, don't you, James?"

"Yuh, sah," said James, "dey need a strong massa."

Edward fell silent.

After what seemed like many hours, they turned north off the coast road at a place called Morant Bay. "It's the capital of our parish, St. Thomas in the East," said Lane. The track was steeper and even bumpier as it climbed steadily higher. When they reached the crest of a hill, Edward looked back and saw the sea.

"Not long now," said Lane.

Chapter Twenty-Seven

It was getting dark when they approached a gate in a stone wall, with a hut beside it. A black watchman with a machete at his belt came out and opened the gate for them. There was a short drive up to a large white house with a wide verandah. It was the grandest house Edward had ever seen.

Lane jumped down off the bench. With unsteady legs, Edward followed. James and the wagon disappeared around the side of the house.

"Mini! Rose!" Lane yelled. "We want supper! Now!"

A slight young woman hurried onto the verandah. "Yuh, Massa," she sang to Lane, before hurrying back inside.

"Come," said Lane, "we'll have our meal. Then I'll show you to your lodgings."

Edward followed him into the house. They passed through a spacious entrance hall and then turned right into a dining room lit with many candles. A white cloth was spread on a long table. Edward hesitated, and Lane called, "Willie! Where is that boy?"

A moment later, a small brown boy ran into the room.

"Willie, show Massa Fraser to the privy."

Edward followed the boy as he led him through another room and outside. The darkness was alive with strange sounds.

The boy led him past a small building at the rear, then down a path to a hut. When Edward emerged, Willie pointed to the well nearby and a bucket of water that stood beside it for washing. They retraced their steps, and Edward found himself back in the dining room. Willie scurried away. Lane was already seated, eating.

"There is roast pork on the platter, plantains and yams in the bowl, and a jug of grog. Help yourself."

They ate in silence. Edward found that he was hungry enough to try the strange food in the bowl. It was not to his taste, but he ate a little of it.

Lane stood up. "You will take your meals here in the Big House with me and the other bookkeepers, unless Mr. Hamilton, the attorney, is in residence. We're a small estate, so I live here in rooms on the main floor. You lodge with the other bookkeepers in a small building near the counting house. Come, I'll take you there now."

Edward followed Lane through the large entrance hall, out onto the verandah and into the night.

"What's that sound?" he asked.

"That is Jamaica," laughed Lane, "the sound of countless insects, and the croaking of lizards."

Edward had only a vague idea of what a lizard was. He was preoccupied swatting at swarms of mosquitoes that surrounded him. They reached a small low building, and Lane led him inside, into a long room.

It was dark, but Edward could make out a large table, some chairs and four cots lining one wall. Two were occupied by men already asleep.

"James has left your trunk at the end by the far cot," indicated Lane. "Don't unpack. Get some sleep. Use the mosquito net on the cot. We start early in the morning. It's harvest time."

Then he was gone. Edward sank onto the cot. He felt lonely and bewildered, but most of all exhausted. Despite his anxiety and the snoring of his companions, he was asleep in minutes.

A harsh sound woke him at dawn. It sounded like a loud horn of some sort. He rubbed his eyes and glanced at the other cots. No movement. Quietly he used the chamber pot under his bed and then washed, using a jug of water and bowl he found on the table. He dressed in clean clothes from his trunk and went outside. It was hot, but not oppressively so. Yet. He could hear a distant drone. He moved toward the sound and, after rounding another building beside his own, saw a line of black people moving away from him toward small buildings in the distance and fields beyond. It sounded as if they were singing.

Knowing Lane was keen to make an early start, he turned back toward the main house and entered the dining room. His boss was seated at the table.

"Good man. Up already, before your colleagues," he said, through a mouthful of food.

Edward sat down. The strange food was there again, as were a jug of coffee and a platter of cold herring. The young woman he had seen last night entered the room. She was small and slight. In daylight he could see now that her skin was a rich toffee colour.

"Ah, Mini, good," said Lane, as she laid a bowl of hot potatoes on the table.

As she left, two men walked into the dining room. Edward judged both to be a little older than he was, but younger than Lane.

"Gentlemen, this is our new bookkeeper, Edward Fraser, from the colony of Nova Scotia," said Lane. "Edward, meet your colleagues, Douglas MacGregor from Glasgow and Thomas Howe from Bristol. The brawnier, fairer one here is the Scot. And both have survived their seasoning!" He laughed at his own joke.

Edward rose and shook hands with them. They nodded, then sat down to eat.

"I am taking Edward for a tour of the estate this morning, gentlemen," said Lane. "This afternoon I expect you two to set him up in the counting house and begin his training on the ledgers."

"Yes, sir," both chimed.

Lane turned to Edward. "Can you ride?"

"Not well, sir, but I have ridden before."

"Good, it will be faster. Willie!" He called. When the boy had not appeared after few moments, Lane yelled louder, "Willie! Now!"

At that point, Willie came running into the room and stopped at his master's chair. Lane struck him hard on the side of his head, which sent the boy sprawling against the wall. Edward was appalled, but the other two did not even glance up from their meal.

"Faster, next time!" growled Lane. "Tell James to saddle up two horses. Now!"

Willie sprinted from the room.

Lane looked at Edward's stunned expression. "A firm hand is all they understand. You'll learn that."

By the time Edward and Lane had ridden out to the fields the heat had become unbearable. It shimmered over the cane fields as far as the eye could see. There were scores of men and women there, cutting the giant stalks of cane, bundling them and hauling the weighty bundles to the wagons. All were dark-skinned, with sweat glistening on their exposed bodies. The women wore brightly coloured clothes and kerchiefs. All kept their heads bent to their work.

Black men walked amongst these slaves, yelling at them and cracking whips. Lane called them drivers. Despite the heat, hard work and threats, the Negroes were all singing.

"They sing while they work, when they grieve, when they are happy," Lane told Edward. "I told you, they're not like us."

He explained that these field slaves were the strongest ones who made up the first gang. They performed the hardest tasks at planting and now, during the harvest.

The second gang, composed of weaker adults and youths, sometimes pregnant women, who cleared cane, carried away cane bundles or brought water to the field workers. They also worked in many other areas of sugar production.

The third, weakest gang was made up of old people or young children, and they weeded, cared for the animals and did anything and everything else required on a plantation.

"We're a small estate," continued Lane, "less than three hundred acres, and we have only seventy-six slaves. So every white man must be familiar with all aspects of work here. You will be called on to do more than just record in a ledger."

From the fields Lane and Edward moved on to a series of small buildings. First was the mill house, where the raw cane was crushed to extract the juice. Next was a boiler house, where the juice was boiled in cast-iron coppers to crystallize it. Edward found the heat there excruciating. Lane explained that this process produced raw muscavado sugar, which was shipped to Britain in hogsheads, or barrels.

"Slaves handle all these tasks. It's too dangerous for white men," Lane said. "Now that it's harvest time, the mill and boiling houses operate twenty-four hours a day."

From there, Edward was shown a variety of other structures and areas: storage buildings, and blacksmith, carpenter and butchering sheds. In every place, Edward saw at least one or two Africans working. Some of the skilled ones, like blacksmiths, Lane said, were freed slaves.

In the animal pens, yards and paddocks, Edward saw only children. As they rode back toward the Big House, Lane pointed to a small building next to the bookkeepers' lodgings.

"The counting house, your workplace, most of the time." He stopped his horse, then gestured around him. "You see, we have everything here we need. We are a world unto ourselves. The only thing we lack is a hospital and doctor; only larger estates have them."

"Where do the slaves live?"

"As far away from the Big House as possible, thank the Lord," said Lane, "over there, beyond the animal pens."

"And the owner?" asked Edward.

"Not here. Mrs. Elizabeth Collard is the owner. She inherited the estate from her late husband. She's an absentee landlord, like most, enjoying her profits in England. In fact, she has never set eyes upon the estate. Jamaica is no place for a white woman."

They rode on and dismounted at the rear of the Big House. Edward was relieved to see Willie already there, so surely would avoid a punishment this time. The boy took the reins and led the horses away.

"Punch time," said Lane, and led the way into the dining room.

Before the overseer could open his mouth, Mini appeared with a jug and set it on the sideboard beside some glasses. Lane poured two glasses and offered one to Edward.

"Lime and rum," he said, "the only drink fit to cope with this place."

Though not used to liquor, Edward drank gratefully. It quenched his thirst. For the first time since he had met the man, Edward felt he could agree with him on something.

Chapter Twenty-Eight

A substantial meal of soup, roast chicken, potatoes and more yams and plantains followed several glasses of punch. Before the jug was empty, MacGregor and Howe joined them.

After most of this spread had been consumed, Lane yelled, "Rose!"

A tall muscular woman entered the room. She was darker in skin colour than Mini, but lighter than the field slaves Edward had seen. Slowly she moved to Lane's chair, glancing disdainfully at the other men. Bending a head wrapped in a bright red kerchief, she leaned close to him.

"Massa want mo?"

He put his arm around her waist and squeezed. "Good dinner, woman!" he slurred.

MacGregor grinned, but Howe looked away, disgusted.

Rose squirmed out of Lane's grasp and sauntered out of the room. Lane said he was going to his study and left.

"To take a nap, no doubt," Howe whispered to Edward.

In a louder voice, MacGregor added, "To retire with his housekeeper, most likely."

The three bookkeepers walked to the counting house.

Desks, tables and chairs were positioned close to the single window in one room. Beyond, in a smaller windowless room, ledger books occupied floor-to-ceiling shelves.

"You start him off, Tom," said the Scot, "I'm to supervise the mill and boiling house this afternoon."

"As you say, Mac," was Howe's reply. It was obvious who the senior bookkeeper was. Howe motioned to Edward to pull up a chair by a desk which held an open ledger. For the rest of the afternoon, Edward watched and listened as Howe described each entry he made and all the records required of a sugar plantation. It was all very overwhelming.

Everything was recorded, from the number of hogsheads of sugar produced each harvest to detailed entries concerning the animals and the status of every person on the estate: slave, of any age; freed African; indentured servant; or European. Details of the health, absenteeism, disciplinary actions and punishments of each slave were carefully noted. Edward was distressed by some of these entries which listed floggings or amputations, even hangings. But he said nothing.

At dusk Howe closed the ledger and stood up. "Enough to addle even the sharpest mind?" he asked.

Edward smiled. "Yes, I fear so."

"Don't despair," said Howe, "I found it so at first, but have come to some proficiency, as you will, too."

Edward felt a rush of gratitude for this gesture of encouragement and understanding. "I appreciate your kindness, sir," he said awkwardly.

Embarrassed, Howe said, "Call me Tom. I remember how hard it was for me when I came to this place."

As they walked toward the Big House, Edward felt bold enough to ask, "What did Mr. MacGregor mean by Mr. Lane retiring for a nap with his housekeeper?"

"Mr. Lane refers to Rose, the cook, as his housekeeper," said Thomas coldly. "It's a polite term here for mistress."

Edward stopped in his tracks. Speechless, he turned to Howe.

"You will learn that this is common," said Thomas. "There are no white women at Stony Gut, of course, and few elsewhere. Most white men are more than happy to... to abuse coloured and black women. There's a great supply, after all."

Before he could stop himself, Edward asked, "And you?"

"I am a Christian, sir," snapped Thomas. "I refer to most men. Not to me!"

They walked on in silence. As they reached the Big House, a young woman came skipping down the steps of the verandah. At first glance Edward thought she was white. Her skin was the colour of milky tea.

When she saw the two men, she stopped, moved aside quickly, lowered her eyes and murmured, "Massa Howe, sah."

Thomas said, "This is Elizabeth, who works in the house, along with Rose, Mini and Mary. She is a seamstress. Elizabeth, this is Massa Fraser, a newly arrived buckra."

Edward, slightly embarrassed, bowed and said shyly, "It is good to make your acquaintance, Elizabeth."

With eyes fixed on the ground, she whispered, "Ah welcomes yuh, sah." Then she looked up, and her eyes met his for an instant. There was no expression on her face, but he was sure that her eyes were smiling at him.

After that, Edward did not see Elizabeth again, even though he saw Mini and Rose every day. And he did not think about her; he was too busy. Harvest time demanded twelve-hour days from the buckras, even more from most of the slaves. Edward spent most days in the counting house, recording all aspects of the harvest, including the daily output of each body on the estate. Most of the time he was alone, as Thomas and Mac were overseeing the work in the mill and boiling houses, while Lane rode through the fields and toured every building, demanding maximum effort on everyone's part.

By the end of his first week, Edward suddenly realized that he had spent full days poring over ledgers, and had not once succumbed to day dreams or distraction.

He hoped that it was the result of his determination to make his father proud of him, but suspected that it was more the fear of making a mistake and incurring the wrath of

Richard Lane. Regardless, he was exhausted each night. He longed for word from home, but had no energy left to put pen to paper and start a letter himself.

He dreaded his days assigned to the mill or boiling houses. Luckily, he was still considered too much of a novice to be placed in either location often. But even one day's placement was pure misery. Both places operated around the clock, each with a gang of slaves.

The noise from the giant rollers grinding the stalks of cane in the mill house was deafening, but the heat of the bubbling sugar in the boiling house created an even worse hell, or so Edward thought. His second time in the mill house convinced him otherwise.

A tired slave, who was feeding cane stalks into the mouth of the grinding stones, managed to get the fingertips of one hand drawn into the rollers, along with the stalks. He screamed and pulled away frantically, but he could not free himself. Edward stared at this appalling scene, paralyzed. Another slave pushed by Edward and, with one swift blow of his machete, cut off the man's forearm.

Released, the injured man fell to the ground, clutching his stump and screaming in agony. Edward finally found his voice and gasped, "Send for a doctor."

The slave who had wielded the machete looked at him blankly.

"No doctah, heah, Massa." He bent down and wound a rag around the man's stump and shook his head.

"Him be a dead man."

Lane, who had heard the screaming, which had drowned out even the thunder of the rollers, strode into the mill house. Calmly he looked down at the injured man.

"Damn! Second slave we've lost in here this harvest." He looked at Edward angrily. "Keep a closer watch on this operation, damn you!" Then he turned to the handful of slaves standing off to the side. "Get back to work!" And to the slave comforting the dying man he said, "Stay with him, then get him out of here."

When he left, the slaves looked over at the remaining buckra. But Edward stood motionless, still stunned by what he had just witnessed.

"Massa?" One slave said softly.

It was only when the injured man ceased screaming that Edward reacted.

"Yes, back to work... please," he mumbled.

That night he relived the events of the day in vivid nightmares and woke screaming.

After that, sleep would not come. Mac threatened to turn him out of their sleeping quarters if he disturbed them again, but Thomas was sympathetic. "I remember my reaction the first time."

Fortunately, Edward did not serve in the mill house again that harvest season, but spent a great deal of time in the boiling house. As punishment, he believed. There were accidents there too, mainly burns from the hot sugar, although nothing as obscene as what he had witnessed in the mill house. But there were other horrors to come before the end of the harvest.

Edward had seen slaves struck often and knew it was commonplace. Lane and the black drivers in the fields were free with their whips, or cowskins, as the slaves called them. But never more than three blows. By law, more than three lashes had to be officially recorded. Edward believed that, in itself, prevented worse treatment.

But slaves could be punished for minor infractions without the whip: they could be shackled, weighted down with irons or confined in stocks.

Toward the end of the harvest, Lane came to Edward one day in the counting house. He slapped his whip handle rhythmically against his leg as he spoke.

"Two field slaves were caught trying to run away this

morning. They are to be flogged. You will be there to witness it and then record it in the ledger. Meet me at the edge of the near field within the hour."

Edward's heart sank. He found it difficult enough to see the house boy, Willie, being cuffed regularly on the side of the head. This was unthinkable. How could he witness such an outrage... and take notes?

Chapter Twenty-Nine

When Edward reached the field, he was surprised to see all the field slaves gathered, with the drivers, as well as many of the children who worked in the stables and paddocks. They parted when they saw him and revealed a Negro woman lashed to an overturned cart, face first. Her naked back and buttocks were exposed. Edward could not stifle a horrified gasp.

Lane glared at him. In a loud voice, so that all could hear, but staring straight at Edward, he declared grimly, "This is a legal punishment meted out for the crime of desertion. Be warned that this will be your fate if you attempt to run away. Massa Fraser is here to uphold the law, as witness and recorder of this action."

He gestured to one of the drivers, who pushed a shackled man forward. The driver unshackled the man's wrists, then handed him a whip.

In a loud voice Lane said, "Fifteen lashes."

At first, Edward was confused by this bizarre turn of events. Then he realized the special cruelty of this punishment. This man was being forced to flog someone close to him. His wife, perhaps?

The man raised the whip, then threw it at Lane's feet, spitting as he did so.

Lane was furious. He struck the man on the side of the

head with his whip handle. "For that, you will receive thirty lashes and she will receive twenty."

The crowd of slaves gasped and started to mutter ominously. The drivers moved among then, striking many. When they were quiet again, Lane raised his whip and said to Edward, "Count out loud."

Edward did as he was told, trying to keep his voice steady, looking not at the woman but at a place above her head. He stopped counting at twenty, but Lane kept going, stopping after two more blows. The woman had stopped crying out, but was twitching and whimpering. After she had been untied and carried off by a group of women, the man took her place. Edward's mouth was dry, and his heart beat so loudly he was afraid that everyone could hear it.

Once again, Edward was instructed to count out loud and he did. This time there was so much sweat in his eyes he could see nothing clearly. But, sadly, he could hear.

He stopped counting at thirty and was relieved when Lane stopped also. Perhaps he was exhausted after double floggings. The victim was limp and silent against the cart. Edward prayed he had lost consciousness.

"Get these punishments recorded immediately," Lane said to Edward. "Both are of the first gang; the man is Benjamin; the woman is Bessy."

Edward turned and, despite shaking legs, walked away from that awful place as quickly as he could. He stopped when he rounded the corner of the nearest building, then leaned heavily against the wall and vomited. As he retched, his mind raced as quickly as his heart. He could not remain here and be party to such barbarity.

And he hated himself for doing and saying nothing in protest. He was intimidated by Lane, he knew that, but despised himself for his cowardice all the same. When his stomach stopped heaving, he launched himself unsteadily from the side of the wall and stumbled on. He had to get to his cot.

He bumped into Thomas near the counting house.

"I've heard of the punishments," his friend said grimly. He studied Edward carefully. "Come, sit down inside. I will get you some water."

While Edward drank, Thomas spoke quietly. "You're outraged and prepared to leave this instant. I know. I felt the same not long after I arrived. But consider this: You have been here a short time. You have yet to earn any wages. Your family has invested in your future here. Do you wish to return to them a failure?" He gripped Edward's arm, and then his voice rose and became animated. "Edward, stay! God willing, men like you, like us, can be a force for good. We must be. If not, we condemn these Negroes to the continued cruelties of men like Lane. Help those of us who wish to change things, each in our own small way. It's our Christian duty. Make your mark here. Make your family proud."

Edward stared at Thomas for a moment. Then he shook his head and spoke quietly, as if to himself. "You're right, of course. The Christian thing to do is to stay, to confront this evil, not run from it. My father, my brother, even my sickly grandfather, would never hide from it. But what can I do?"

"Come with me to Sunday service at the Trinity District Church as soon as the harvest is over," said Thomas eagerly. "Reverend Stearns, our curate, is one who speaks for change."

Edward nodded vigorously. "I will."

"Good," said Thomas. "Change is slow, but it has happened. In the old days, slaves regularly endured frequent, severe floggings. Now thirty-nine lashes of the whip is the legal limit, but most, like Lane, will not inflict that many. Not out of any feelings for the slaves of course," he added bitterly, "but for the sake of practicality, because he cannot afford to lose the slave's labour."

Edward stood up. He put out his hand to the other man. "Thank you, Thomas."

Thomas shook his hand warmly. "It's good to have the company of a like mind."

That night, despite his exhaustion, Edward began a letter to Alex. Along with descriptions of the plantation, its workings and people, he poured out his feelings about the horrors he had witnessed.

At the end he wrote:

> "I have found a purpose now greater than my desire for adventure and a different life. With Thomas's help, I hope to work for change. I know that you, of all people, will understand and support me in this. Please pass on any advice or wisdom you may have. I send my love to you and all in the family. I intend to make all of you proud of me.
>
> I remain your loving brother, Edward."

Finally the harvest was over. To Edward it seemed to have lasted a lifetime. He had known only the crushing schedule of work since his arrival. Now there was free time. Even the slaves were given a few days off. Harvest's end was known as cropover, and it was embraced as a welcome respite, a festival which included an evening of dancing and music.

After a sumptuous dinner with the estate's attorney, from Kingston, George William Hamilton, Edward and the other buckras moved onto the front verandah.

Below, black fiddlers played, while some of the slaves, in their best clothes, danced and sang. Edward noticed Mini and Rose watching from just inside the front door. When he gazed at the large front windows, he saw two other faces peering out, studying the festivities. He was sure one was Elizabeth and he wondered again about her precise role in the household, especially now that Hamilton was visiting.

Later, as he lay on his cot, he fell asleep to the lulling beat of drums, the gumba, which lasted in the slave quarters long into the night.

Lane and Hamilton left the next day for Kingston, leaving

Mac in charge. Cropover was an opportunity for whites to visit friends in Kingston and Morant Bay and on other estates.

MacGregor would do the same once Lane returned. For Thomas, it was an opportunity to visit his friend, Reverend Stearns. Edward accompanied him that morning.

As they walked north toward the blue hills in the distance, they came to an area filled with Negroes, along with roaming pigs and chickens.

"What are they doing in this place?" he asked Thomas. "I thought they would be resting."

"This area is known as the provision grounds," said Thomas. "It's unwanted land, set aside for slaves to grow their own food."

"A new, enlightened measure?" asked Edward.

Thomas laughed, "No, just good sense. This system has been in place for years. If the slaves grow most of their own food, the owners have to provide less. Cropover gives the Negroes extra time to work in their kitchen gardens."

Edward shook his head; even after all this time, he was still discovering more about the appalling system of slavery.

It was a long uphill walk to the Trinity District Church, and both men were bathed in sweat when they arrived. Reverend Stearns greeted them warmly, ushered them out of the sun and into the wooden church, and offered fruit juice. He was delighted to learn that Edward wished to join them in their cause and spoke enthusiastically of the visit of Reverend William Knibb at the next Sunday service.

"He is a Baptist preacher, a powerful speaker and a major anti-slavery champion. Not only does he hold great influence in Britain, but he is already famous throughout this island. He may prove to be an agent of great change. Both of you must come to hear him."

The following Sunday, Edward sat in the small church beside Thomas. They were the only individuals from Stony Gut amongst a small congregation. Thomas pointed out owners, overseers, buckras and even a white woman with two children from other estates. Isolated so long at Stony Gut, Edward gazed with interest at this other white society that existed close by.

All other thoughts were banished when Reverend Knibb started to speak. Edward was familiar with the serious, measured tones of Presbyterian ministers, so was startled by the theatricality of this man's presentation. He spoke in a loud, excited manner, sometimes in anger, leaning forward from the pulpit to make a point, arms waving and eyes blazing.

Edward could sense that the congregation was uncomfortable as Reverend Knibb exhorted each to do his part to "bring down the great evil of slavery." He added that he hoped the British Parliament would soon move to ban it outright. When he asserted that even Negroes had souls and were God's children, too, like whites, Edward heard a few gasps and knew that not all agreed. There was silence when he finished.

Afterwards, Reverend Stearns admitted to Edward and Thomas that he, as a Church of England curate, was ill at ease with the animated delivery style of his Baptist colleague, but felt that it was necessary to the crusade. "I, too, believe that Negroes are God's children and baptize as many of their offspring as I am allowed."

In the months that followed, Edward attempted to show any small mercy he could to the slaves he managed. He ensured extra water and rest breaks for the slaves working under his direction. He showed them a respect many had never known. Edward became a well-liked massa. But it was all done covertly. Thomas had warned him that if Lane, or even Mac, suspected what they were doing, they would be denounced and summarily dismissed. Edward was tense and anxious at the beginning of this mission, but as their secret work seemed to pass unnoticed, he began to relax.

Chapter Thirty

Finally, just when fall clearing and planting began in new cane fields, Edward received his first letter from home. His hands trembled as he took the envelope, recognizing Alex's writing.

He had waited so long and so impatiently for this day. But the news from home was not what he had anticipated so eagerly. His beloved grandfather was dead. Shock buckled his knees. Alex had enclosed a copy of the death notice from the Halifax Nova Scotian of August 3, 1826. Hugh, the patriarch of the Fraser family, had died on July 26. Alex reported that he had been buried with Sophia in the cemetery beside the river, where most of the early settlers were laid to rest. Many *Hector* passengers had followed his funeral procession on foot to the cemetery.

There was more in the letter, other news of the family, of a possible newspaper in Pictou, of schools in the county that now numbered sixty and the continued prosperity of his father's businesses. Edward took none of this in. All that mattered was that Granddad was dead. When he had been ill and failing, his grandson had sailed away. When he had died, his grandson had not been there with him.

I should never have left when I did, thought Edward.

He sat for a long while, leaning up against the counting house. The sun was directly overhead, and he was drenched in sweat.

Edward wiped his face with his jacket sleeve, then folded the letter and put it in his pocket. As he was about to get up, he caught a glimpse of movement behind a tree. Someone was watching him.

He stood up slowly and called out, "Who's there?"

Elizabeth stepped forward. She was carrying a large basket of sheets, as white as her blouse.

"Ah begs pardon, sah. Yuh be poorly?"

Edward shook his head. "No. Just sad. Very bad news. From home."

"Someone done die?" she asked in her soft lilting voice, looking up at him.

Edward nodded. "My grandfather."

She pursed her lips and her voice shook. "Mah granmama, her die las harvest. Ah stills aches fo' mah Missy Queen."

With alarm, he noticed a tear drop down her cheek. He moved toward her.

"I did not mean to upset you, Elizabeth. I'm sorry."

She flashed him a wide smile. "No, Massa, ah t'inks o' her an' ah be happy. Yuh musa t'ink o' yuh grandaddy and be happy, too."

"Yes, you're right," said Edward, slowly. "I will remember him always and his goodness." Then he added, "Tell me about your grandmother."

But, before she could answer, a female voice called out from the direction of the Big House, "Sistah! Where yuh be? Get dem sheets heah!"

Without a word, Elizabeth quickly shifted the basket to her other hip and hurried away down the path toward the house.

Because he rarely saw her, he was surprised to come upon Elizabeth again the following day at the rear of the Big House, near the kitchen building. She and another woman were draping large curtains over tree branches. The other woman was slightly taller and sturdier, but shared similar features with Elizabeth: a sprinkling of freckles on an oval face, a honey complexion and dark, expressive eyes. The other woman lowered her eyes immediately and stopped what she was doing.

But Elizabeth smiled and said, "Massa Fraser be fine, t'day?"

"Yes, thank you."

Elizabeth touched the other woman on the arm and said, "Dis be mah mama. Dis be Mary."

Edward was surprised. He did not recognize the woman and had not imagined Elizabeth as having a mother on the estate. But why ever not, he thought to himself.

Then he nodded at Mary and said, "How do you do?"

She bowed in his direction but never raised her eyes. He lifted his hat to both women and continued on his way.

Intrigued, he asked Tom about them.

"The mother, Mary, was the daughter of a previous overseer here, William Bishop. She was allowed to work in the household and was trained as a seamstress, rather than being sent into the fields. Rumour has it that Elizabeth, her daughter, may be the child of Collard, our deceased owner. You will have noticed she has even lighter skin than her mother, almost white. Collard doted on Elizabeth, but never acknowledged her as his own. She was his personal attendant and trained as a seamstress, too. She is undoubtedly a pretty thing. Why this interest?"

"I am interested in the house servants as people," Edward replied stiffly.

"Oh no," cautioned Tom. "Remember, they are not *servants*, they are *slaves* and you can't develop friendships with them. Of course, Mac would say you are free to bed one, but having one as a friend is unthinkable."

Edward was offended by Tom's words. But he said nothing, realizing that his friend was speaking only of the realities of plantation life. But he intended to ignore the advice. He felt drawn to this slave girl and believed a friendship was possible. He hoped another opportunity would present itself, so that he and Elizabeth could share stories of their grandparents.

Within the next few months he came upon her on several occasions with her baskets of laundry, by the trees. She was usually alone and seemed at ease with him. While she worked, he spoke to her of his youth and how his mother and grandfather had supported him.

She reciprocated with stories of a tall, strong, dark-skinned grandmother who had encouraged her to be proud of her heritage.

"Missy Queen Ibo name Zicora, mean sent by da Lord. Da Lord surely sent her t' me," Elizabeth said.

Edward noticed that her voice became warm and animated when she spoke of her grandmother. He formed the impression that Mary, Elizabeth's mother, was more docile, and Missy Queen poured all her energies into creating a tough and determined granddaughter. Edward was both fascinated and horrified to learn Elizabeth's great-grandmother, Adamma, had arrived in Jamaica at only fourteen, having been kidnapped by slavers in West Africa. Both Adamma and Missy Queen had known the harsh life of the field slave, but the birth of a daughter by the overseer, Bishop, had transferred Missy Queen from field to house and so to an easier life. Thanks to her, Mary and then Elizabeth had been born into work in the Big House.

By the time of the next harvest, Edward was more at ease with his life at Stony Gut. He felt better prepared to face the hardships and vigilance that the season demanded. He and Thomas had been careful, and Lane had not learned of their work with the slaves. That had encouraged both of them. Edward was determined that on his watch no slave would die in the mill house.

Cropover was once again a time of celebration. But for Edward the relief at harvest's end turned to consternation when he learned that Elizabeth had been sold to Coley, a neighbouring estate.

Edward did not see Elizabeth before she left. By the time Tom passed along the news, she was gone. Tom said she was given little warning. She was permitted an hour to gather her belongings together in a hamper and say goodbye to those closest to her. Then James appeared in a cart to transport her north and west to Coley Estate.

"Happily for her," Tom added, "Coley is not far, perhaps a distance of five or six miles. She may visit her mother and others here on occasion. For her this is a great mercy, far better than if she had been sold to an estate in the west, on the other side of the island."

Edward, who had been reduced to silence, finally found his voice. "But why?"

Tom laughed. "Only you would ask such a question about a slave. I don't know the reason. Neither did Mac, who told me, but then he would not be interested."

Edward tried to imagine Elizabeth's anguish at being torn from her mother and the only home she had ever known. He had to find out more.

He could not ask Lane. No, Lane would tell him to mind his own business. Mini? Yes, friendly, chatty Mini.

Mini did know and was happy to tell him. "De seamstress at Coley done die, so dey need new one dere. So Lizbet go."

It was that simple. Although it could not compare to the past cruelties her ancestors had suffered, Edward was still dazed by this casual act of human relocation.

Mini was watching Edward's face. "Don' worry, Massa. Her not far. An' dat gal be lickle, but her be tough."

Edward wished he could accept it as easily as Mini did, but he could not. He tried to find Mary, Elizabeth's mother, but she was nowhere to be found. Eventually he gave up looking, convinced she was avoiding him. He was mystified by his own reaction. Surely he should not be so upset by the transfer of a slave, even if she were a friend?

If Elizabeth ever visited Stony Gut, Edward did not learn of it. Although he came to think of her less often, she lingered at the back of his mind, like a nagging piece of unfinished business.

Chapter Thirty-One

In his letters home to Alex, he had never mentioned Elizabeth, so said nothing of her departure. Instead, he wrote of his growing confidence in his work, his continued struggle with the Jamaican heat and his dedication to help the slaves as much as he could.

"My impact may be small, but I hope that future advancement might place me in a position where I can affect greater change."

He received a letter in return. In it, Alex reported that coal was replacing timber as the primary industry of the area. "These are times of great change," he concluded.

Great change proved to be true the following year for his faraway brother, too. Edward was offered a position at Coley Estate. While the post of bookkeeper was not a step up, on a larger estate it was a more demanding job and implied greater responsibility and the chance for advancement. Edward did not hesitate to accept.

"I shall miss your friendship," said Tom, "but you are wise to go. You'll advance quickly at Coley; I hear that the two senior bookkeepers will retire soon."

Stony Gut's size had allowed Edward a relatively smooth transition to plantation life and had demanded that he perform a variety of tasks, so he was grateful for the experience.

He was sad to leave a like-minded friend and confidant like Tom. But the greater, restless part of him was enthusiastic about a change and the chance to prove himself in a new setting.

And it was like moving from a village to a well-appointed town. Though only a few miles farther north and west, the estate's setting on the Negro River was attractive, with a view of the nearby Blue Mountains. Everything was larger, and there was more of it. Coley boasted almost nine hundred acres of cultivated land, employing more than twice as many slaves as Stony Gut. There were a separate overseer's house and other buildings not present at Stony Gut: one for a doctor and one for a catechist-schoolmaster.

Another feature of his new home that was different was the presence of a white woman and children. He had seen them at church, but their daily presence on the estate was startling at first.

Edward had met few of his colleagues before, as they did not attend church. His immediate superior, head bookkeeper Robert Guthrie was a quiet man and a widower. James NcNab was also an older man who, Edward suspected, enjoyed his drink a little too much. He had a black mistress and children, as did another man, Charles MacKenzie. And lastly, there was David Taylor, whom he had glimpsed in church. He was like Edward: young, unmarried and apparently without a mistress.

The overseer was a refreshing change from Richard Lane. Archibald Drew was a dour Scot and a strict master, but a fair one.

He even demonstrated some humanity to the slaves on the estate. It was his white family that Edward had seen in church and now saw daily.

Edward penned an enthusiastic letter to Alex soon after his arrival. He described a much larger, grander Great House and more spacious quarters for bookkeepers. "I have a room of my own with a desk and bookshelf." He listed the estate's absentee landlords, Davidson and Jennings, then his many colleagues. He spoke admiringly of John Eccles Ward, the doctor, "a warm man, who invites my conversation," and of the catechist, "Joshua Wood, who ministers to slaves and whites alike. I have offered to help him in the reading instruction of Negro children, once a week, on the Sabbath." He ended his letter by suggesting he saw a bright future for "my advancement and for the cause of abolition."

What he did not mention was another person he had seen and whose presence had affected him dramatically. While touring the estate with David Taylor, he had caught a glimpse of a familiar figure in the slave provision grounds. As he stared at her, she turned to look in his direction. Their eyes met. She gasped and dropped the basket she was holding. Edward rushed over to gather the fallen okra and yams, while she stood there astonished and wordless. He rose and handed her the basket.

"I presume you hang the sheets out here, too," he said.

She nodded, and he turned back to David, who looked at him in a quizzical manner but said nothing. They walked away.

The very next day before dinner, he scouted the grounds around the Great House wondering if he might see Elizabeth, and he found her. She put her hand to her mouth when she saw him.

He smiled nervously. "Elizabeth, I am so pleased to see you again."

But she was tense and unsmiling. "How yuh be heah?"

"Well... I was offered a position here," he replied. Then asked uncertainly, "You are not happy to see me, too?"

She started to cry. Without thinking, he moved forward and gently enfolded her in his arms. She felt like a fragile bird against him.

She sobbed softly on his chest. Eventually she looked up at him and said, "Yuh bin in mah heart ev'ry day."

He kissed her softly then. As she nestled her body closer to his, he felt a rush of happiness he had never known.

When he found his voice again, he whispered, "You are so precious to me, dear Elizabeth. Would you... perhaps sometime...?"

"Ah will come t' yuh dis night," she interrupted, then laughed when she saw the amazement on his face. "It be fine. Now ah know ah be in yuh heart so strong, too."

The rest of the day passed in a blur for Edward. He was excited and uneasy in equal measure. She was deep in his heart that was true, but was this right?

Their first night together erased any reservations Edward may have had. That her passion matched his own was thrilling, but it was her tenderness that captured him. He knew his heart had found its home.

Each night while they were together, Edward was blissfully sure of himself. During the day, however, his mind was disturbed by doubts. On one side, guilt argued that what he was doing was sinful and abusive. He felt sure that Granddad, Father and Alex would all disapprove. But on the other side, his heart answered strongly. He was not just another buckra preying on a slave woman; she came to him willingly. They loved each other, and he respected her.

So Edward determined to banish his doubts so he could focus on his work. It would be a test of character, of his mettle as a Fraser. He would prove his worth to himself and to his superiors by exemplary work.

And he was largely successful. He worked harder than anyone else. He surprised himself with enough energy to assist Joshua Wood regularly in his mission with the slaves. If the catechist knew of Edward's relationship, he did not let it interfere with his grateful acceptance of Edward's help. From this volunteer work, Edward learned of the rising expectations of many slaves for major reform. Joshua was concerned about these expectations, which he told Edward were being fuelled by itinerant Baptist ministers.

"I fear the slaves are being duped into believing that slavery will end tomorrow.

I know there is a mood for abolition in Britain, but it will not happen overnight. I worry that these preachers will falsely inflame the hopes of the Negroes, to what end I don't know."

Edward, in his bubble of happiness, did not share Wood's gloomy outlook. For him the days sped by in the twin glows of Elizabeth's love and his meaningful work. And at Coley he did not have to hide his kindness to the slaves.

With Christmas came the festival of Junkanoo and a chance for everyone to relax and celebrate. It was to be a grand affair this year at Coley, with many invited guests for the Christmas feast. Some attorneys and merchants from Kingston, as well as planters and overseers and their families from several neighbouring estates, had been invited. To cope with the large number of guests and the added work, extra house slaves were brought in to Coley from some nearby plantations.

Elizabeth's mother, Mary, was one of the many on loan, to Elizabeth's great delight. They were among five house slaves who were selected to serve at table on Christmas Day.

By the time the guests sat down to their evening meal, the wine was flowing freely, and the mood was festive. All looked forward to a special feast that would include turtle soup, pigeon pies, boiled ham, turkey and stewed duck.

Even as he watched with pride as his Elizabeth moved gracefully around the dining room, Edward strained to hear some unsettling conversation. Down at the other end of the table, a Kingston attorney spoke of serious slave unrest.

A merchant replied that a rebellion was not out of the question, thanks to the provocation of those "damned Baptist ministers." But Edward did not wish to hear more, so turned away. That subject could spoil his mood, let alone his appetite. Instead, he turned his attention to the serving of the next, delicious course.

Following the meal, the ladies adjourned to the parlour, while the men regrouped on the verandah for cigars and brandy. Edward was relieved to be out of the stuffy dining room and outdoors, even though he had no interest in either brandy or cigars. Unfortunately, the talk about rising slave tensions on the island persisted here, too. Mary and Elizabeth moved about the verandah filling glasses.

Uninvolved in the conversation, Edward became aware of the sound of an approaching horse. He stared into the inky blackness of the night, but saw the horse and rider only as they pulled up sharply, just short of the house. As the rider slipped from the saddle, Edward recognized George, a free black from Stony Gut Estate. George approached the verandah steps, looked up at Archibald Drew and drew a paper from his jacket. Drew moved quickly down the steps to join him. After a brief conversation, Drew dismissed George, then read the message. When he rejoined the silent group on the verandah, his face was grim.

"It's a message from the authorities in Kingston, forwarded from Stony Gut. A full-scale slave revolt has broken out in the west of the island. At first the slaves refused to work in protest, but now it is all-out violence. Thousands of them are burning and looting all over the west."

There were shocked gasps all along the verandah.

Drew continued. "Every able-bodied man must ride out with the militia to quell this revolt. Now. This night."

"Is there any trouble here in the east, in this parish?" asked the Kingston attorney.

"No, not yet," replied Drew, "but we must act quickly to prevent it spreading." He paused. "But I won't leave this property unprotected in our absence." He studied each face of the men present. "A few of you must remain here," he said.

As Drew pondered his selection, Edward caught Elizabeth's eye. She stared back at him, with a look of horror on her face.

Drew made up his mind quickly. "Mr. Wood and Mr. Guthrie will remain behind to manage and defend Coley. All the women and children will remain here; the house slaves will see to their needs. The rest of us will ride west to face the rebellion. Elizabeth, you and the others must go now to prepare provisions for our departure."

With rising panic, Edward watched Elizabeth hurry from the verandah, without a backward glance. It took him a few moments to realize that he was expected to ride out with the others, into the midst of a slave rebellion. He was terrified. He could not fire a pistol at another human being. It was unimaginable. And how could he leave Elizabeth, his dear, sweet Elizabeth?

In the uproar that followed, everyone seemed to speak or cry out at once as they hurried off in all directions. Before Edward could go after Elizabeth, Drew grabbed his arm. "No, Edward, do not follow her. She will be safe. The sooner we leave, the faster we will return. I, too, am leaving loved ones." His tone had been gentle, but his eyes and grip were steely. "Come!"

Edward allowed himself to be led away by Drew and soon found himself on a horse, with a pistol in his belt and a pack of provisions on his saddle.

Almost at once, the dozen riders in their party were off on the road south to Morant Bay. There they met another group of riders from their parish. As darkness fell, this larger body, almost three dozen strong now, galloped westward along the coast road.

Chapter Thirty-Two

They stopped once that night to rest themselves and their horses, but Edward could not sleep. His fears about Elizabeth and what he might face in the following days kept his mind racing.

Mercifully, the first two days were uneventful. The roads were unnaturally quiet, with no donkey carts, gigs or carriages to clog the way. Some blacks had gone to join the rebellion, some had taken the opportunity to escape into the hills, and the rest remained on the estates. Some whites had already sailed for home, while others had gone to the relative safety of the towns.

Toward noon on the third day, Edward's group began to notice the smell of smoke. The peaceful countryside gave way to torched, smouldering cane fields. They crested a rise and saw spectacular flames in the distance. As they rode closer, the men could see that the source was a newly torched boiling-house. Through thick flames and smoke, they saw a group of slaves armed with machetes and shovels battling a smaller number of whites. The slaves ran off when the militia men rode up. Edward was among those who stopped to aid the whites, while the rest of the party rode after the slaves. A few of the whites were horribly wounded by machete blows.

Edward and Ward quickly dismounted to help.

Thrusting bandages into Edward's hands, the doctor

shouted instructions above the roar of the fire. Gratefully, Edward followed his lead, willing himself to focus only on staunching blood and binding wounds.

One thought ran through his head: thank the Lord I do not have to fire my pistol. As if to reinforce that horrific alternative, he heard the sound of gunshots and screams in the distance, as the militia caught up with the fleeing slaves. One of the wounded whites died that day, but many more slaves were killed as they tried to flee.

As they moved westward, Edward's group saw more and more devastation: burned buildings, vandalized Great Houses, destroyed cane fields and terrified animals wandering everywhere. And there were dead bodies. Other than the wounded man who had died in that first skirmish, Edward saw only one other white fatality. But he saw countless black bodies in the ruined fields and by the roadsides, left rotting in the sun and picked at by carrion crows. As a result of that very first skirmish, Edward was assigned by the militia captain to assist the doctor in future engagements. The relief he felt to be spared the fighting itself was overwhelming. A few men in their militia unit sustained minor injuries, but none of them was serious.

The militia's orders were to punish the guilty without mercy when they were caught. But Edward suspected that the innocent were being punished just as ruthlessly.

In the ruins of slave villages, he saw the bodies of children and old women and wondered what role they could have possibly played in the rebellion. Though he never fired a shot, he could not shake his despair. What was happening around him was barbaric and unchristian. And Edward tortured himself with worries about the situation at Coley. Was Elizabeth safe? It was unbearable to think otherwise.

By the tenth day, the rebellion was over, successfully quashed, and he and his weary Coley companions headed home.

At sundown on that first day travelling east, they

approached a very large tree by the roadside. Despite no command given, the group reined in their horses. Disturbed crows squawked angrily at their presence and flew off, and then the only sound was the night drone of insects. From the sturdy branches five black bodies, including one small one, hung motionless. The adult ones were terribly mutilated. All five were barely recognizable as human beings. Dr. Ward, ashen-faced, turned in his saddle to face Edward. "I fear that hundreds of men, women and children have been slaughtered just like this," he whispered hoarsely, "many undoubted innocents, not even suspected of being rebels."

Edward reached out to lay a hand on his friend's arm. There was nothing to say. He was sure that the haunted look he saw in Ward's eyes mirrored his own.

They continued on their journey home, exhausted, filthy and relieved that it was over. They were a silent group, not a jubilant one.

When they arrived at Coley, they found it the same as they had left it, untouched by any of the turmoil in the west.

Elizabeth raced to Edward's side as soon as he entered his room. He crushed her to him, caressing her shoulders, her hair, her face repeatedly, as if to convince himself that she was unharmed.

"Mah heart be back," she whispered into his ear. "Mah prayers be answered. Sleep now."

He did as he was bidden, happy to surrender himself completely to her care. He slept for almost two days.

When they spoke again, Edward was relieved that she had neither the need nor the interest to hear of his experiences. News had travelled quickly from estate to estate, over the entire island; she was well aware of the awful events that had transpired. He was surprised when she claimed she had not been afraid. Instead, his small, dainty Elizabeth shook with anger as she railed at the reprisals of the whites.

"We never be free, dose white devils kill us all first!"

"I'll protect you always, my dearest, you know that! And Joshua Wood believes that this terrible event will only hasten the end of slavery. He is convinced that in Britain the public will be appalled by what has happened here."

"Bah!" was her indignant response. It was obvious that she did not believe that possible. Edward had little faith in white intentions himself.

And what if there was more trouble? Legally, he could not marry Elizabeth and he dare not return to Nova Scotia with her. He must find a way to protect her.

A few months later, Guthrie and MacNab announced their plans to return to Britain, and Drew offered Edward the position of head bookkeeper. Edward was thrilled and hoped that his new status would mean more security for Elizabeth. He rushed to tell her, but she in turn greeted him with news of her own.

"Ah gon' have our very own chile, Edward," she beamed. He was elated.

The situation on the entire island continued to deteriorate. Archibald Drew had earlier returned from Kingston to report the revolt's aftermath. The loss of white lives during the ten-day uprising was limited to fourteen. Baptist minister William Knibb had been charged with inciting revolt and was to be exiled to Britain. However, for the slaves the news was grim. More than two hundred blacks had been killed during the rebellion, and over three hundred rebels, including the leader, Sam Sharpe, had been tried and executed. Many others had been flogged and some were imprisoned for life. While many believed that the harsh punishments were justified, Edward, Ward and Wood were sickened by them. Edward absorbed all of this with a sinking heart. The punishments were bad enough, but it was not over.

The revolt may have been contained in the west, but the

poison had spread over the whole island. Coley, in the peaceful east, was not immune. The mood on the estate was tense between the races. The slaves were sullen, frightened and distrustful, even of the whites who, like Edward, had been sympathetic toward them in the past.

Some slaves had been shipped away to fill the labour shortage on western estates, so those remaining were forced to work even harder. While the blacks seethed with resentment, the whites feared them and were terrified of another uprising.

Finally, more than a year later, there was momentous news from Britain. Parliament passed the Abolition of Slavery Act. Slavery would end on August 1, 1834. Wood had been right in his prediction.

When Edward shared this news with Elizabeth, she collapsed on the ground, sobbing over and over again, "Mah chile be free, mah chile be free." For the first time in a long, long while, Edward permitted himself to feel a sliver of optimism.

He wrote to share some of his joy with Alex. Proudly he announced his promotion and then talked of the new act. He told his brother that while it was an answer to so many prayers, he was troubled by the inclusion of a clause about an apprenticeship period. It was as if slaves had to earn their freedom first.

"I do have concerns as to how this will be accepted by the Negroes, and work in practice." What he did not mention was the upcoming birth of his first child, much as he longed to.

The letter that followed from Alex praised his brother, passing along their father's congratulations, which touched Edward deeply. Alex echoed his brother's sentiments about the new act, then went on at length about their exciting local news, the first Atlantic crossing of a steamship. The *Royal William* left from Pictou, carrying Albion Mines' coal and was seen off by a cheering crowd of thousands.

Edward scowled as he read this. How could his brother devote more lines to a steamship than to Abolition, the most dramatic event of the century? But his irritation was short-lived as his son was born soon after. This birth and aftermath were frustrating for Edward, because a nana, or midwife, had taken over completely, barring him from the room for eight days. True to slave ritual, mother and child were isolated to protect them both from spiritual and physical harm, with nana keeping guard.

At the end of the seclusion, Elizabeth and her baby were released to greet the world and announce the baby's name as Edward Coley Fraser.

As the new mother sang to her infant, "Mama gon' rock, mama gon' hold, lickle boy-chile mine," Edward gazed at both of them, believing he could never again be as happy or fulfilled.

"You know," he said, "I would marry you this instant if I could, my love."

Elizabeth returned his gaze tenderly. "Ah know yuh be mine, mah heart." She caressed the baby's soft curls. "An mah pickney knows he can count on his daddy."

The absence of a sanctified union continued to bother Edward, as much as it did not seem to matter to Elizabeth. Her pride and happiness could not be diminished; her baby was not only beautiful, but his flawless, milky skin was almost white. Best of all, he was no slave and never would be. The Abolition Act stated that all children under six were free.

The year that followed was one of great anticipation and excitement, as the date of Emancipation drew near. Early on the morning of August 1, Joshua Wood held a service on the estate to mark the occasion. Every slave at Coley attended, as did some of the whites. Elizabeth and Edward stood side by side, with young Edward nestled in his mother's arms. Tears of joy rolled down many faces, including Elizabeth's.

Joshua spoke of a new era of justice and brotherhood. Edward prayed silently that it would be so, though he feared the aftermath would not be as promising as Joshua suggested.

Chapter Thirty-Three

It did not take long for Joshua's predictions to be proven overly optimistic. Edward had been right to be sceptical. The terms of freedom were there to appease the planters, not the newly freed slaves. Under the Act, newly freed slaves were apprenticed to their former owners for a period of up to six more years. They were to devote forty hours of work per week to their former masters in exchange for food and lodging. They could receive wages for additional work.

As Edward feared, most Negroes were very unhappy with these terms, believing that the owners had betrayed them once again. Elizabeth echoed the common sentiment when she grumbled to Edward, "If we be free, we be free to work how we want."

Without slavery's punishments, former slaves were unwilling to work as brutally hard in the cane fields. Production fell. Edward heard that on some estates owners were taking drastic actions to coerce their workforce. Negro villages and provision lands were burned and their livestock killed in an effort to force them to work as before. Some were cowed and remained; many others deserted and settled in the hills beyond the borders of any plantation. Although these tactics were not used at Coley, sugar production continued to fall.

Edward and Drew struggled hard to encourage their workforce with reasonable working hours and decent treatment. Even so, many cane fields remained unplanted.

The one happy event during this chaotic time was the birth of a sister for little Edward. But the joy was short-lived, as sickly Mary succumbed to a fever after four months. Elizabeth was inconsolable, refusing to let little Edward out of her sight, as if fearing he, too, might be taken from her. For his father, as well, the baby's death was heartbreaking.

Edward was frustrated, too, by his unravelling dream of making a difference. Now that he was finally in a position of some influence, all his efforts seemed to be in vain.

By 1838, the British Parliament admitted that the apprenticeship system was a failure and ended it. All slaves were finally, truly free. However, the situation did not improve. Many Negroes simply quit the plantations, and others were turned out by the white planters who could not, or would not, pay them. The result was a wandering mass of thousands searching for any land that could support them. Whole estates ceased to operate and were abandoned.

In a letter to Alex the following year, Edward described the situation on Coley. He related one incident, though there had been more than one, when a group of former slaves had appeared. After denuding the provision grounds, they had rampaged through the slave village, stealing and vandalizing, and then approached the Great House.

Only the armed presence of Edward, Drew and their colleagues was successful in driving them off. This time Edward joined the others in discharging pistols and muskets over the heads of the marauders.

An appalled Alex had written back to say that Edward must return to Nova Scotia immediately. Edward never acknowledged this advice. How could he suddenly reveal a secret family, the tie that bound him to Jamaica?

A year later, Elizabeth was expecting again, and they were both uneasy after the tragic death of daughter, Mary.

But in December, 1840 Elizabeth delivered a healthy baby, another girl.

Elizabeth Ann was baptized the following April, a great relief to both parents. Her brother, Edward, almost eight, was enchanted by his sister, whom he called Annie. And he became a trusted helper to his Mama.

The struggle to keep the estate running was onerous, but Edward's spirits had been lifted with the birth of Annie. And he was buoyed further the following year by his appointment as Coley overseer, on the retirement of Archibald Drew. With great ceremony, he introduced his family to their first proper home, when he moved them into the overseer's house. Elizabeth was thrilled by her new home and her elevated status on the estate. Best of all, Edward arranged for her mother, Mary, to move to Coley and live with them as part of their family. It was a gesture that amazed and touched Elizabeth.

Edward was delighted not only by a congratulatory letter from Alex, but also by a rare separate letter from his father. Edward had kept his promise. At last he had made his father proud.

Despite Edward's best efforts, the estate's fortunes continued to decline, and that brought a visit from the owner. William Davidson arrived from England to discuss plans to rescue the estate by using indentured Asian workers.

Other estates had adopted this practice of replacing their ever-dwindling supply of freed slaves. It would be Edward's job to make this new venture work. He worked harder than ever before, spending precious little time with his family. He had started teaching his nine-year-old son bookkeeping skills, but found he no longer had the time. Young Edward was relieved. Restless like his father at the same age, he much preferred wandering the estate when he could escape his mother's watchful eye. Most of all, he loved observing and helping the carpenters.

The family grew again a few years later, when Alexander was born. Edward named his new son after his beloved, steadfast brother. But like Mary, Alexander was a sickly baby and although he survived his baptism, he died of a fever before his second birthday.

While Elizabeth's sadness led to her becoming more protective of her two remaining children, Edward's reaction was different. He grieved for the son he had lost, but also for the absence of the far-away family who might have comforted him.

He struggled to put aside his grief and focus on the enormous task of incorporating the new indentured workforce. Stress and overwork gradually wore him down. By early 1848, he had lost weight and was having difficulty sleeping. Elizabeth became increasingly worried and sought out John Ward. The doctor prepared tonics to help Edward sleep and boost his strength, to no avail.

When Edward complained of nausea and an aching body one evening, Elizabeth believed it was no more than his usual malaise. With alarming speed, however, he developed a high fever and became wracked by chills, followed by delirium and vomiting.

Dr. Ward came, but had little to offer in the way of treatment. He prescribed spoonfuls of broth and water and wipe-downs with a cool wet cloth. He told Elizabeth he suspected yellow fever. In desperation, she called her nana, who put mud packs on Edward's mosquito bites hoping to draw out the poison.

For almost a week Edward was in the terrifying grip of the disease. Then, on the sixth day, released from delirium and fever, he awoke with a clear head. Elizabeth was speechless with relief.

But Dr. Ward warned her that this might be only a temporary reprieve and that a second, more dangerous, stage of the disease might still follow. Edward was very weak but began to take food. Even as he seemed to recover, Ward warned him, too, of the possibility of relapse.

"You honour me, dear friend, with your honesty,"

Edward whispered weakly. "I must make my will... and send word to my brother in Nova Scotia. He needs to know about my family, finally... I fear it will come as a mighty shock... I will need your help in these matters, John."

Ward nodded in assent, agreeing to write to Edward's brother Alex with a request.

Then Edward asked to see Elizabeth. She sat by his bedside caressing his hand. It pained him to see the exhaustion and worry on her face, but he smiled at her. "You have been everything to me. I loved you from the very first moment I laid eyes on you, on the verandah steps at Stony Gut. Do you remember that day, my love?"

Elizabeth squeezed his hand and nodded, as tears streamed down her cheeks.

"I have to ask you now to do something that I know will be unbearable, impossible... but it will be for the best... for our children."

He stopped to catch his breath and saw that her face had become wary, her eyes fearful of what was to come.

"After I am gone, I want you to send our children to my brother Alex in Nova Scotia. They will have a better, more secure future there with him and his family—" He stopped, as she yanked her hand from his, a look of incredulity and horror in her eyes.

"Mah pickneys be took fro' me?" she gasped, shaking her head. "No, no, no! Dis not be possible. Edward, yuh not mean dis!"

"Please, my love, think about it. I would not ask such a terrible thing of you... unless I thought it was the only way. There's too much unrest here... violence... disease... it's too dangerous to live here," he gasped. "You must want better for Edward and Annie."

"But Edward, ah die wi'out mah pickneys!"

Marshalling all the strength he had left, Edward voiced a final plea. "In Nova Scotia, our children will be white." Then his head fell back on the pillow, all energy spent.

When he blinked away his tears, he saw that she had vanished. He closed his eyes. He knew that what he was asking of her would devastate her. The asking itself had been an agony for him, a knife to his own heart.

Later, he called his son to his bedside. They spoke alone for a long while, Edward pleading, young Edward crying. As his son rose to leave, Edward pushed a leather pouch into one of his hands. "This is yours... to keep," he said. "Remember who this belonged to. Remember all I have told you. I'm putting my trust in you, my son." Shaking, young Edward stumbled from the room. Elizabeth had still not returned.

She did not reappear for the rest of the day. Mary nursed him silently in her daughter's absence. When Elizabeth did return, she sat down at his bedside and stared calmly into his sunken eyes.

She placed a finger on his lips, then straightening her shoulders, she looked down, focusing on her hands in her lap.

"Yuh be silent, now. Yuh musa heah me out," she insisted, in a strong, clear voice. "Ah have listened t' the spirit of mah Missy Queen an spoke t' mah mama. An ah have listened t' mah heart. Dey all tole me t' same t'ing. Don fight. White man get his way ev'ry time." She paused then as she pursed her lips. "But dey say yuh man speak da truth. Best t'ing fo' mah pickneys is t' leave dis place. Dey be safe wit Uncle Alex." She hesitated, then took a deep breath. "Missy Queen say yuh musa be tough, sistah, like Adamma. Let dem go."

There was silence when she finished. As she wept quietly, Edward reached for her hand. She looked into his eyes through her tears and he knew she would read the message there: his gratitude, his relief and his love.

They gazed steadily at each other until finally he closed his eyes. She leaned over, kissed him on the forehead and sat very still watching him sleep.

Despite the return of fever, on September 2, 1848,

Edward was able to sign his will in the presence of his executors, John Eccles Ward and neighbouring planters, Edward Bainbridge and Thomas Henry Richardson.

On the thirteenth of that month, Reverend Stearns, Island Curate, conducted a simple bedside ceremony.

Feverish and in pain but aware, Edward Smith Fraser married Elizabeth Bishop in the presence of their children. The bride wore a green silk dress she had made herself.

From his sick bed, the groom wore a look not seen since the disease had struck. It was one of peace.

He died four days later, on September 17, with his wife clinging to one hand as if to hold him to this life. He was forty-three.

Part Four

1848 – 1860

Chapter Thirty-Four

Under a warm December sun, seven-year-old Annie sat sobbing on a stout trunk on the Kingston wharf. Her cloth doll, M'randa, clutched against her face, was absorbing some of the tears. Nearby her Mama and brother were once again deep in conversation, another one that she was not privy to. Ever since Papa had died it had been like that. Mama and Edward whispering together, Mama pleading and crying, and Edward listening. Sometimes arguing, once even storming off. He had never sassed Mama before. Papa's dying had been bad enough, but the anger she sensed in these conversations was scary. It felt like something even worse was going to happen.

All the misery of these last weeks had finally led them to this wharf, to this great ship. The ship that would carry them across the sea to a place called Nova Scotia. It would take them away from Jamaica, away from home. Worst of all, it would carry her and Edward away from Mama. She was not coming with them. It was Papa's wish for them to go, said Mama, said Edward. They would be happy there. Jamaica was too unsettled.

They would live with Uncle Alex in a place called New Glasgow, a real town. They would meet a host of aunts, uncles and cousins. They would be part of a big family,

Papa's family. Mama had promised Papa. Edward had promised him, too. Besides, Mama said she would come. But later, not now. Annie must say goodbye. Today.

She traced the doll's smiling lips with a finger, then the bright red scarf wrapped around its tiny head. Mama had made M'randa, just as she had all of Annie's clothes that were packed in the trunk: her embroidered dresses and petticoats and her underthings. And most important of all, Mama's gift of her own beautiful green wedding dress. They were carefully packed, as were other treasures: Annie's delicately carved wooden sewing box and a beautiful clock of Papa's. It was Edward's now. Edward! He would be with her, to care for her and to comfort her. He might be only fifteen, but he was as dependable as a grownup. He was even more important than M'randa.

Feeling guilty, she looked down at her loyal friend. "Ah do love yuh, too, ah do," she reassured the doll.

When Annie looked up, Mama and Edward were beside her. Edward motioned for her to rise. Most of Mama's face was hidden by a scarf pressed against it.

"It's time to board," said Edward.

Panic seized her then, and she grasped her mother around the waist.

"No, Mama, Ah want tuh stay wi' yuh! Please!"

Edward pulled her away, gently but firmly. "Yuh will see Mama again. But now, for her sake and for Papa's, we must go."

Annie pulled the scarf away from her mother's face and saw only grief and pain there.

"In mah heart always," Mama sobbed, as she drew her children close in a fierce hug.

Swinging Annie's bundle and his own leather satchel over one shoulder, Edward coaxed Annie up the gangway and onto the ship, following the sailors who were carrying their trunk. He held her tight against the railing as they looked down at their mother on the wharf.

"Yuh must smile and wave. For our dear Mama, yuh must do this!" demanded Edward through gritted teeth.

At that moment his voice cracked, and alarmed, Annie saw tears streaming down his face. She had never seen him cry, not even when Papa had died.

He gripped her tightly, and she felt his panic. "Please, Annie, yuh must help me."

Never had he asked for her help! For a moment she was confused and then she squeezed his arm.

As the ship moved away from the wharf, both of them waved at their mother and tried to smile, despite the tears that would not stop. Annie blew kisses and yelled, "Ah love yuh, Mama," over and over again, long after their mother could possibly hear the words. Together Elizabeth's children remained fixed at the railing until they could no longer see the tiny speck that was their gentle, loving mother.

After they had stowed their small bags under their bunks in the passengers' cabin, Edward persuaded Annie to rest on her bunk.

"Yuh look so tired," he said gently. "And yuh will feel much better after some sleep."

She clung to his hand as she lay there, afraid he too might disappear. She looked up into his weary, tear-stained face. "Yuh should sleep, too," she remembered saying before she drifted off.

Their first five days at sea were fair, and the sun followed them in their northward journey. Edward and Annie spent as much time as possible on deck, avoiding their dreary lodgings below. There were only a handful of passengers and no other young people, aside from an infant and the woman who suckled him in the bunk beside Annie's. Edward used this time to tell Annie all he had learned about their new home and family.

"Papa and Uncle Alex have always been close, and Papa trusted him, Annie," Edward began. "Our uncle is a merchant and a tailor, a skilled man with cloth, like our Mama and yuh, too." He smiled encouragingly at her. "Also, he is a religious man, who is much involved with the church, much like Mr. Wood. He has four children, and one is a girl close to your age, Annie. "

Annie could tell he was trying to sound enthusiastic about their new home.

"They live in a town called New Glasgow, perhaps like Kingston. It is not always warm like home," he went on. "It can be very cold, with strong winds and lots of snow."

"Snow?" wondered Annie. "What's snow?"

"Papa says—said—it falls from the sky, like rain, but it's white and soft and very cold."

Annie shivered. "Ah won't like that."

Edward's voice became serious then. "Annie, yuh must do something for me when we get there. Promise me yuh'll not say much about Mama. Do not say what she looks like, just say... just say only... that she is a good Mama and a very good seamstress."

"Why?"

"She wants it to be a surprise when she comes. What she looks like. Just like we'll be a surprise to them! Yuh must promise me!"

Annie promised. She would promise him anything, especially now as his face looked so sad. She was worried he might cry again.

The weather turned the very next day. Strong winds created swells that caused the ship to roll and heave. Heavy rain followed. The air grew bitingly cold, as if to remind them where they were headed.

The last ten days at sea were a misery for both of them, but Annie suffered more. She held down little food once the stormy weather started.

The ship's arrival in Pictou on December 17 was not the happy relief they had both imagined. It was late afternoon and almost dark, and the area was in the grip of a blizzard. Annie was too frail to walk down the gangway, so Edward carried her. He murmured encouraging words in her ear, but she heard the uncertainty in his voice. Annie was afraid of the swirling white mass that bit at her skin and tried to invade her eyes. She kept them tightly shut. Then she heard a deep voice beside them.

"Poor souls! Here, put on these coats and boots, quickly now."

Annie remembered little of what happened after that. Bundled like a baby, laid on the wooden bench of a carriage without wheels, she was covered by heavy blankets. Blissfully, she was lulled to sleep by the motion of the sleigh as it slid over the snow. When it finally stopped, she was lifted out and carried indoors.

It seemed almost as dark inside as out. Smoke from a fire in the hearth and the flickering of candles and oil lamps made everything hazy, a room of shadows. She stumbled instinctively toward the warmth of the fire.

At her side, Edward whispered, "Greet our aunt and uncle."

She turned in the flickering light to face two large adults. The man was tall, with more hair on his head and face than she had ever seen on a man, but he was smiling.

"Welcome, wee niece, to Nova Scotia."

She smiled and, in a weak voice, replied, "Pleased t' meet yuh, sah," as Mama had coached her.

The woman beside him was as tall, too, and very thin, and her hair was pulled tightly away from her face. It made her look stern. She was not smiling.

Annie stepped forward, dipped her head and repeated Mama's greeting. Then she looked up at her aunt.

Aunt Margaret's thin lips remained in a disapproving line as she studied Annie closely and said, "The child speaks in a strange manner."

"A Jamaican accent," said Edward lightly.

But Aunt Margaret's voice was cold in response. "Not suitable. She will have to learn to speak properly."

There was a silence, and then Uncle Alex hustled them to the back of the house. Edward was to share a room with his two cousins, John Robert, twenty-four, and William, sixteen.

Next door was the girls' bedroom, where the Fraser trunk had already been placed beside a small cot. A large bed was on the opposite wall under a window. Annie, who had always had her own large room, would be sharing with Christiann, twenty, and Louisa, ten, in a much smaller space.

It was not until later, at supper, that Annie and Edward met the rest of the family. It was crowded as they sat around the table, but it was a quiet meal. After Uncle Alex said a prayer, everyone kept their heads bowed, seemingly intent only on eating. There was little conversation, and none of the others seemed interested in the newcomers. Only the youngest, Louisa, glanced quickly at Annie and smiled, a wide smile much like her father's. Annie returned the smile. Louisa had long, straight light-brown hair, so different from Annie's dark-brown curls.

Annie was not hungry and would have found the food unappealing even if she had been. It was mushy and bland, nothing like the strong flavours and crisp tastes she was used to. After supper, Annie watched Louisa closely, then copied her in clearing away the food and utensils. Edward had accompanied William outside to feed and water the two horses in the stable.

Later, while Aunt Margaret and Christiann sewed, Annie sat with Louisa, and Edward with William, while their cousins did their school work. Annie wondered why it all felt so strange, and then realized it was because so many people in such a small space were so quiet. Drowsy from the fire, she fell asleep quickly at bedtime but woke in the night. It was freezing and impossibly dark. She was used to moonlight and the hum of hundreds of insects. Their absence was unsettling, reminding her that she was in an unfamiliar place, a place without Mama.

She began to cry, stuffing M'randa against her face to

muffle the sound. Suddenly, someone was by her cot. A soft hand touched her hair and then stroked it. "I'm here, Annie," said a voice. Even though Annie could not see clearly, she knew it was Louisa and reached out to her. Eventually she fell back to sleep holding Louisa's hand.

Chapter Thirty-Five

The next morning when she saw Edward, he grinned at her and said, "It's your birthday, Annie!" She felt a momentary thrill but it died quickly when no one else made mention of her special day. Mama would be making a fuss over her if she were at home. Home.

That thought brought fresh tears, but Edward came over and hugged her. "No more tears, for Mama's sake," he whispered, so she did her best to wipe them away. Her control was broken, however, later that morning. After the younger Frasers had left for work and school, Annie and Edward unpacked their trunk.

When Aunt Margaret saw the elaborately embroidered dresses and petticoats laid on Annie's cot, her face reddened. "We are good Christians in this family and dress simply. We do not wear such fanciful garments," she spluttered. "I will not have them in my house!"

Annie and Edward glanced at each other. What did she mean?

"These are simply Annie's clothes. Our mother made them." Edward's voice shook slightly, but he looked directly at his aunt. "As yuh can tell, she is a very fine seamstress."

"Be that as it may, these things speak of a love of ornamentation, not of purity. They will go to the mission box at the church." Aunt Margaret leaned over to pick up Annie's clothes, but Edward stood in her way.

Taking a deep breath, he said in a determined voice, louder than he had intended, "This child has just said farewell to her mother. Yuh can't take away the only part of her mother she has left."

Aunt Margaret glared at Edward. "How dare you speak to me like that!"

That brought Uncle Alex to the door. "What is the matter?" he asked anxiously.

Nervously Annie looked from one angry face to the other.

Her uncle listened to both his wife and Edward and then, in a gentle tone, said the garments must go. But Edward was not giving ground.

"Uncle, please show some Christian charity. Surely it's not too much to ask that this child may keep a remembrance of her beloved mother?" Edward looked at his uncle.

Uncle Alex's face darkened. Angrily he said, "Do not dare to lecture me on Christian charity, I who have taken you in, despite..." His voice started to shake then, and he stopped, as if he were too upset to continue. But Aunt Margaret was not finished. She stepped in front of her husband and faced Edward.

"How dare you!" Her voice was steely. "Your father thought so little of his older brother that he didn't mention he even had a family in Jamaica. After all these years! Why was that? Had your father something to hide? Your uncle agreed immediately to your father's last request. To take you in, to oversee your education, despite his shock and hurt. That shows the great depths of his Christian compassion. If it had been up to me..."

Even Annie could tell how that sentence was meant to end. She looked up at her brother for some reassurance, but his stricken face frightened her more. In the unbearable silence that followed, she inched closer to Edward and took his hand. Then she stole a quick glance at her uncle. He looked back into her tear-filled eyes, and his shoulders slumped.

Quietly he said, "She may keep one dress and one petticoat for special occasions and her mother's wedding dress. All the others must go."

Edward realized this was the best he could hope for in the circumstances. In a subdued voice he mumbled, "Thank you, Uncle."

But the older man left the room without acknowledging him. Aunt Margaret straightened her shoulders and, without a further glance at either of them, gathered up Annie's clothes and followed him out. Edward sat Annie on her cot and put his arm around her. She sobbed into his chest.

"Ah want Mama! Please, Edward, take me home. Ah hate it heah!"

Edward stroked her hair the way Mama used to. "Annie, I know it's hard now, but we'll get used to it in time," he murmured.

Annie said angrily. "Mama will hate da cold an' da mushy food and mos' o' all she'll hate Aunt Marg'et!"

"Then we must be strong so we can help her when she comes," said Edward. "Will yuh do that for her, and for me?"

When Annie nodded, he got up and placed M'randa beside her pillow. "Keep her close to yuh. She'll help."

But M'randa did not help enough. Annie tried to hide her tears from Edward, but he saw them too often. He grinned broadly each time he saw her and reminded her that Christmas was only a few days away. Until then, they were kept busy with household chores. Not until the New Year would Annie start school and Edward his apprenticeship.

Christmas was another disappointment. Unlike the joyful Jamaican festival that incorporated Junkanoo, the celebrations in Nova Scotia were a serious religious affair. They went to frequent church services, full of prayers and sermons.

But at home, the usual quiet was broken by a stream of

visiting relatives, curious to meet their exotic kin from far away. For Annie, it was an unhappy blur of strange staring faces and unusual accents.

She overheard unwelcome comments about her dress and odd speech, even her hair and freckles. A special guest, John Fraser, known as John Squire, who was Papa's father, was a stern old man who frightened her. He did not seem to be anything like Papa. Only the presence of Louisa at her side made those times bearable. Louisa held her hand, speaking gently as she introduced Annie to her many relatives.

It was on one of these visits that Annie met her two youngest cousins, children of her father's youngest brother, John McPherson Fraser. She was enchanted. Margaret, aged three, had an infectious giggle, and Annie found herself playing peek-a-boo with the little fair-haired girl. Margaret's brother, six-year-old Edward, presented Annie with a gift, a carved wooden bird. When Louisa told her that he was named Edward, Annie started to cry. But they were happy tears. It was nice to know that Papa's name lived here, too.

She relied on Louisa even more when school started in the New Year. Annie, who had been tutored at home, was very nervous about another new experience and more strangers to face. But Louisa never left her side.

The young teacher was happy to turn over the orientation of a new pupil to such a competent assistant. Both teacher and Louisa were surprised to learn how advanced Annie was. Louisa seemed proud of her little shadow and Annie, in turn, was thrilled by Louisa's admiration. One night, under her cot covers, Annie embroidered a heart onto a handkerchief, using the contents of her sewing box.

"Yuh be mah angel," she said shyly to Louisa, when she presented it to her next morning.

Louisa's eyes grew wide, and then she hugged her cousin. "Will you teach me to do this? Your needlework is so much finer than mine!"

Annie nodded, delighted she was able repay her cousin's kindness, even in such a small way.

Edward did not have a friend in William, as Annie did in Louisa, but he told Annie that he could rely on his quiet cousin's help to show him what was expected in the household.

Annie had been anxious about starting school, but Edward admitted he was eager to escape the house and start his apprenticeship in carpentry, training that Uncle Alex had promised his dying father. He was determined to become independent as soon as possible. It was more than the desire to be treated as an adult, he told her. Ever since the confrontation over Annie's clothing, a permanent tension had existed between Edward and his aunt and uncle. Annie could feel it, too.

"Don't worry, Annie," he reassured her. "It doesn't trouble me. I love my carpentry work, and when I master it, I'll earn a good living. That will mean a secure future for both of us."

During that long first winter, Annie pestered Edward repeatedly with "When is Mama coming?" But Edward's replies were always vague. Sometimes he said that the weather prevented her from making the sea voyage, sometimes he said that she had things to take care of at Coley first and sometimes his reply was an unconvincing "soon."

As winter dragged on and the frigid snowy days seemed unending, Annie's pleas became desperate.

Edward had resorted to mumbling "I don't know" each time she asked. He tried to compensate with a big hug each time, but Annie would pull away. She did allow Louisa to comfort her. Her cousin had noticed the tension between brother and sister.

"You mustn't blame him," she said gently to Annie. "It's not his fault your Mama can't come yet. Perhaps it's taking longer than she thought to finish up all your father's business affairs."

"Ah know," said Annie, "but..." She could not finish. All she knew was that she was hurt and confused.

Annie saw so very little of Edward anyway. As spring approached, he spent long hours with the master carpenter in New Glasgow, and then was usually so busy at home with household chores that he had little time for her.

At least Uncle Alex always had a kind word for her, and Louisa was there to help her with chores and rescue her when Aunt Margaret found fault. Annie noticed that no one was there to help Edward when he was criticized. She had her sewing. She had school. And she had Louisa. All of them helped take her mind off her homesickness.

The arrival of spring brought relief. For Annie, the sun's warmth was disappointingly weak, but it did lift her spirits. She and Louisa were able to go on frequent visits to nearby cousins' homes. Not only did she escape her aunt's critical eye, but she loved playing with the young ones in her extended family.

When Louisa mentioned more than once that she would make a grand teacher, Annie was thrilled by her cousin's praise and with the idea itself. Yes, that's what she wanted to be.

The onset of summer raised Annie's spirits even more. The heat could never match Jamaica's intensity, but it rid her of the chill she hadn't been able to shake since arriving. The season meant that she and Louisa were often assigned outdoor chores: tending vegetable gardens and animals, collecting plants and picking berries.

She still missed Mama, but asked Edward about her less frequently.

Uncle Alex and Aunt Margaret seemed untroubled that Mama had not yet arrived and that there had been no word from her. Strangely, no one even mentioned her.

Then one morning, Uncle Alex asked Annie and Edward to meet him in the parlour before they left the house. Annie could tell by his voice that something had happened. And she had a feeling of dread. When they sat down opposite their uncle, Edward reached for Annie's hand and held it. He feels it, too, she thought.

"I received a letter yesterday from Jamaica, from a Dr. Ward, dated a few weeks ago," began Uncle Alex.

"He was Papa's doctor!" interrupted Annie. Edward squeezed her hand.

"Yes," continued their uncle. "And I am afraid he sends bad news. Your mother contracted yellow fever last month and has been very ill."

"Oh no, no," wailed Annie. "Will it make her dead, like Papa?"

"Hopefully not, Annie," replied Uncle Alex. "She is recovering, but it will take a very long time. She cannot think of taking a sea voyage anytime in the near future."

Annie looked desperately at Edward. What did this mean? But the look on his face was calm. He turned to her.

"She's getting better, Annie. Dr. Ward says that. Perhaps she can make the voyage later. It's not truly bad news. I'm happy that at last we have heard some news of her."

Annie looked at him gratefully. Yes, of course, he was right. Edward was always right. Mama would get better. She would still come.

But another letter followed six weeks later. Uncle Alex shared the latest news from Dr. Ward with both of them. The letter said that Mama's illness had made her an invalid. She would never be well enough to travel to Nova Scotia to be with them. Never. Ever.

Once again Annie turned desperately to Edward to make sense of this news. This time she read only despair on his face.

"We musa go t' Mama!" she cried. "We musa go t' be wit' her, t' help her. Please, Edward. We musa go back!"

Her brother just shook his head helplessly over and over again. Their uncle quietly slipped out of the room as she cried and shrieked and beat her fists against Edward's chest. He held her tightly until she wore herself out and went limp in his arms.

Chapter Thirty-Six

Annie avoided Edward after that. She could not look at him or speak to him. He has been mean to me, she thought. And to Mama, too. Because of him, we will not do the right thing. We will not go back to Jamaica to take care of Mama like she took care of us. I will never forgive him for that. Never!

Annie decided to write her own brief letter to Mama to say how much she loved her and would be with her if only she were allowed. Mama must know that her Annie would do anything to help if she could. She asked Louisa to plead with Uncle Alex to ensure that her letter was sent to Dr. Ward. Uncle Alex agreed.

Annie was grateful for Louisa's help, but did not want to talk about her feelings with anyone, not even her best friend. It was too painful. And how could sweet Louisa possibly understand?

Annie waited and waited. She waited all through the winter and into spring. But still there was no reply to her letter.

In the summer of 1850, Annie's grandfather, John Squire, died of pneumonia on July 31, at McLellan's Brook. He was eighty-four. The grief and mourning touched everyone, even

Annie, who did not know him well and had remained a little frightened of the old man.

But he was the father of her father. His passing brought back the death of Papa and all the pain of the loss of Mama and of a precious Jamaican childhood. She needed to talk to Edward. She waited for him to return from work one warm August evening. When he caught sight of her waiting near the front of the house, he quickened his pace and greeted her with a wide smile. "Annie!"

"Oh, Edward, there are so many things I need to say. Only to you."

"Of course, Annie. I want to talk like we used to. Sit with me awhile on the front step."

As soon as they were seated, she said in a rush, "I want to feel sad about grandfather, even to cry for him, for Papa's sake, but I can't. Am I a bad person?"

"No," he said, "I feel the same. The sadness I feel is for our Papa... and for Mama, too. I hardly knew Grandfather."

"I miss Mama and Papa, too," said Annie, "and I think of them... of home... but it seems so long ago now."

"Yes, it does. But we must never forget them and how good they were to us. I'm so relieved that you can speak of them now without crying."

Annie laughed and hugged him closer. "Remember when I cried all the time, when we first came here and you were there to comfort me?"

He nodded and his face became serious. "Annie, I know you blamed me for refusing to go back to Jamaica to take care of Mama, but we couldn't go. It wasn't possible."

"I know that now, Edward. I'm sorry I blamed you. Perhaps one day when we're older we can go back. You know I wrote a letter to Mama?"

"You didn't!" he cried.

"Yes, I did!" She shot back. "I wanted her to know how much I love her. But I got no reply. Nothing," she said sadly.

"Oh, Annie, what a disappointment. But you know

Mama loves us and always will. Promise me that you will never, ever forget that."

The intensity in his voice surprised Annie, but she nodded. "Of course, Edward, I know that and will never forget her love. Ever."

They spoke easily after that, and Annie realized how much she had missed her brother.

At the same time, she repaired her friendship with Louisa. Louisa said she understood.

Annie spent little time with Edward because he was so busy, but they sought each other out when there was an opportunity.

Annie suspected that he needed the companionship more than she did. She had a following of little cousins who adored her, she had friends at school and she had Louisa.

But six months later Edward confronted her with news that seemed likely to shatter their relationship. The mourning period for grandfather had long passed, and the New Year had arrived. Edward caught Annie's eye at breakfast and motioned to outside. She nodded, and as soon as she and Louisa had cleared and washed the dishes to Aunt Margaret's satisfaction, she found her coat and boots and dashed outside. It was another dreary, overcast day with the threat of more snow. Surprisingly, Edward was not waiting on the step, but at the end of the lane.

"Perhaps you have a secret for me?" teased Annie when she reached him. "One not for anyone else's ears?" She did not notice the serious look on his face.

"Annie," Edward began, "you know that my apprenticeship will soon be over. Mr. Gillies cannot keep me on as a partner in his business and there do not seem to be any openings in the area. Uncle Alex agreed to help me find a post elsewhere and he has." Edward stopped. Annie had been nodding. She knew all of this already, but the word elsewhere caught her attention. She tensed. What was he trying to tell her?

Edward took a deep breath. "Papa's half-brother, Uncle Hugh is a carpenter, and he has agreed to take me on. He has been in business a long time, and some of his sons, our cousins, also work in his shop. It's an excellent opportunity for me to—"

"But where does he live?" asked Annie apprehensively.

Edward answered slowly. "It's not very far. He lives in a town called Fall River. It is in Massachusetts... in the United States."

Wild-eyed, Annie shouted, "Edward! You can't leave me! You can't go so far away!"

When Edward reached out to her, she pushed him away and stepped back.

"You promised Mama you would look after me!" she continued, still shouting. "You promised you would never leave me. How can you do this? Edward, you promised!"

He hung his head. "Annie, you know I would never leave you if it were up to me. But Uncle has wanted to be rid of me ever since we arrived. You know that. I have no choice. I can't find work here. I have to go. Perhaps you can join me once I am settled, sometime later."

"Sometime later!" echoed Annie bitterly. "That's what you said about Mama! That she would come later, and she never did! You lied to me then and you're lying now!"

When Edward tried to reach for her, she pushed him away, turned and ran. Instead of running toward the house, she ran down the snow-covered road and kept going until she could no longer hear his cries of "Annie!" She ran until her lungs ached and she was out of breath, then sank down on her knees at the base of a tree and poured her tears into the snow.

Only when her legs started to throb with cold and she became aware of her wet stockings did she struggle to her feet. Her life was coming to an end. She had to go back to find Louisa.

Louisa listened patiently. Finally she looked into Annie's eyes.

"I know this is terrible, terrible news for you, but I fear Edward has no choice."

When Annie started to protest, Louisa stopped her.

"No, please listen. I hate to admit this about my own parents, but I know they have never been fond of Edward. Now that he is of age, they feel their duty is over and it's time for him to leave. They honoured your father's wish to take him in, to help him become a carpenter, but now the debt is cleared. He must go. Haven't you noticed their feelings toward Edward?"

Reluctantly Annie nodded, as the tears started to flow again.

"This is a good opportunity for him," Louisa continued. "He will be freed from a place where he never felt welcome."

"But Louisa, he promised me. When we left Jamaica he said he would stay with me always... I hate him!"

"Oh, Annie, you are angry and hurt. I understand. I'm sure Edward understands, too. I think leaving will hurt him just as much as it will hurt you."

"But can he not work here in New Glasgow? He could do something else until he finds work as a carpenter. He's choosing to go. To break his promise. To leave me."

"I don't believe he has a choice. Father—"

"No! You're wrong, Louisa. I'll never forgive him!" Annie took a deep breath and continued. "But thank you for being my friend. I'm very glad I have you."

"Remember," said Louisa tenderly, "you'll always have me, who loves you just as much as Edward does."

Annie hugged her cousin tightly as if afraid she, too, might disappear at any moment.

The next day, she sought out Edward before he left for work. Together they walked outside into a sunny though freezing morning.

"Perhaps I can take you with me," he said straight away, but she put a finger to his lips.

"No, let me speak first," she said.

He nodded.

"I was hurt and very angry by what you said yesterday. I'm still upset that you lied to me."

Edward opened his mouth but she stopped him once more. "Let me finish! I know this is what you want, what you must do. Our aunt and uncle have never been kind to you. I could tell. Louisa told me she could see it, too. It's not the same for me. Uncle Alex is kind to me, but not Aunt Margaret. I'm not sure if Aunt Margaret likes anyone."

Annie looked at Edward with a hint of a smile and continued. "But I must stay here and go to school with Louisa. Perhaps I may visit you sometime."

Edward smiled, relieved by Annie's words. "How can I have such a sister like you, so understanding, so grownup?"

Annie smiled. "Because I am grownup. I'm eleven now!"

Chapter Thirty-Seven

Edward left on June 12, 1851, taking a ship to Boston. Annie could not face another dockside farewell, so did not accompany him to Pictou Harbour. Despite her words of acceptance, Annie had continued to feel hurt and unsettled in the six months since Edward had made the decision. So a quick hug at the house was all that she could manage.

The next month was hard for Annie. Despite the warm weather and her favourite summer activities beginning, she could not summon up her usual enthusiasm. The loneliness she felt at Edward's departure was more than she had believed possible. As ever, Louisa was her comfort, saying little but at her side most of the time.

Edward's first letter arrived about a month and a half later. It was a very brief message, but Annie could read his mood within the opening lines.

> "Uncle Hugh met me in Boston and we journeyed the considerable distance south to the large town of Fall River. He and his family have made me feel very welcome. I have started working in Uncle Hugh's carpentry shop. It is very busy and I am gaining valuable experience. This is a pretty

> town, much bigger than New Glasgow, and a booming one! Perhaps one day you will be able to see it."

Over the next four years, Annie wrote occasionally, and Edward replied when he could.

Each of her letters included a reminder that Edward had broken his promise to stay with her and that she missed him terribly. Every letter concluded with a stream of questions: When could he come to visit her? How far away was Fall River? Could she visit him there?

Edward's letters in response were always the same: news of his exciting life in Fall River, but no mention of visiting. The carpentry business was growing. He had met a girl, Ellen Cameron, and was hoping to court her. She had come previously from Nova Scotia. Every new letter spoke of a new development. Annie began to feel a touch of envy. Her life was routine in comparison.

But when Edward wrote of news of his marriage, and a year later of the birth of his son, Annie became determined to go. She wanted to see her brother and meet her little nephew. And so, with Louisa's encouragement, Uncle Alex made the necessary arrangements for Annie to travel to Boston. Edward would meet her there, and they would continue to Fall River together.

Annie was overwhelmed when she saw Edward again. He was stronger, more handsome, and with a glow she had never seen before. He seemed truly happy, she thought. His wife, Ellen, was kind and welcoming. And little Edwin was enchanting!

"He looks just like you!" she told her brother. "He has your eyes, your mouth, but thankfully not your tight curls. His are soft."

As she spoke, she noticed Edward staring at her. "I see great change in you, little sister! You're all grown up now at fifteen! I must keep my eye on the men of Fall River!"

Annie just laughed. "The only man I have eyes for is Edwin. May I hold him, please?"

Annie stayed only a month with Edward, but it was a wonderful visit. She had a chance to spend time with Edward, Ellen and Edwin and to meet her Fall River relatives. Annie still felt a little resentment toward Edward for abandoning her four years earlier, but refused to let those feelings spoil the happiness of her visit.

As Annie's departure date drew near, she wondered how many more years it might be until she would see Edward again. And then, good fortune, as he arranged for Ellen and Edwin to accompany her home to Pictou. Ellen would visit her parents there. Annie felt better able to face yet another separation from her brother.

Annie's return was a joyous one. She was surprised by how happy she was to return home. She was welcomed warmly by many, including her young cousins, her school friends and Uncle Alex.

But her sweetest reunion was with Louisa. It was tearful and heartfelt. They confessed to missing each other terribly and promised that they would never again be parted for so long.

Annie continued to write to Edward, but her longing to see him had been satisfied for now. She felt more settled, ready to think about her own future. When she completed her studies at sixteen, she applied to become a teacher at the school in New Glasgow, hoping to realize her long-held dream. The school had expanded since she had started there, and now boasted two rooms, one for older students and the other for the very young. Annie was hired and was delighted to be put in charge of the younger pupils.

She wrote to tell Edward that teaching was all and more than she had hoped it would be. "Although, of course, I will always miss you, the joy I find in my work takes some of the sting out of our separation. However dear brother, we must never again wait so long to see each other."

After school in the afternoon, Annie often went to Uncle Alex's shop to help him. If he did not require her assistance that day, she would visit shops in town to buy household supplies for Aunt Margaret before returning home.

One of her regular stops was the bakery in New Glasgow, owned by John Miller. When he took on a new young apprentice, Duncan Ross, Annie's visits became more frequent. Duncan would rush to assist Annie the moment she entered the shop. He always managed to include an extra bun or pastry in every order and then would run to open the door for her. On the rare occasions when he had time off, he waited by the school door at dismissal, to walk her to her uncle's shop or wherever she had to go.

Annie was charmed by his attention, his enthusiasm and his thoughtfulness. She told herself he reminded her of Edward.

Duncan sought Uncle Alex's permission to court her. He told Annie that he had been very nervous in doing so. Her uncle had a reputation. But to Duncan's relief, Uncle Alex gave permission readily. John Miller's assessment of his apprentice's prospects had been very favourable.

Annie was thrilled by Duncan's commitment to her. She wrote to tell Edward all about him and admitted that she was in love. But she did not mention Louisa's uneasiness.

Louisa had cautioned her. "I have heard say that he has a quick temper."

"Never with me," declared Annie. "But I know he professes strong feelings on many subjects."

"Perhaps, but please be careful, Annie. Be sure of your suitor's character. I love you and just want you to be happy. As happy as I am in my marriage."

"Dearest Louisa, I know that," laughed Annie. "I promise to be careful and cautious!" Then more seriously she added, "Duncan is very loyal, Louisa. I can count on him. Like I have always counted on you."

Their eyes met. "I know how important loyalty is to you," said Louisa softly.

Despite Louisa's reservations, Annie accepted Duncan's proposal.

But they had to wait for more than a year to marry, as Uncle Alex decreed that a wedding could not take place until Duncan could support his wife properly by owning his own business. When Annie wrote to tell Edward, she was surprised by his reply.

"Uncle Alex was never my champion, but he has always been yours, Annie. I am happy that he has placed those conditions on your suitor. Well done, Uncle Alex!"

Within a year Duncan had satisfied Uncle Alex's terms by opening the Ross Bakery in New Glasgow. Wedding preparations followed. Annie had dreamed of wearing her mother's green silk wedding dress, brought all those years ago from Jamaica. She was disappointed to find, when she tried it on, that it was too short for her. But when Uncle Alex said he thought that together they might be able to alter it, she was overjoyed. Once it was ready, Annie tried it on in front of Louisa. "Oh, Annie, you look so very beautiful!"

"I feel special in this dress because I feel close to Mama in it," said Annie, wiping away a few tears. "And I feel so close to my Papa, too. I'm so happy at this moment I feel I might burst!"

"Don't do that," laughed Louisa, "or my father may need to do even more alterations!"

Annie laughed and reached for Louisa's hands. "I have your father to thank for this and everything. He's always been so good to me."

"My father has always been your champion, Annie." agreed Louisa.

"That is exactly what Edward said in one of his letters!"

Elizabeth Ann Fraser married Duncan Ross in the Fraser home in February 1860. Reverend George Walker of the

Presbyterian Church officiated. The bride was nineteen years old, with her best friend at her side. Her only disappointment that day was the absence of her brother Edward. He had written to say that he could not attend. It was too great a distance, after all. But was that true, Annie wondered. Was he really unable to come, or was he simply unwilling?

Epilogue

September, 1888 Boston, Massachusetts

I sat in stunned silence for a long time. The candles had burned down, but it was no longer dark in the room. Morning sunlight was starting to creep in around the edges of the curtains. The only sounds were the soft tick-tock of the grandfather clock in the hallway and, to me, the much louder thudding of my heart.

My thoughts were chaotic. What Edward had revealed to me was unbelievable, impossible surely. I was not the person I had thought I was. My mother, my own dear Mama, was a coloured slave! How could I not have known? I tried to remember Mama's face, her hair, her eyes and the colour of her skin. But the image was blurred by time and love, and a young girl's perspective. The truth was shocking. I felt heartbreak, too. How Mama must have suffered, the pain she must have felt that day on the wharf, knowing she would never see us again. As a mother now, I could only imagine her agony. And that made me think of Sophia, another mother who was forcibly separated from her child. Mama and Sophia shared more than they would ever know. But at least Sophia had been reunited with her son. Why did the mothers in our family have to suffer so?

But Edward had known about Mama. All this time. He

had plotted with Mama and Papa to keep the truth from me... promises and lies... years and years of lies. I was paralyzed by a jumble of emotions: anger, shock and grief. I could not move or speak.

And then a soft voice from across the room broke into my thoughts. "Annie dearest, I am so sorry. I know I have caused you such heartache all these years. But you can understand now why Mama could not come with us. Without her beside us, we were accepted as white. But if she had come, our background would have been obvious. As a mulatto, a former slave, Mama would have suffered prejudice in Nova Scotia. And we would have suffered along with her."

"But we are white, Edward!" I exclaimed.

"Yes, outwardly so, but in many places one drop of Negro blood makes you a Negro. Would Uncle Alex have taken us in if he had known?" He paused, then continued. "I knew Mama could never come to Nova Scotia, but we had agreed to let you believe it was possible, to make it easier for you. And we were afraid you might let the truth slip out if you knew. You were so young then, Annie. I hated keeping this from you, but I had made a solemn promise to Papa and Mama. I hope you can forgive me some day."

Then suddenly a new thought shot me bolt upright. "Dear Lord, Edward, that means our children are not white! They carry Negro blood, too!"

"Yes, that's true. But like us, they appear white. They are white. I have always classified myself as white on official documents and, as long as you keep the secret about Mama, your children are also white."

Edward paused, then added firmly, "Annie, the secret must die with us."

I nodded, as I tried to understand the implications of everything I had heard. No one must ever know that Mama was a slave.

But I felt a twinge of guilt as well. "Poor Mama. I feel like... like we are rejecting her, like she never existed," I stammered.

Edward crossed the room to sit beside me. "We are not rejecting her! We have her freckles and curls, and so do some of our children. And I like to believe that inside we carry the best of her, her quiet strength and loving nature."

We lapsed into silence then, each of us sifting through thoughts of the past. Then a painful memory came to the surface, and I felt cold. "Edward, remember that letter from Dr. Ward, telling us that Mama had yellow fever and could not come to us? Did she really have yellow fever, or was that another lie?"

Edward looked guilty as he answered me. "Another lie, Annie. Part of the plan. Remember, we had to give Aunt and Uncle a valid reason why Mama could not come, could never come. That was just as important as trying to protect you."

I thought about all the pain behind those lies and I asked in a small voice, "Did you ever find out what really happened to her?"

"No, I never did. I wrote to Dr. Ward several times, but never received a reply."

"She must have always wondered about us," I said softly. "And I have wondered about her all my life. I hope she was able to find some small measure of happiness again."

Edward nodded. Then, slowly, he got to his feet and moved to the desk. "Do you remember last night that I mentioned I had something for you, a piece of Fraser history?" he asked. "Now that you know who you are, this will mean much more to you."

When he sat down beside me again, he placed a small leather pouch in my hand. "Open it," Edward encouraged. I loosened the string and peered inside. I saw... sand? Soil?

"Can you guess?" he asked.

"No—yes! Is this Hugh's pouch of soil from Scotland?"

"Aye!" Edward answered, with a grin.

"Why did he give it to Papa and not to one of his older sons or grandsons?"

"I think I know why. Hugh had a special bond with Papa. He, like Papa, risked his future in a new place across an ocean," Edward paused. "But now the soil needs to go home to Nova Scotia. With you, Annie. Pass it on to one of your children. Please. For me, for all of them."

"Oh, Edward! Thank you. I will take care of it always."

As I held the well-worn leather, I thought of all the Frasers I had learned about. Our Grandfather, John, of whom I had been a little afraid, but understood better now. Like me, he had been torn from his family at a young age and had suffered for it. And of all those Frasers I had never known.

Then it struck me how much Edward was like the man he had so vividly described, our kind and steadfast great-grandfather Hugh. How proud Hugh would have been of Edward.

"Edward, I'm sorry for the distress I caused you when we were young. I was hurt when you left and could think only of myself. I've waited far too long to apologize."

"Oh, Annie, there's nothing to apologize for. I never stopped loving you and hoping that some day we could be close again."

A sound at the door surprised us, and we both turned to see a sleepy Josie stumble into the room. I looked at her now with different eyes.

Was there any feature that would mark my daughter as coloured? No, despite the freckles and curls, she appeared as white as me. Whiter even. Could anyone see that she carried a few drops of Negro blood? No, there was no way to tell. Perhaps some time in the future there might be... but for now, I would keep the secret.

Afterword

What do we know of the real people and events in this story?

We know that Hugh and Sophia had four children born in Scotland, and that John contracted smallpox shortly before the family was to leave, and remained in Scotland for six years. We know that Hugh took a letter with him attesting to his character and occupation as a weaver.

The *Hector*'s voyage is based on fact, including the smallpox outbreak and deaths, and the storm which blew the ship back toward Scotland. Many real *Hector* people have been included in our story: Captain John Speirs, agent John Ross, and passengers John Patterson, John William MacKay, Walter and Christie Murray, and Hugh and Christina MacLeod among them.

The arrival in Pictou and the early years there would have been much as we have portrayed them. Many *Hector* families, including the Frasers, left during the first winter to work in Truro or other established communities. We required a family to employ Hugh and Sophia, and so created the Blairs.

The Frasers' neighbours, John and Jane MacLellan were the first *Hector* people to settle on McLellan's Brook, a tributary of the East River in Pictou County. (Note that the spelling of names often changed incidentally. MacLennan became MacLellan on McLellan's Brook.)

John Patterson was the only *Hector* settler known to have

returned to Scotland, even temporarily. We do not know if he was a friend of Hugh, but chose to make him so, and give young John Fraser the means to immigrate to Pictou.

Reverend James MacGregor, a highly respected Presbyterian minister, played a significant role in the advancement of religion and education in Pictou County.

John became a successful businessman. His first wife, Jannet, died tragically at age seventeen, a year after her marriage, and just months after their son, Hugh, was born. John married two more times; his second wife was Catherine Fraser Ross.

Records show that Edward Smith Fraser worked at Coley Estate in Jamaica and before his death married Elizabeth Bishop, a former slave of Stony Gut and Coley Estates. His children were sent to Nova Scotia "to be educated". Edward C. Fraser, Annie's brother, went to Fall River, Massachusetts to work as a carpenter and became a naturalized American citizen. Annie remained in New Glasgow and married Duncan Ross. Duncan bought property on Provost Street in New Glasgow where the family lived, with the bakery and stables in the back.

As reported in *The Eastern Chronicle,* Annie did not see her brother, Edward, for thirty-three years, until she went to Boston in 1888. This newspaper article gave the story its Prologue and Epilogue.

Duncan died in 1892 and Annie followed him less than a year later at age fifty-four.

Family lore describes Annie as the little girl who came from Jamaica with beautiful clothes, considered sinful by some of the family.

The green silk dress did exist and was Annie's wedding dress, although it did not come from Jamaica. It was made for her in 1859 and later remade as a child's dress for her daughter, Louise.

The story of the Frasers ended for my family in 1860, when Annie took the surname Ross, but that year also marked a beginning. Annie Fraser and Duncan Ross had six children, the second one born in 1862.

That child was Louisa (usually called Louise), named after Annie's cousin, Louisa, with whom she grew up in New Glasgow. Louise Ross was my great- grandmother. The tradition of naming the eldest daughter Louise has continued for 153 years. Lou Six was born in 2015.

Annie was right when she suggested to Edward that someday there might be a way to find out, to see inside a person and determine their racial heritage. But it would be more than one hundred and twenty-five years before Annie's family, or anyone, could have their DNA tested. Surely Annie must have known that she was descended from a slave, but true to her promise, kept the secret. Or perhaps she never knew? It seems that her descendants were unaware that they carried those drops of African blood.

In the late 1800s, racial discrimination and prejudice were common and many white families would have thought it a scandal to admit to a trace of black blood in the gene pool. There was certainly no hint of that "scandal" in mine. Once I dug into my family's roots using genealogy and found Elizabeth on a slave record, I wanted the confirmation that only DNA testing could provide. I was tested in 2014, and the proof was there.

Mitochondrial DNA, which is passed directly from a mother to children, is carried in the maternal line to all future generations. My DNA indicated that I was part of a group of people from Africa, within the last four to five hundred years. This would align closely with the Atlantic slave trade.

The people I have discovered who share most closely my mitochondrial DNA are of African heritage, and live in the southern United States, the Caribbean and Brazil.

The final question remains: what happened to Elizabeth after Edward died? It has been suggested by some that she must have died shortly after him, and the orphaned children were sent to Pictou. That is possible, but we have chosen another alternative: Elizabeth made the incredible sacrifice to send her children to a better life in Nova Scotia.

The Fraser story is one of great courage and perseverance.

Hugh was an illiterate farmer and weaver who arrived in Nova Scotia with almost nothing, an early immigrant to a country of immigrants. He and Sophia established a family and, against great odds, tamed a toehold in the land that would be Canada.

—Ann Louise Stevens

To those readers whose ancestors appear in this story, please understand that they have been given imagined personalities and woven into a fictional narrative. We extend our apologies if you feel they have been characterized unfairly.

The terms used and descriptions of those of African and Indigenous descent reflect the time and setting, and do not represent our views or what is acceptable today.

—Pamela Edwards and Ann Louise Stevens

Acknowledgments

Many people have contributed generously of their time and talents in making *Children of the Hector* a reality. Their knowledge and insights helped us in the writing of this story. Any mistakes, however, are those of the authors.

Anne Gorham Blakeney researched the Frasers before the internet made genealogy relatively easy. With assistance from her sister, Eileen Gorham Paton, she laid the foundation for our story. Her interest and enthusiasm for *Children of the Hector* are greatly appreciated.

Michelle Davey, Curator/Manager, and Teresa MacKenzie, Researcher, McCulloch House Museum and Genealogy Centre, Pictou, Nova Scotia, provided ongoing assistance and answered many questions.

Teresa MacKenzie, Art and Design, made the wonderful maps which appear in this book.

Brenda Hutchinson, Project Researcher, Hector Descendants Project, Pictou, Nova Scotia, provided enthusiastic help in bringing *Children of the Hector* to our readers.

Barry MacKenzie shared his extensive knowledge of Pictou, New Glasgow and McLellan's Brook with Ann.

Rosemary McDonald and Kirsten McDonald walked the cemeteries of Pictou County with Ann and shared their love of genealogy.

Dr. Elizabeth Ritchie, Undergraduate Programme Leader,

Centre for History, University of the Highlands and Islands, Dornoch, Scotland, kindly provided information about eighteenth century Highland life.

C. Anne Fraser, Family Historian, Highland Archives Centre, Inverness, Scotland, and Dr. Alice Glaze, Research Director (Ottawa), Know History, Ottawa, Ontario, helped with Scottish history and genealogy.

Susan Hughes, author and freelance editor, read opening chapters of the novel and pointed us in the right direction.

Brian Henry, book editor and creative writing instructor, evaluated an early draft of the novel.

Janice Hamilton, author, provided a welcome review of a later draft and offered valuable tips on the mechanics of publishing.

Kate Barlow, author, made valuable suggestions about style, content and publishing options, in addition to providing constant encouragement.

Sally Keefe Cohen, literary consultant, generously offered advice on the mechanics and legal aspects of writing for publication.

Joann Egar, Copy Editor, edited our manuscript and offered us an encouraging review.

Patty Osborne, Vancouver DeskTop Publishing, helped guide us from manuscript to finished novel with patience and professionalism.

John Ashton, Ashton Creative Design, Pictou, Nova Scotia, brought *Children of the Hector* to life with his beautiful cover art.

And thanks to all the others who have helped, supported and encouraged us in writing this book.

Finally, special appreciation is extended to our most loyal supporters, the Stevens family: Larry, Scott, Todd, Brooke, Rebecca and the grandkids; and the Edwards family: Bob, Ian, Victoria, Andreea and Rob. They have read, reread and proofread, and have been there for us for seven years. Heartfelt thanks.

Further Reading

Many books and materials provided invaluable genealogical and/or historical information. Among those which may be of special interest are:

Abbott, Elizabeth, *Sugar: A Bittersweet History*. Toronto: Penguin Canada Books, Inc., 2008

Abraham, Carolyn. *The Juggler's Children*. Toronto: Random House Canada, 2013

Levy, Andrea. *The Long Song*. Toronto: Hamish Hamilton, 2010

Mackay, Donald. *Scotland Farewell, The People of the Hector*. Toronto: Natural Heritage/Natural History Inc., 2001

Patterson, George. *A History of the County of Pictou, Nova Scotia*. Montreal: Dawson Brothers, 1877

Winkler, Anthony. *The Family Mansion, A Novel*. New York: Akashic Books, 2013

www.shiphectordescendants.ca

Bannocks

Oats and barley were staples of the Highland Scots, as they were readily grown in the harsh climate of the North. They were ground in different ways to produce meal and flour. If there was no mill nearby, the women used the laborious quern, or hand mill to grind the grains. Oatmeal was served in some form at most meals, usually as porridge, or baked into bannocks or oatcakes. Even the early Highland soldiers depended on oatmeal. It is said that each carried a pouch of oatmeal, which was mixed with water, and cooked on their shields over the open fire.

Bannocks were also eaten by the First Nations peoples of Canada. The Mi'kmaqs' diet was largely meat, fish and native plants, but they also ate bannocks using corn or nut meals, which were cooked in pits or on green sticks over the fire.

About the Authors

Pamela Edwards and Ann Louise Stevens are long-time friends who have known each other since they were young mothers. Their first major collaboration was founding a book club which just celebrated its 40th anniversary. Their second was writing this book.

Pam, a graduate of Carleton University, is a retired elementary school teacher. As a child and Army brat, she moved frequently and lived in different parts of the world, experiencing many ocean voyages in the process, none as horrific as the *Hector*'s. At retirement, she was free to work on her first love, writing. Her children's picture book, *Oliver Has Something to Say!* was published in 2007.

Ann, a graduate of McMaster University, is also a retired elementary school teacher. She made a career change to interior design and has pursued many interests in the creative and performing arts. Through her passion for genealogy, she found Hugh and Sophia Fraser, and multiple trips to Scotland and Nova Scotia brought them to life.

We welcome your questions and comments about *Children of the Hector*. If you enjoyed it, please pass the word. If you, too, are a *Hector* descendant, we'd love to hear from you.

childrenofthehector@gmail.com

Manufactured by Amazon.ca
Bolton, ON

34905005R00157